NO
BEAUTIES
OR
MONSTERS

TARA GOEDJEN

DELACORTE PRESS

Text copyright © 2021 by Tara Goedjen
Jacket art copyright © 2021 by Jack Hughes

Visit us on the Web! GetUnderlined.com

Educators and librarians, for a variety of teaching tools, visit us at
RHTeachersLibrarians.com

Library of Congress Cataloging-in-Publication Data
Names: Goedjen, Tara, author.
Title: No beauties or monsters / Tara Goedjen.
Description: First edition. | New York : Delacorte Press, [2021] |
Audience: Ages 12+ | Audience: Grades 10–12. | Summary: Even though she is suffering from memory loss and hallucinations, Rylie must unravel her family's secrets in order to save herself and find her missing friend.
Identifiers: LCCN 2020050033 (print) | LCCN 2020050034 (ebook) |
ISBN 978-1-5247-1480-2 (hardcover) | ISBN 978-1-5247-1482-6 (ebook)
Subjects: CYAC: Space and time—Fiction. | Missing persons—Fiction. |
Families—Fiction. | Deserts—Fiction.
Classification: LCC PZ7.1.G62 No 2021 (print) | LCC PZ7.1.G62 (ebook) |
DDC [Fic]—dc23

The text of this book is set in 11.5-point Janson Text LT.
Interior design by Ken Crossland

Printed in the United States of America
10 9 8 7 6 5 4 3 2 1
First Edition

For Cora and Ella,
the girls who changed my world

Of all base passions, fear is most accursed.
                    —William Shakespeare

*Is not this world an illusion? And yet it fools
everybody.*
                    —Angela Carter

PROLOGUE

THE BEES ARE GONE, BUT Ethan's knife isn't. It's clean from last time and tucked under his bed. Other sleeping bags are in the room—the kid his age is sprawled out on one of them—but everyone else is at morning chores. Today Ethan's chore was the beehive. The bees had left, vanished completely, and it scared him enough to send him inside.

But even inside there are too many windows and doorways. All the openness makes it hard to think. He needs to hurry; he can feel them coming. He needs—*what?* The beekeeping veil is hot and he yanks it off, then glances outside. It's still dark—the sun hasn't risen yet. That's when they like to come.

Ethan hauls up his bag; he has water in it, food. Enough to give him some time until it's all clear. And then he'll come back and sleep next to the others and do his chores, and he'll be happy with that, even if it's his turn to scrub toilets. But now he has to hurry.

He shoves the last of the broken pill into his mouth, choking down the bitterness as he grabs his phone and the card. A tiny hexfoil's on it, a number to call for help.

1

He starts to dial, but the phone slips. He's sweating again; sweat's beading over his arms and legs. There's a sound at his ears like rushing water, a tap turned on full blast. Then something slams against the door and the other kid in the room startles, sitting up.

It's too late.

"Run," Ethan whispers. "Run!"

When Ethan rolls over and opens his eyes, he sees the bruising on his arms, over his hands. The sleeping bag next to him is empty. There's blood on the floor.

Another one. Ethan's stomach heaves, but nothing comes up. They'll lock him away again.

He gets to his feet. He grabs his backpack, his knife. The beekeeping veil and gloves. To keep himself calm he recites the name. *Caruso. Caruso.* Then he shoves everything into his bag and heads to the door.

There's nowhere to go except into the desert.

CHAPTER 1

"OUR TURN," RYLIE SAYS. SHE nudges the jeep up to the guard post. A sign's hanging from the new razor wire fence: VEHICLE CHECKPOINT, TWENTYNINE PALMS. The name sounds tropical, but it's a lie—Twentynine Palms is a Marine Corps base surrounded by desert. A *lot* of desert.

"Here." Rylie holds out their IDs for the guard. He scans their cards but doesn't open the gate. Instead, he turns on a flashlight and aims it at the jeep.

"We're with my mom, Major Caruso," Rylie says. "In the U-Haul that just went through? She was assigned—"

"Got it." The guard's flashlight hits her in the face, and she blinks, her eyes burning. A second later it's on Ben. Her stepdad's sitting too straight in the passenger seat, his tracksuit sleeves pushed up to his elbows, his forearms flexing. Behind him, Owen's holding down a growling Castle, their rescue terrier.

"Castle doesn't want to move here either," Owen whispers, and Rylie turns to squeeze her brother's knee.

"He'll be fine," she whispers back. This time they'll all

be fine. She glances at the guard—he's taking too long. "How come there's a checkpoint here? We're not even at the base yet."

"Heightened security. It's temporary." He clicks off his flashlight. "You're all clear."

She wants to ask more, but it's probably better just to keep driving. The gate swings outward, and she quickly accelerates—following her mom, just like always. Because no matter what they're heading into, they have each other. *A triangle has strength*, her mom used to say. *Me, you, Owen*, she'd say. *We're strong*. But they aren't a triangle anymore, not with Ben and Kai, and they're going straight into the one place Rylie never wants to see again.

"Well, that was interesting," Ben says, clutching the door handle like she's going too fast. His gaze flicks from the speedometer to the window. "So far the desert seems fairly . . ."

"Warm and welcoming?" It's another lie, but maybe it's not a lie to Ben. All he would see right now is an inky highway and a scattering of lights in the distance. No memories to go with them. Nothing to keep him awake at night, hoping there'd been some mistake. Hoping they weren't actually going back.

"Welcoming, huh? I could use some of that," Ben says, giving her a tired grin. "After San Diego, living out here will take some adjusting."

"We used to come here every summer," Owen pipes up. "So you're the only one who's new, Dad."

Dad. Rylie's heart twinges, and she tightens her grip on the wheel. It's good that Owen's calling him that. It's a good sign. The wedding was only last month, but her mom met Ben a few years ago and used to joke that she wanted Owen to fall in love first.

"I'm looking forward to seeing this place in daylight," Ben says. "You can be my tour guides. After everyone gets a sleep-in." He attempts to hide a yawn. "All the packing really took it out of me. Thanks for driving, Rye."

"Wouldn't have it any other way." Rylie feels her shoulders ease, just a little. They can do this. *She* can do this, for her mom, for Owen. The blended family, the move back to Twentynine Palms. There are upsides to living in the desert too. Wildflowers so blue they shame the sky. Sun-baked rock for climbing. The Joshua Tree cabin. And Nathan and Lily.

"Not much longer now," she says, switching on the radio. The anchorwoman is loud, anxious. ". . . just outside Twentynine Palms, where earlier today, a teenager was found dead. The identity of the victim remains unknown. . . ."

Rylie stiffens. For a second she's thirteen again and her eyes are stinging, and a too-sweet scent is in the air. She reaches over and snaps the radio off. It's just a coincidence. She gets her breath under control: breathing out slowly, breathing in even more slowly. Ben doesn't notice—he's asleep now, with his head resting against the window. In the seat behind him, Owen's playing with the voice recorder, their dad's old Talkboy that still has life.

"It feels funny here, doesn't it?" Owen twirls his headphones. "Do you feel it too?"

"Feel what?" Her voice catches, but she pulls herself together. "The freedom of the open road?" she jokes, but she knows what he's really getting at. The truth is, she's always felt off in the desert, not exactly herself. Not *normal*. It happened every summer vacation they spent here, every holiday visit. "All I feel is the hum of the tires, O."

"Then you're not paying attention," Owen says, his face solemn, his curly brown hair in his eyes like usual. "It's not like I can hear better than you. I just pay attention." He's only eight, but sometimes he seems older. "And being quiet helps."

Rylie grins. "That your way of telling me to shut up?"

"Nope." Then he grins back. "Maybe."

"All right," she says. "If the desert could talk, what would it tell us?" It's a game their mom invented when Owen was a toddler. *What would the plant by the window say if it could talk? What would the window say?*

"'Weeelcome baaack,'" Owen drawls out. Ahead of them, the U-Haul careens around a dark curve, and then the jeep's speakers start to crackle; the radio isn't switched off all the way. Rylie's just reaching for the dash when there's a blur ahead, something darting across the road. She slams the brakes, but there's a thud and a sickening lump under the tires as the jeep jerks to a stop.

No.

"What did we hit?" Owen whispers.

For a second she can't find her voice, can't unclamp her fingers from the wheel. Point A to point B. That's all she needed to do. And now this.

She opens her door. It feels like there's a hand on her chest, pressing down. It feels like it's happening all over again.

"Rylie?"

She forces herself to talk. Forces a lightness into her voice. "I'll get out to check, O."

There's nothing in sight except for the highway and a roadside bar that looks abandoned. She glances over at their stepdad. Ben's somehow still asleep in the passenger seat, a peaceful look on his face. No way is she waking him up. She turns, making sure Owen's white cane is in reach.

"Back in a minute," she says. But now it's getting harder to breathe—the bad feeling is spreading under her ribs. "Stay here, okay?" Then she steps outside.

CHAPTER 2

RYLIE ROUNDS THE FRONT OF the jeep, its headlights searing her eyes. *If I hit a person . . .*

But nothing's lying in the road. There's no blood on the metal. No fur, no hair, no snatch of cloth.

The window creaks, and Owen calls, "Everything fine?"

"Yeah. Maybe it was just a rock." *Liar.* When it went under the tires, she felt how big it was. "Just stay in the car."

She touches the hood. The metal's wet, almost sticky, and she shoves her hand into the headlights. Her skin looks dry; it looks fine. But her fingers are still shredded from last week's climb, and it feels like something's seeping into the tiny cuts on her fingertips. She wipes them on her shirt and kneels down, the pavement scraping her knees as she looks under the jeep.

At first she can't tell what she's seeing. Something dark and shadowy is behind the front right tire. She slowly reaches out. It's a sleeve. A black sweatshirt sleeve. Limp fingers, slightly curled.

No. Rylie yanks her hand back. *Please no, please no.*

She stumbles around to the other side of the jeep. Lying

on the ground is a boy about her age, a hiking backpack beside him with a tire mark streaked across it. The boy's face is turned away from her, and there's blood on the pavement. She clamps a hand over her mouth. A wave of dizziness hits her, but she leans down to touch his neck anyway, gropes desperately for a pulse. His skin is wet. She can't feel *anything*. Then the sound of a jagged breath slices the air. Hope flares in her chest, but the boy's not moving.

The jagged breath comes again—it's her own lungs, heaving. *I did this. I did this.* She stares down at him for another breath and then jerks into action, pulling her phone from her pocket with numb fingers, her hands shaking as she dials. The phone's still ringing as she straightens fast, pounding on her stepdad's door.

"Rylie?"

It's not Ben calling her name; it's her brother.

"Stay *inside*." Her voice sounds too harsh to be hers. Then the phone connects.

"Nine-one-one," the operator says. "What's your emergency?"

Rylie staggers away from the jeep, away from Owen and the body on the ground. She shuts her eyes and sees a black sweatshirt sleeve, pale fingers. "There's been an accident," she chokes out. The weight of what she did presses down on her throat. "I hit—" A loud crackling noise drowns out the line, and she pushes the phone against her ear. "Hello?"

Nothing but silence. The line's dead. Rylie fumbles the

phone, dialing again as she turns back to the boy. And then she freezes.

He's not there.

She blinks. He couldn't have gotten up without her hearing; he couldn't have walked off. But he's not under the car anymore. Her fists tighten as she scans the highway. Nothing. No one. Even the nearby bar looks abandoned, empty. There aren't any lights on, and its sign is covered with huge graffiti: LIVE ON TIME, EMIT NO EVIL. A shiver prickles down her neck. The bar's parking lot is empty too—no cars, no people, no one. Same for the desert scrub around it.

He couldn't have gone far. She turns back to where the boy was lying, and her stomach clenches. The blood she saw under his head—it's not there either. No smear, no wetness.

It's happening again. She rubs at her eyes, so hard, they burn. The road's empty; the blood is gone.

Because it was never there in the first place.

The relief should come, but it doesn't. Instead, panic floods her. Seeing the boy on the ground, *touching* him. None of it was real—only a memory. His face was wrong, though. All of it was wrong.

Rylie presses down on the fleshy skin between her thumb and forefinger—one of Ben's tricks to help her relax. There's a creak behind her as the jeep's door opens, then footsteps over the pavement.

"Rylie?"

She can't turn around, can't face her brother yet. "It's all good, Spaghetti O," she says. She resists the urge to reach out and hug him. He'd ask what's wrong.

Get it together, she thinks. *You'll scare him.* But it's this place—it's the desert. It's messing with her head. She stares down at the empty pavement and takes a breath, willing herself to relax. Because nothing happened. Nothing happened. It's not Yucca Mesa. She's not thirteen again.

Nothing happened. She looks up and finally glances toward Owen, and her heart skips a beat. He's standing at the edge of the highway.

"Owen!" Rylie rushes over to him, catches his elbow. The highway's empty, but he shouldn't be out here at night. No one should. "What are you doing?"

"I'm recording that humming sound," Owen whispers, holding up his Talkboy. "Besides, there aren't any cars."

"Doesn't matter. It's hard to see out here."

"I'm used to it."

"You know what I mean, O." She pulls him close. "Come on, we should get going. It's just the next exit."

When she turns, a figure's in the headlights, looking toward them. "Hey, you two all right?" Ben calls out, and Rylie lifts a hand to wave, and then runs through excuses in her head as she leads Owen back to the jeep.

"Can't believe I was dead to the world." Ben takes off his glasses to rub at his eyes and starts peering at the tires. "My phone's not working. Do we need Triple A?"

She shakes her head and climbs in behind the wheel. "We're good." The headlights are still shining over the empty highway. The dry, dark asphalt. "I thought we hit something, but we didn't." There. That didn't sound so bad, and she didn't even have to lie. She waits for Ben to get in and checks that Owen is buckled before throwing the jeep into gear. "It's not much farther."

"Hey, I hope you're really all right," Ben says quietly. He's looking at her across the console. "Your mom wasn't sure about taking the job here, because of—"

"She's in the military. She doesn't get much choice." Rylie's mom is good at what she does: analyzing numbers for government projects that aren't supposed to exist. Projects that are perfect for isolated bases like Twentynine Palms. When she got the assignment, Rylie told her it was fine. That she'd be fine.

Ben nods. "Just talk to us if you need to. I know you haven't been back since the accide—"

"I still don't get why we have to move into Grandpa's house," Owen cuts in, and Rylie silently thanks him. "Besides the saving-money part," he adds.

"There's that, and the house has just been sitting empty," she says. "Wait till you see it, Ben." Her stepdad is checking his phone now, so she glances at Owen. "Remember all the balconies, O?"

"I remember," Owen says. He rubs his shirt against the Talkboy to clean it. "Mom thinks that I don't, but I do."

"All right, my service is back on." Ben holds up his phone victoriously, a map glowing on the screen. "Take a left." He points, but Rylie's already seen it. She's already turning into the small neighborhood, her grip tight on the wheel. Behind the few spacious houses is a dark expanse of desert. And there, at the very end of the road, is her grandpa's house— a vast Spanish Colonial looming over the high fence that surrounds it, every window lighting up its wide pale walls. She reaches for her leather necklace, clutches the jade figure eight around her neck.

"Are we here?" Owen asks, and then a coarse humming noise suddenly fills the jeep. "Sorry," he says, punching a button on his Talkboy as Castle starts barking. "I think the volume's stuck, Rye." The humming gets louder—the small speakers are going tinny with it, the kind of sound that crawls its way down her spine.

"Did you record the wind? Must be strong out here," Ben says loudly, just as Owen presses another button and the noise snaps off. Rylie parks behind the U-Haul and cuts the engine. No one gets out.

"Mom and Kai are probably waiting for us inside," she says, but she doesn't rush to move, and neither do Owen and Ben. Instead, she stares past her stepdad and up at the house. It looks just like it did four years ago, the last time she saw it. If it could talk, it wouldn't be saying "welcome back." It'd be telling them to stay away.

She glances at Owen and does the only thing she can. She slings open her door. "Ready?"

CHAPTER 3

FROM SOMEWHERE CLOSE, AN ALARM sounds, and Rylie sits straight up in bed. But it's too soft—the mattress is softer than it should be. Around her is an enormous room: white walls; ornate, overly large furniture; Castle curled up beside her. *Where . . . ?*

The blaring continues from somewhere outside, and then yesterday comes rushing back. They're here, at 5115 Sundown, the house she was once kicked out of. For good, supposedly.

She slides off the mattress and opens the door to the private balcony. The view is Nikon friendly, a serene stretch of rocky desert and the mountains beyond, everything ablaze with the morning sun. There are no window screens, so there's easy access to the roof, just how she likes it. Behind her, Castle whines, his little brown ears lifted.

"At least we're allowed inside now." When she pats him on the head, her fingers still feel sticky, even after scrubbing them last night. She pads across the thick carpet to the bathroom, wanting to wash her hands again, maybe shower. After the drive she was too exhausted to do much of anything before collapsing into bed. Now that it's light enough to see, she can tell the bathroom's bigger than her old bedroom in San Diego, everything fitted out in white tiles and chrome.

Rylie shoves her hands under the faucet and then holds them up. Her fingertips are still split from the climbing gym, but other than that, her skin looks normal, clean. The tight feeling in her chest comes back as she thinks of yesterday's drive. She swears she felt the thud against the jeep, the body underneath it. The body that vanished seconds later because it hadn't been there in the first place. She bites down on her lip, hard, then tugs her phone from her pocket. The scratched screen has a missed call from Lourdes, followed by a string of text messages: *Did you make it? Is it as bad as you thought?* Lor's next text is a YouTube link, Stevie Wonder's "Superstition." Then: *Seriously, are you alive? Also, I can't believe I kissed Barista Barry on New Year's. Whyyyyy.* Rylie quickly texts her back a row of scream-face emojis and then looks up hospitals. She calls Desert Heights Hospital first.

"Did a teenager show up at the ER last night?" she rushes out. Then she holds her breath till she gets an answer: no one. The operator asks why she's calling, and she hangs up. Next she tries the base hospital, and after that Bear Valley, where a sympathetic nurse tells her "informally" that the only teenager admitted had a gunshot wound to the head. The news shouldn't make her feel relieved, but it does. Nothing happened last night. And today will be fine. Everything's always better in the morning; her dad used to say that. *Even grading papers,* he'd say, holding up his latest stack of tests and his favorite coffee mug—THE PHYSICS IS THEORETICAL, BUT THE FUN IS REAL. Rylie shakes away the memory as she slips on leggings and a sleeveless shirt, then hears a knock on her door.

"It's not exactly a humble abode, is it?" Her stepbrother is leaning against the doorway in jeans and a faded *Twin Peaks* T-shirt, his black hair long enough to frame his face. "Rumor has it you're one of those sunup, wake-up kind of people," Kai says. "I'm surprised you slept in."

"And I'm surprised you're here." His smile drops away, and she backpedals. Kai has never seemed the sensitive type, but she doesn't really know him—he started college last year and was hardly around before the wedding. "Hey, in a choice between Yale and the desert . . ."

"I prefer chilling in the desert. If you can even do that," Kai says, smiling again. One of his arms has pen marks across it, comical devils that are wickedly charming—a little like Kai himself, especially when he's carrying around his guitar like he is now. "And I'm deferring next semester. Didn't my dad or Eve tell you?"

Ben and her mom didn't tell her much of anything, except that she shouldn't ask questions until Kai is ready to talk. The alarm's still blaring, a low droning noise. "Lucky you," she says. "I want to defer too."

"Ah, the joys of moving to a new high school as a senior," Kai jokes. "At least there's a week left of winter break, right? Should be pretty relaxing out here, minus that alarm."

Rylie ducks past him and into the hallway. "What *is* that, anyway?"

"Mom says it's an exercise on base," Owen calls out from his room, the door wide open. "We can hear it since we're so close." Lying on his bed is an open suitcase, his clothes folded into neat piles that Castle's sinking his jaws into, fearlessly killing them like he's clearing a pit of rats.

"You're quick to move in," Rylie says. "Looks good." Owen's already hung up the climbing posters she gave him for his birthday: tactile shots of Ashima Shiraishi on a route in Spain, and his hero, Justin Salas, winning a Paraclimbing World Championship in Austria.

"I really don't get the appeal of hanging out on cliffs." Kai sits on Owen's bed and clangs out a chord on his guitar. "Seems like there's enough danger in the world, right?" Kai adds, and his voice almost sounds tense, until he starts half singing, "Without adding cliffs to the *miiix*. Without going looking for *iiiit*."

"You sound like a medieval minstrel," Rylie says, and Kai bows, strumming faster and making her brother laugh. She might not know Kai that well, but she likes how he is with Owen.

"You should come with us, Kai," Owen says. "Rylie's taking me climbing outdoors soon." His chin juts up. "Aren't you, Rye?"

"Soon as you're ready, Spaghetti." She understands why Owen wants to do it so much—because after he lost his sight, most people assumed he couldn't. "I was thinking we'd start with hiking first, though. Maybe at the old cabin."

"What cabin?" Kai asks.

"It's near Joshua Tree, close to some trails," Rylie says. "Our grandpa used to live there, before he built this place." She tousles Owen's curls. "Come on, let's get some breakfast."

"Count me in." Kai strums the guitar to a crescendo. "This traveling bard is famished."

They head out of the room and down the enormous set of stairs, which reveal soaring wooden ceilings, ceramic tile floors, security cameras in every corner. The entire house still feels off-limits. Here the commands are practically echoing from the walls, she heard them so much before. *Don't open closed doors. Don't answer the phone. Don't talk to guests.* Worst was the argument that last summer they came to visit. Having Owen around was "too much" for her grandpa. And then the accident pretty much sealed the deal, and they hadn't visited since.

"Do I smell doughnuts?" Owen asks, rounding the corner into the kitchen.

"You certainly do. And croissants, and those little egg things, because they're moderately healthy," Ben calls out, beaming at them from the island. It's strange to see him here, in this house. But it's not her grandfather's home anymore. It's *theirs*—and not just her mom's but her mom's and Ben's. This time, things will be different. They'll be better. They already are—not once did the kitchen ever smell like powdered sugar before. "I stopped at the bakery this morning after my jog," Ben goes on. "Place called Italy Mine?"

"Jogging for pastries," Rylie says. "I like your style."

"It's the hunter-gatherer in me." Ben pushes a tray of steaming drinks toward them. "Got some coffee too. You don't drink it yet, do you, Rye?"

"I do with milk." She reaches for a cup. "It doesn't actually stunt growth. You know that, right?"

"True, but it *does* stimulate the central nervous system," Ben says, switching to his soothing therapist voice, "possibly causing anxiety."

"I'll have my daily dose of anxiety before work, thank you." Her mom appears, already in uniform.

"It's the weekend," Rylie points out, right away knowing what she'll hear.

"Just need to get my footing. I've got some big meetings coming up." Her mom pecks Ben on the cheek as she tugs away the last of the coffees.

"Hey, what's with the steel shutters?" Kai asks, nodding at the covered windows. "A little excessive, right?"

"Like everything in this house." Rylie flips a switch, raising the exterior security shutters and letting in light. The backyard still looks the same: the slim saltwater pool bordering the deck like a moat, a second pool next to a sauna they were never allowed to use, and a stretch of cacti-heavy landscaping leading to a high stone fence. Just as she's peering at the iron spikes on top of it, there's a thud against the window. Then another. Two bees are crawling on the glass.

She nudges her mom. "Remember how I'd get stung every summer?"

"Maybe the shutters knocked down their nest," Ben says, gazing out.

"Maybe they want their honey back." Kai reaches for the pastry box as Rylie's brother grabs a bear claw and then plops down on one of the couches.

"You know what I remember, Rye?" Owen takes a huge bite. "The echoes," he says, his mouth full.

"The echoes?" Ben repeats, but the irony is lost on him. Despite his running shorts and the puff pastry in his hand, he looks like he's about to grab his notepad and psychoanalyze her brother.

"Grandpa would argue with himself in his room," Owen explains. "Out loud, like there were double voices."

Rylie doesn't miss the shadow that falls across her mom's face. She's probably thinking of that last summer they came to visit, when her grandpa would disappear to his cabin for days at a time. If he hadn't wanted visitors, he shouldn't have built so many guest rooms.

"Hey, let's all get outside today, after we unpack," Rylie suggests. "This house is a little claustrophobic, isn't it?"

Ben grins, catching on. "It really could be more spacious."

"I can't believe there are only two pools." Kai shakes his head in mock-sadness. "And a hot tub is so cliché."

Rylie's mom cracks a smile. "In that case I'll have it all to myself after work." She adjusts her service uniform, its tan color matching her brown eye, her ribbons matching her blue one. She always looks like this—completely together, ready to take on the world. "Oh, and I forgot to tell you, Rye," she adds. "Thea Seguin left a note on the door for us. There's a party tonight, at her place near Joshua Tree."

Thea Seguin? Rylie sits down on a stool. Hearing the name feels like an electric current, tingling and quick. "That means Nathan still lives here," she says. "Lily too."

Her mom stiffens. "I thought I told you about Lily," she says, almost hesitantly. Her mom is never hesitant.

"Told me what?"

She starts twisting her new wedding band around and around, and Rylie's overcome by a sudden, sharp awareness. "Is Lily—"

"She left," her mom says quickly. "That's all." But she's still twisting her ring.

"What do you mean by 'left'?"

"Thea isn't in contact with her. Neither is Nathan."

Rylie locks eyes with her mom, wondering what else her mom isn't saying in front of Owen. It wasn't like Lily Seguin to cut herself off. "How long has she been gone?"

Her mom breaks their gaze, scoops up her keys. "About a year."

About a year. So Lily left home a year ago. Around the same time Rylie's grandpa died. Around the time that Nathan called her in San Diego and she ignored him. Rylie stands, suddenly wanting to flee into the sunlight. Kai and Ben look uncomfortable, like they're not sure what to say, and Owen has gone rigid with stillness—he's stopped chewing his bear claw, he's listening so hard.

"I better go," her mom says softly, her hand on the door. "I'll try to make it back by five. That sound okay?"

Rylie knows what her mom is really asking. She's really asking if *she's* okay. And it's not just because of Lily. It's because they're here again, in Twentynine Palms.

"Good luck today, Mom," she says, and then she forces herself to take an apple tart from the box. She bites down, but the tart's too syrupy and sticks to the roof of her mouth. Last night is in her head again, how she thought she'd hit someone. How she felt something wet on the front of the jeep, then saw the body underneath it. The body that disappeared, reminding her how she couldn't trust herself here. The news about Lily has set her on edge, and the sweetness on her tongue is turning acidic. Then there's a sudden tug on her sleeve, and Rylie feels like she's been pulled back into the too-big kitchen.

"So are we going to the party tonight?" Owen asks, letting go of her shirt. "It'll be fun, Rye," he says. As usual, he sounds hopeful, and there's only one way to answer if she wants him to stay like this. There's only one way to answer if she wants to find out more about Lily too.

CHAPTER 4

JUST BEFORE SUNSET THEY DRIVE out to Joshua Tree. Rylie is wedged into the back with Owen and Kai, who's playing "When Can I See You Again?" on his guitar with a little too much angst. She lowers her window, letting the wind hit against her face and drown out the sound. The fresh air feels good after spending the day unpacking and talking to Lor on the phone about Twentynine Palms and the news about Lily Seguin. And just like that, her mind goes to Nathan. It's been four years since she last saw him, and she has no idea what to expect, or how to ask him about his sister, or whether she even *can*.

"Rye?" Owen nudges her with his shoulder. "Thanks for going to the party."

She nudges him back. "I can't ever tell you no," she says, and he grins and then slips on his headphones again. In the front, her mom looks tense as she talks about her first day of work, and Ben reaches out to hold her hand across the console. Rylie glances away, down at her own hands. They still feel strangely sticky, and for once she's glad not to be behind the wheel—she still can't get last night's drive out of her head, the thud and then the hard lump she felt under the tires. What she *thought* she felt.

A second later her mom pulls over, and Kai finally sets down the guitar. "Looks like a place you could get lost in," he says, gazing out at Joshua Tree. The desert sky above the park is strewn with deep reds and pinks, and the granite rock formations are practically begging to be climbed. "I thought your grandpa had a cabin nearby too?"

"He does. That's how we met Thea," Owen says.

Rylie grabs her Nikon as she gets out, and then points to an outcropping of rock. "His cabin's just past those boulders. You can't really see it from here, which is how he wanted it."

"Unlike Thea's." Ben nods. "You could see her house from space right now."

He's right—Thea Seguin's home is glowing. Fairy lights are strung up everywhere, and there's music, and laughter, and a sudden ache of longing hits Rylie in the chest. The house looks just how she remembers it, and all the memories come rushing back. Her dad always said that sometimes you don't miss what you have until it's gone, but that's not it, not exactly. Sometimes you don't miss what you have until it's right in front of you again and no longer yours.

"We're late," Rylie's mom says, that military clip in her voice whenever she talks about the time. "Come on, Leap," she says to Owen, and Rylie's surprised to hear the nickname. It's what their dad called Owen because of his February 29 birthday. Being back here is making the old memories surface, for all of them, maybe. Her mom must realize the slip too, because she glances away from Ben and then hustles Owen past the huge firepit that Thea uses to chase away the coyotes. Next to a garden full of pointy aloe vera plants is a claw-foot bathtub for steaming and stargazing, currently filled with ice and drinks. A pack of kids races past, while most of the adults mill around the picnic tables. A few people are drinking near an open cooler, their voices carrying.

"It's becoming the norm around here," a man's saying. "The assaults, the murders. They think expanding the base is going to change things."

Rylie turns to her mom, her eyebrows raised, but her mom looks at Owen and then shakes her head. "You know I can't talk about it, Rye."

"Hey," Ben says. "Absolutely under no circumstances is anyone allowed to talk shop while we're at a party."

"You seem to be taking this party very seriously." Kai nods at the two giant bags that Ben is carrying. "Sure you brought enough?"

Ben jostles him with one of the bags. "You know how long it takes to judge someone? A tenth of a second." He snaps his fingers. "Nothing wrong with a good first impression."

Rylie clenches her camera strap and then charges up to the door. "What about second impressions?"

"Don't get him started," Kai says, stepping in front of her and then waving them all inside as if he's the host. Rylie scans the noisy crowd as she weaves her way through the house. And then old habits kick in and she makes a sudden turn up the stairs. At the top, all the doors are open in the hallway, and there's the faint sound of voices.

"Anybody here?"

The voices are coming from Lily's room. Maybe she's home; maybe the news about her was wrong.

Rylie taps on the open door and peers in, expecting Nathan and hoping for Lily too. But the room's empty; a radio's on. The DJ from Mojave Mix is talking about a murder at a commune near Twentynine Palms. Rylie steps inside, half chilled, half perversely interested.

"The seventeen-year-old suspect is on the run," the DJ says in his low, radio-smooth voice, "and was last seen just outside Joshua Tree." He goes on about how big the national park really is—almost eight hundred thousand acres—and the window in Lily's room seems to prove it. It overlooks the desert, the miles and miles of rocky scrub filled with boulders and canyons and caves.

A peal of laughter rings out, muffled by the glass, and Rylie leans forward to look. Just below, Ben's standing next to Owen in the barbecue line and making him laugh, and she rubs the goose bumps off her arms and then turns. The black walls in the bedroom are intense—a lot like Lily herself. She was always into photography too, mostly Polaroids of nature, and her photos are taped everywhere, with elaborate captions written underneath each picture. There are close-ups of prickly cholla plants and spiky lupines, and pale blue Mojave asters that you can find on rocky hillsides just before the summer heat kills them.

Rylie's about to leave, when there's a hand on her arm, fingers squeezing. She whirls. Thea Seguin is beside her, her dark hair streaked with white now, her brown eyes so much like Nathan's.

"Hi, Thea," Rylie says, suddenly feeling awkward. "It's me."

For a moment Thea doesn't seem to recognize her—and then she shakes her head roughly like she's shaking off fog. "I never thought you'd be back, not after . . ." She suddenly pulls Rylie into a hug, patting her hard between the shoulders as if she's choking, and it takes Rylie a second to speak. It's been four years, but she has to say *something*—she has to start somewhere.

"I missed you, Thea." It's nowhere close to what she wants to say. "I should have stayed in touch."

"Leave your 'should'ves' at the door." Thea's voice is gravelly and low, but soothing too. "What matters is that you're here, Little Lee."

Little Lee. No one calls her that anymore. Rylie's throat clenches up and she can't talk at all now, can't even manage a word. Thea gives her one final pat and then pulls away. "Come on, my dear. Other folks have been asking about you. Let's get downstairs."

She's moving fast for her age, and Rylie hurries to follow her, back into the throes of the party, where jazz music is playing loudly from the speakers. Rylie still isn't sure how to ask about Lily. She's not sure she wants to hear the answer either. Just then, a girl with short hair and a long flowy skirt steps in front of her.

"Rylie Caruso-Evers," the girl says formally. Her whole look is bohemian—she's even got a silk purse. "I've been looking for you."

"Have we met?" Rylie stares at her for a second, trying to place her face.

"We've hung out a couple of times," the girl says, and then it's her pale blue eyes and even paler lashes that make things click.

"Sara," Rylie says. Sara Mazur was Lily's friend. As close to Lily as Rylie was to Nathan—the two girls always running off to Lily's room every time Sara came over.

"I need to ask you about something," Sara says, lowering her voice.

Rylie hesitates. Usually when people say they need to ask something, it isn't anything good. She glances at the crowded kitchen. Near the back door, her mom is deep in conversation with Thea, and both of them are crying, either the happy tears of seeing an old friend or the type of tears that come from sharing news that pulls at the heart. Then she glances back at Sara, who's watching her with a hint of expectation in her eyes. The music in the house gets louder, too loud for them to talk, but Rylie wants to ask Sara if she knows where Lily is, why Lily left.

"We could go out back?" Rylie offers. Sara nods and then

smiles—it's quick and dazzling, and gone a moment later as she reaches for the door and holds it open, the smell of barbecue smoke thick in the air. Rylie steps out first, heading toward the cluster of boulders in the yard that she used to jump from, until she broke her tibia one summer. The boulders are a little like ocean waves: you don't realize how high they are until you're at the crest and it's too late to back down. That's how Lily got her to jump the first time, Nathan grinning up from below. *Jump or else*, Lily said, but she was smiling too. *Jump or else*. Lily was barely two years older but she would have been in charge anyway. That was the kind of personality she had.

"Thanks for coming out here," Sara says. She opens the silk purse she's wearing, her long skirt swaying. "Our parents used to be friends," she adds. "So I always heard a lot about you, even after you stopped visiting." She tugs out a small piece of paper from the purse and starts absently folding it. Then the paper transforms—it's origami, a bird with pointed wings. "Thea used to talk about you too, before she got sick," Sara goes on.

"Sick with what?" Rylie asks, a tingle of unease spreading through her. "What's wrong with her?"

"My mom says it's dementia. My mom's a nurse, so she would know." Sara's blue eyes are back on Rylie. "I think Nathan's in denial about it," she says. "He's stopping by later after work, actually. He's got guard duty today."

Guard duty. Rylie's thrown off center. Nathan was ahead of her in school—he would have graduated last year—but it still doesn't make sense. "He'd never join the military. Lily maybe, but not him."

Sara looks at her curiously. "Why not?"

"Because he—" Rylie can't picture the skinny, sweet kid she once knew holstering a weapon or taking orders from a drill instructor. He didn't even like video games with guns in them. "It's not his thing, that's all."

"But you don't know him that well anymore," Sara points out, and Rylie feels her lungs clamp tight. Maybe Sara is dating Nathan now and wants to know what was between them before. But everything between them happened so long ago that it doesn't matter. It *shouldn't* matter. They were friends; that's it. Summer friends.

"So you want to talk about Nathan?" Rylie asks, her voice sounding more defensive than she wants it to.

Sara shakes her head. "No," she says. "I want to talk about the let—"

"Aperitifs, anyone?" Kai calls out, striding up to them. He divvies out red Solo cups, oblivious to the fact that he's interrupting. "Sounds more sophisticated than calling it punch, right? I'm Kai, by the way." He nods at Sara and then takes a huge gulp of punch. "Man, I don't know about you, but being in the desert just makes me want to drink more. Get in all I can *while* I can."

Sara narrows her eyes. "Don't do the same thing with your showers."

"You want to know about my showers?" Kai asks, grinning. "But we just met."

Sara's face goes pink, and Rylie steps forward. "Don't listen to him. Half the time he's joking."

"And half the time I'm very serious," Kai says. "Which begs the question, are you a glass-half-full person or a glass-half-empty?" It's unclear who he's talking to, but Sara answers first.

"I *want* to be half-full." She turns abruptly, pointing toward the backyard. "The home videos are on. You're in them, Rylie."

"Thea's still doing those?" Rylie can't help it—she's already walking around the side of the house to look. Kai catches up and then beats them both to the large projection screen in the yard, an old church pew stationed in front of it. The screen's glowing with an image of Rylie at thirteen, with Nathan and Lily beside her. They're all sitting, stiff and cross-legged on the ground, staring at something in the sky.

"You look utterly terrified," Kai says. "Like me at a park without my EpiPen." He's the only one who takes a seat on the pew, then makes a big show of sliding away from a bee that's crawling on it.

"What were you looking at, anyway?" Sara asks, nodding at the screen.

"I'm not sure." The video ends too soon, ripping Rylie from the memory. Another video starts up, this one more recent. It's of Lily, her black hair long on one side and shaved on the other.

"Stand still, you grunt!" Lily shouts on the screen

between laughter. "Stand still, I say!" She's knuckling Nathan on the head, only he's taller, so she's on her tiptoes. "Get off me, Lil," Nathan says, but he's laughing too.

Rylie tightens her grip on her Nikon case. If she could just talk to them both, tell them why it hurt too much to stay in touch . . .

The camera pans to a man sitting next to them, hunched over an outdoor table. "There's no reason to be laughing," he snaps, and her breath catches. Her grandpa looks nothing like she remembers.

"Hey, you have the same eyes," Kai says. "And the same nose, only yours is smaller. Slightly."

"Oh, his head was a lot bigger," Rylie says. "Trust me on that one." She sips the sugary punch and turns away from her grandpa's image on the screen. It's easier to look at anything but him; it's easier to *talk* about anything but him. "So why did Lily leave?" she asks Sara.

Sara folds her arms across her chest. "Who told you that?"

Rylie shrugs. Her mom usually isn't one to make mistakes. "I just—"

"I heard someone bring it up inside," Kai cuts in. The easygoing smile on his face is gone now. "She didn't run away, or leave or whatever. They said that she's . . . missing."

Missing. Rylie sits down on the pew. *At least it's Lily*—that's the next thought she has. *At least it's Lily and not Nathan.* The wrongness of it makes her feel sick. She can still see Lily in front of her on that day four years ago: Lily's dark amused

eyes, her knotted T-shirt and arms akimbo. *I'll go with you,*
Rye, she said. And she did, and she saw it all—the accident
with Rylie's dad and grandpa and Owen—everything that
happened. Lily was there the whole time. And now she's
missing. Guilt leaks into Rylie's stomach, and more questions tumble out of her. "What happened? Where was she
last seen?"

"Right here, Rylie," Sara says. Her pale blue eyes are
suddenly sharp, accusatory. "She was last seen here, on the
trail by your grandpa's cabin."

CHAPTER 5

RYLIE HURRIES AWAY FROM THE smoke-scented spread of food, away from Kai and Sara and the party lights that seem too bright now, too desperate.

With every step, a little warning in her head keeps repeating itself: *We shouldn't have come back, we shouldn't have come back.* She passes the cluster of boulders and makes her way over the rubble, favoring her good ankle, the one she hasn't broken before, steering herself forward until the sounds of the party fade.

And then her grandpa's small cabin is in front of her, blending in with the rock and stone around it, the setting sun flushing it red.

She has to go inside. She has to go inside and check—just in case. When she runs her hand along the window ledge, her skin hits metal. The spare key's still there, where he's always left it. All of a sudden there's a prickling at her neck like she's being watched.

"Hello?"

Cabin, juniper, boulders, the red sun dipping off the side of the earth. A shadow near a boulder too. "Is someone there?" Rylie makes her voice firm, unafraid. No one answers. For a second the Mojave Mix newscast comes back to her, the suspect on the run. But Joshua Tree is huge, and the party is so close. Close enough for her to shout for help if she needs to. She reaches into her pocket for her phone, its solid frame reassuring as she slides it out. One bar of service, and a text from Lourdes is on the screen: *How's desert life?* She also sent a GIF of a skeleton in sunglasses, pulling itself out of a sandy grave. It doesn't seem that funny.

The prickling is still at Rylie's neck, and she checks around the back of the cabin. More rocky desert and a view of the mountains. A hiker's out, moving quickly, probably trying to beat the dark.

If what Sara said is true, then this is the last place Lily was seen. This trail, right here. Her grandpa called it the arroyo trail, even though it was always dry.

Rylie turns, holding the key so tight that it digs into her palm as she walks around to the door. A number is etched into the wood—16—and there's a small circular flourish underneath it. The key makes a scraping sound in the lock, and dust hits her lungs as she swings the door open. The last of the daylight streams in behind her, and her hand goes to the jade figure eight around her neck.

Here it is.

The place her family used to love—for a while, at least. Now there's only dust and the faint stench of something rotting. Maybe an animal found its way inside. Rylie steps in, leaving the door ajar behind her to air out the smell. There's a poker by the small fireplace, and she grabs it, just in case, then looks around the main room. It's sparsely furnished with a desk and a single couch. One wall has built-in shelves full of books, another has a shelf full of antique cameras, and the window has a view of the hiking trail. If her grandpa was at the cabin the day that Lily disappeared, he might have heard something, even *seen* something. . . .

Rylie sits down at his desk and pulls out every drawer, but his journals aren't here. She peeked at one before, when she was younger, until he slammed it shut on her fingers. They were like ledgers: a daily record of his schedule, his thoughts. Who he talked to, what he did, what he saw, and he never missed a day. She turns to the bookshelves and starts searching them, but the Moleskines aren't there either. The cabin grows darker as she checks the bookshelves again, just to be sure. If they aren't here then—

"Rylie?"

She whirls. Standing in the doorway is a guy in camouflage with dark hair and tan skin. A face that's both familiar and not, at the same time.

"Hey, sorry." Nathan Seguin's voice is lower than she remembers, but four years would do that. He's nearly a whole head taller than her now, his hair is cut short, and he has muscles and broad shoulders where he was all scrawniness before. "You okay?" he asks. "Didn't mean to scare you."

"You didn't." Rylie can feel her heart beating hard, but not for the reason Nathan assumes. She once heard about a girl who'd had her heart replaced, and after she'd been stitched back up, her new one was so loud that everyone around her could hear it beating. That's how hers sounds, even though it's just Nathan in front of her. *Just Nathan.* His eyes seem more coppery than brown now, and she can't look away. She swears her heart thuds louder. Who's she kidding? When was he ever *just* anything? Not before, and not now, even though he looks different: his jaw is sharper, more defined, but he still has his grandma's high cheekbones, traces of her Mi'kmaq heritage, the culture she was stolen from as a child in Canada. Rylie heard about it plenty of times from Lily. But Lily isn't here now, shouldering between them like she used to. It's just Nathan. He's staring at her too, and her cheeks go warm.

"What are you—how did you know I was here?" There's so much to say, but it's the first thing that comes out of her mouth. If he expected her to say something else, he doesn't show it.

"I followed you." Nathan glances over his shoulder; the door is still wide open. "I mean, I didn't follow-follow you. I just heard you were out here. Didn't even set down my bag." His voice is rough and gritty, almost like the wind in the desert, and he turns back, smiling a little. "Not that I'd mind following you or anything." Now it's *his* cheeks that look like they're flushing. "You know, as long as you didn't." He grins wider, and she can feel herself start to smile too.

"Well, if it was dark out and we were in an alleyway, then yes. Yes, I would mind."

"Same for me," he says. "Don't surprise me in an alleyway. Especially if you're in a clown suit."

"Don't worry, I grew out of mine."

Nathan laughs, and she thinks about hugging him like she used to, and then suddenly she *is* hugging him, as if no time has passed at all, and he crushes her back. For one long breath she feels like she's thirteen again because he smells the same too, like the cinnamon and menthol toothpicks he used to chew on, after swiping them from Thea's purse. There's another scent flooding her too: soap and laundry detergent, and then Nathan drops his arms at the same time that she does, and even that reminds her of how he used to be, how *they* used to be.

"I was way taller than you before," she says.

"And way faster, unfortunately for me." Nathan smiles at her again. He's wearing the same leather bracelets he used to, and he's twisting them as he talks. "It's been too long, hasn't it?" He nods at the window. "Remember that night we camped out back? And we both had those dreams—"

"More like nightmares," she says. "And we got in trouble for leaving the yard and wandering around in the dark?"

"It's still not a good idea." Nathan's eyes are on the window again. "The Sandman and all that. Remember?" He's talking about the stories her grandpa used to scare them with—about creatures who stole away children at night—but he's also talking about Lily. He's seeing if she knows about Lily.

"Nathan, I just heard. I'm so—"

Footsteps, and they both turn. Standing in the doorway are Owen and Kai, Sara in a wool parka behind them. Kai's looking between her and Nathan with a half-raised fist like he wishes he had knocked. "Oh, hey. Owen wanted to show us the cabin. We got a key from your mom. Didn't mean to interrupt or anything."

"Nothing to interrupt," Nathan says, glancing her way. When his eyes hit hers again, the heat from her cheeks rushes down her body. She steps forward, her pulse loud and fast.

"Kai, did you meet—"

"Sara already introduced everyone," Owen cuts in. "She gave me an origami bird too. A forest owlet. It's endangered." Her brother's talking too loud, like he always does when he's excited. He steps inside with his cane and then runs his hand along the desk chair, probably noticing that it's warm. "What were you doing in here?"

"Just taking some photos." Rylie doesn't look at Nathan as she says it. She can't mention her grandpa's journals to him, not until she finds them. Not until she knows whether he mentioned Lily. Nothing is worse than false hope—she learned that a long time ago. False hope swoops you high and then dashes you against the ground, leaving you shattered. She doesn't want that for Nathan. Not for anyone.

"Why don't we head back to the party?" she asks.

There must be something tense in her voice, because Owen is out of the cabin first without protesting, the others right behind him. She's the last one out, the last one to see what Kai's staring at, immobile, just outside the front door.

"Unreal," he says, and then she's staring too. Arcing across the sky is the Milky Way, its trail brighter here than anywhere else she's ever been. For a second she forgets to breathe, she feels so small.

"Perfect night for a hike," Sara says, staring too. "Visibility from the moon, but not enough light to block out the stars." She starts working another piece of origami paper in her hands, glancing between it and the night sky above them. "Anybody up for taking the long way?"

"Me!" Owen shouts, the excitement back in his voice. "Can I come too, Rye?"

"I don't know. It's getting late." She doesn't want to tell him no straight out, not after she promised to take him hiking. Their dad always said that you could lie about a lot of things, as long as you kept your promises. But he also said to be careful, especially out here, and Owen is her responsibility.

"We could turn back in a half hour," Nathan offers. "It's a pretty easy trek." He shrugs. "Plus I have a backpack full of bear spray, if that makes you feel any better."

Rylie laughs. "What about flares?"

"Got those too," he deadpans. "No way we're getting lost."

"But that's when it gets fun." After being away from Nathan for this long, she doesn't really want to leave him. Hiking is a chance to talk some more. It's a chance to find out more about Lily too.

"Let's go fast then, work up some body heat." Kai rubs his hands together and then turns, looking out over the terrain, and Rylie notices the small notebook in his back pocket. Her dad used to carry one too, to write down song lyrics. "I thought this was a desert," Kai goes on. "It's cold out here."

"It's January out here." Rylie shrugs off her jacket. "You can come if you wear this, O," she says to her brother, and he practically beams as he puts it on.

"Ready?" Sara waves them toward the trail, and Nathan starts up first, his boots crunching over the rock. Rylie lets Owen take her wrist and then starts forward too, guiding him. The moonlight's glowing over the sand and rock around them, and the wind picks up as they go along.

"That looks ancient, Owen. What is it?" Sara asks, and Rylie turns to look. Beside her, Owen's holding up his Talkboy with his free hand, the red dot glowing.

"I like to record people with my dad's old Talkboy," he says. "But sometimes I use an app on Rylie's phone, when she lets me."

"You used to make up stories too." Rylie lags a little to match his pace. "For a while you narrated everything I did."

"Like a scribe," Kai says.

Owen nods, grinning over the attention. "I like recording sounds too. The noises the desert makes are different from anything I've heard before."

Nathan glances back at them. "Lily used to say that. She used to . . ." He trails off, as if he's struggling to find the right words. "I just . . ." He clears his throat. "I want to forget sometimes," he finally says. "But I can't keep away either."

He nods at the path ahead, and Rylie realizes exactly where they are. It's the same trail that Lily took. The arroyo trail, the one she went down and never came back from. That little warning voice goes off in her head again: *We shouldn't be here. Owen shouldn't be here.* But she forces herself to keep walking. No matter how beautiful it is at night, no matter how many call it home, the desert will never shake its reputation. Life-taker, destroyer. It's because of the hit-and-runs from drivers speeding across intersections too few and far between, and because of the people who die in the heat, and the tourists who get lost hiking.

But Lily knew her way around. And then Rylie can't stay quiet anymore, she can't *not* ask him. "Nathan, did Lily ever—"

"How about we talk about something else," Nathan says. He manages a smile, probably to soften shutting her down. He used to do that around Lily too, smooth out every stunt his sister pulled. He's the kind of person who never wants anyone to feel left out, never wants confrontation. Owen's a lot like him, actually.

"All right. Want a fun fact, Leap?" Kai rallies, trying out the nickname on her brother. "I heard on this documentary that the Joshua tree only grows in two places on Earth. Here and Jerusalem. One is the gate to heaven and one is the—"

"I heard that before too," Sara cuts in, "but what about the facts that count? Like that assho—I mean, that company out of Los Angeles trying to bottle up what little water the desert has? They're taking *water* from the *desert*," she says, hardly stopping for a breath. "And what about the tourists who litter everywhere, or cut down the trees for firewood? And don't get me started on the tour companies."

"Leave no trace," Nathan says casually, stopping at a small clearing. "It's not that hard." He unzips his backpack. "I've got water, if anyone's thirsty." He glances at Rylie first, holding her gaze too long. Maybe he realizes it too, because he suddenly looks away, a small smile at the edge of his mouth like they're sharing another private joke. "And I've got Sara's tea," he adds, pulling out a thermos. "She sells it at the local cafés. It's that good."

"Here, try it." Sara offers some to Kai, but he's already sitting on a rock and drawing on his forearm, and he doesn't hear her. Rylie takes out her Nikon and snaps a few shots of the group, then leans toward her stepbrother for a better look. He's sketching a surprisingly good profile of a girl on his skin.

"Who's that?"

Kai glances up sharply, like she startled him. For a second she doesn't think he'll answer. "Roza Shanina," he finally says.

"Girlfriend?" Sara asks.

Kai shakes his head. "She died a long time ago."

Nathan freezes, his pack only halfway zipped. Then he finishes and turns to Rylie, a forced smile on his face. "Try that tea. It's the best I've had."

"In that case . . ." Rylie takes a sip, and it's warm going down. "It's like Goldilocks tea."

Sara nods. "Not too bitter and not too sweet?"

"Right. But sweet enough for an eight-year-old," Rylie says, walking the thermos over to Owen. She sets it down just shy of him because he's standing near a boulder, talking into his recorder about the hike, and it's a perfect moment for her Nikon. She backs up to get him and the boulder and the stars in the frame when there's a rattling sound close by. She instinctively goes still. "Don't move, O," she says, forcing her voice to be calm. "It's just a warning."

"I'm not moving," Owen whispers, and then the sand lightens around them and she turns, expecting Nathan with a flashlight. But it's just the moon, low in the sky, shining over the empty clearing. The rattling has stopped.

Rylie lets out a breath and turns back to Owen. But he's not there. He's not where he was standing a second ago. "Owen?" She rushes forward, veering around the large boulder. All around her is moonlight, a silver sea of cholla plants. No Owen.

She has to find him. She hurries back around the boulder, back to the clearing. "Kai? Nathan?"

No one answers—they're gone. The clearing looks different somehow. There's no trail. Instead, there's a sign she doesn't remember seeing before: KEEP OUT. MILITARY FIRING RANGE. The sign blurs as a wave of dizziness hits her.

"Owen?" Her stomach feels wrong, like she's eaten something bad, but she's hardly eaten anything. The punch that Kai brought her, the tea from Sara. The thermos is missing too. It's not where she put it.

Rylie stumbles into the empty clearing. Her feet feel like they're too far away from her body. "Owen!"

Height, she needs height. She needs a better view. She turns back to the boulder, eyeing it, finding the first hold with her fingertips. A rush of adrenaline gets her moving. If she can reach the top, she'll see Owen and the others, or at least the glow of lights from the party.

The climb up is hard. The rock is slick for some reason, or maybe her hands are sweating even though there's a chill in the air. She nearly slips on the last hold, but she pulls herself up, stands.

Nothing. There's no one. Rylie turns a full circle. Her heart starts to thud louder. The moon is bearing down on her, so close and bright, it's almost blinding. She doesn't see Owen. She doesn't see anyone, just open desert. Way in the distance is a plume of smoke.

The warning is back in her head as a hot panic floods her stomach. *We shouldn't have come here. We shouldn't have come here.* The desert air crackles across her skin, and the sounds are sharp around her—loud, crisp. The scuttle of a scorpion. Snakes slithering across the ground. The fluttering of wings. A growl.

At the base of the boulder is a coyote, eyes yellow-green in the moonlight.

Rylie shifts closer to the edge. A second coyote is watching her too. She stares back at it, and for some reason she thinks of Lily. Then another sound makes her turn, and fur and flesh and teeth swarm her right before she slips.

Reasons for Admittance:
Altered mental status with presumed
head trauma.

History of Present Illness:
Patient separated from friends while
hiking in Joshua Tree. Found hours
later, incoherent, severe headache.
Patient unable to recall events. Mother
reports some subtle changes in behavior
in days preceding incident but no
personal psychiatric history or history
of drug abuse.

Hospital Course:
Head CT negative for skull fracture or
bleeding. Mild abrasions on physical
exam. Toxicology screen negative. EKG
normal. Patient regained baseline
mental status, alert and oriented x 3,
within 12 hours of admission.

Discharge Diagnosis:
Concussion from presumed head trauma,
resolved. Lack of cardiac, metabolic
and neurological explanation suggests
an accidental fall while hiking.

CHAPTER 6

THE NEXT DAY, RYLIE'S HEAD is fuzzy with painkillers. She stuffs her discharge papers into her pocket as her mom pulls away from the base hospital, the same one she went to as a kid. It looks smaller than it did before, and she was in more pain back then too. This time she came out relatively unscathed—a few scrapes on her arms and a small bruise on her forehead. But because she'd been found unconscious, they kept her overnight for observation. Her mom stayed with her in her room, and Ben and the boys showed up first thing in the morning. It was sweet but also a little stifling.

"Anyone can wander off the trail," her mom says, catching Rylie's gaze in the rearview mirror. "Even seasoned hikers."

"Mom told us that it's the top reason for needing search and rescue," Owen adds.

"Well, I'm glad you rescued my Nikon too." Rylie makes a show of pulling it out to check it for damage. She doesn't want to rehash what happened when they found her, not as if she remembers it. All morning, Ben and her mom quizzed her, but she keeps coming up short. Her memory feels slippery, like a dream, and the Nikon isn't any help. Part of last night's hike in the desert is there: Owen with his cane, Nathan's thumbs hooked under the straps of his backpack, Sara raising her thermos, Kai sketching on his arm. The last one's a blurry photograph of the rocky ground, and then the pictures end.

Rylie shoves the camera back into its case too fast, and a jolt of pain shoots up her elbow. She tenderly unravels the edge of the gauze that the nurse wrapped around her arms. The crisscross of scrapes doesn't really look like the cuts she's had from bouldering before, and the veins along the undersides of her wrists are darker somehow, almost swollen. She hurriedly wraps them up again, accidentally bumping Kai in the process.

"So nothing's coming back to you?" he asks. He's wearing a red Volcom baseball cap, and he pulls it off to peer at her. "Nothing at all?"

"The specialist wasn't worried," Rylie says, shooting him a look.

"Yeah, but could he even *assess* you?" Kai shakes his head, and then thumps the guitar crammed in front of his legs. "That guy was ancient."

"Sara's mom told us that Dr. Singh has a great reputation," Ben says, turning in his seat. "It's nice that she could fit you in with him this morning. Feeling a little better about everything?"

"Better" would be an overstatement, but Rylie sits up straighter and feigns it anyway.

"He basically just said to follow up if I have any more symptoms." She pulls his card from her pocket. On it is the familiar US Marine Corps emblem—eagle, globe, and anchor—and the number to call if needed. "He said the memory loss was probably from the dehydration, or the mild head trauma."

"Which still makes me wince when you put it like that," Kai says. He picks up his guitar and then starts strumming. "What you need is some R&R," he sings in falsetto, "or else you won't get very far." If he weren't overdoing it, it would almost be ominous.

"The wandering bard returns," Rylie says, just as her phone beeps with a text. As usual, Owen snags it from her and turns on VoiceOver.

"It's Lourdes," he announces just as an automated voice comes over the speaker, reading out Lor's text. When Lor demands an update, Owen brushes back his curly hair with a quick swoop of his hand and grins proudly. "I messaged her when you were in the hospital. I bet she wants to hear about yesterday."

Rylie reaches for the phone. "I just wish I remembered."

"I, for one, wouldn't mind forgetting," Kai says, and Owen nods.

"Yeah, especially when we found you, and you didn't want to come with us, and—"

"Owen." It's a warning from their mom, but he keeps talking.

"You started hitting Mom—"

"Owen, enough."

"And then you told us we were all going to die."

She said they would *die*. Rylie feels her cheeks go warm. It's obvious that her entire family's trying not to stare at her.

"Hey, we all know that's unlike you. You were disoriented," Ben says quickly. "You'd hit your head."

"The good news is, you don't even remember it, right?" Kai says, and Owen lets out a sudden laugh. The pressure on Rylie's chest lifts, just a little. She forces a smile, and Kai takes her lead and clangs out another chord. "If a tree falls in the woods and no one hears it, does it make a sound?" he half sings.

She smiles, a real one this time. "Does the moon exist if no one's looking at it?"

"It does, doesn't it?" Owen asks, his eyebrows narrowing with concern.

"I don't know. I don't remember," she says. It's meant to be a joke but it falls flat, and then Ben turns in his seat again.

"You know, I've been thinking about the memory loss," he says, pushing up his sleeves. "If it's really bothering you, there are some avenues you could consider. Hypnosis, for instance."

Kai shakes his head. "When you throw around words like 'hypnosis,' I always think of that old Sinatra movie *The Manchurian Candidate*. Brainwashing. That sort of thing."

"Remember that comedian in San Diego, Rylie?" her mom asks, glancing at her in the rearview mirror. "He hypnotized everyone onstage, made them think they couldn't even move. They all saw their worst fears."

"Brainwashing? *Stage comedians?*" Ben looks aghast. "I'm talking about hypnosis for noble means. Like when we used it to curb your nightmares, Rye. It works for memory regression too."

"What's that?" Owen asks, switching on his voice recorder and pushing it into Ben's face.

"Let me use an analogy," Ben says, clearly happy to explain. "May I?" Without waiting for an answer, he leans to pluck the pen from behind Kai's ear and starts sketching on his own palm. He draws a large diamond shape, then slashes a horizontal line through it.

"Imagine an iceberg, half-submerged in the ocean." Ben taps his palm, showing Rylie. "The tiny visible portion of the iceberg, the part above the surface, is your conscious mind. And the rest—"

"Is your subconscious," Rylie finishes.

"Don't encourage him," Kai says, smirking.

Ben thumps him on the knee with the pen. "I could talk shop for days. Mind-icebergs in particular."

"We know," Kai and Rylie's mom say at the same time.

"So the key to memory regression is really just about relaxing into the right state of mind." Ben's still using his therapist voice. "If done properly, hypnosis can help you access your subconscious, where repressed memories are stored."

Rylie leans forward. There's usually fine print. "And if not done properly?"

"It's possible to implant false memories in a subject." Ben glances at her mom as they pull into the driveway next to Kai's battered Volvo.

"Please don't implant any memorieeees," Kai sings. "Very confusing, that would *beeeeee*."

"Which is why your mom and I think you should wait a bit, let your memory return organically," Ben says, ignoring Kai. "We discussed it with Dr. Singh too."

Rylie shifts in her seat. So her mom and Ben have been talking about her, privately. It's starting to feel too much like before: the hushed whispers, the concern.

"Focusing on the last thing you remember might help. Just give it some time," Ben goes on. He flashes her a reassuring smile that looks genuine. He's always genuine, actually, and at least he's being straight with her.

"We found you, Rye; that's what matters." Her mom cuts the engine. "Just think of . . ."

She trails off, but Rylie knows what she was going to say. *Just think of Nathan's sister. Just think of Lily Seguin.* And Rylie has been—she was thinking of Lily right before the hike. She'd been looking for her grandpa's journals, but they weren't in the cabin. That's her last clear memory. Her last clear memory that makes sense, anyway. Her stomach churns with unease just as her phone beeps. It's Lourdes again. *Who was there when I got sixteen stitches from the Vespa accident? Who was there when I puked at the opening night of* Macbeth *last year?*

Another beep and a picture of a road sign comes through,

with the mileage to Twentynine Palms on it, the sprawl of the desert in the background. *I'm already on my way,* Lor texts, but there's a dark smudge in the photo that makes Rylie do a double take. At the very edge of the picture is something that looks like roadkill. After she enlarges the photo, it seems more human than animal—dark hair, flesh. A *person?*

She blinks, and the thing transforms back into fur. It's just her head, messing with her again. She can't trust herself here. The drive from San Diego proved it, and the hike did too, and then her fingers are already typing a text before she thinks it over. When she glances down at her screen, she's almost surprised to see her message:

Don't come.

She's waiting for Lor to reply when she hears her mom call out. "Ben," her mom says in an odd voice. She's standing just outside the jeep, staring up at the house. "The front door is wide open."

CHAPTER 7

"WE WERE IN A RUSH to get back to the hospital," Ben says as they get out of the jeep. "One of us must have forgotten to close it."

"Let's make sure that's all it was." Her mom marches up to the house, the boys trailing behind her. Rylie grabs the painkillers and her Nikon and is just locking the jeep when her phone rings—it's Lourdes on a video call.

"Hey, I—"

"Of course I'm coming," Lor interrupts, flashing her an indignant look. She's wearing one of her vintage dresses, this one tea-colored and sleeveless, and she's standing next to a gas pump. "You need a nursemaid."

Rylie laughs, but her head starts to hurt. "I don't."

"Well, I've got a couple of days before my next audition, so I'm coming anyway." Lor gets into her car. "Also, my aunt wants me to see my cousin, so there's that. He hasn't been home since starting college out there."

"I want to see Iggy too," a guy with a British accent says, and Lor angles the phone. Miles Giroux, Iggy's boyfriend, is sitting in the passenger seat and pulling his hair into the man-bun he always wears. "Iggy's been so busy working with his professor and studying the desert *bees* that he never comes to visit," Miles says, "so now I've got to get a lift there, even with the"—he lowers his voice in mock fear—"*commune killer* on the loose."

Rylie grins. "Come up with a better name than that if you're trying to scare me, Miles."

"You didn't hear?" Lor says, turning the phone back on herself. "That's what the news is calling him. They found another body last night."

"Just outside Joshua Tree," Miles adds. "So let this trip be a testament to how much we adore you and Iggy, right? And to our bravery."

"Wait," Rylie says, walking toward the house. "You don't—"

"We're coming," Lor cuts in. "See you soon, my little Rye." She ends the call just as Rylie steps inside, letting her eyes adjust to the dim light.

"You all right?" It's Ben, but he's not talking to her—he's pulled Kai aside in the kitchen. "I know last night was hard on you," he says quietly. "The police and the search party and . . ."

"Rylie?"

She turns to see her mom, who's already back in uniform, her laptop wedged under an arm. "The open door was all clear," her mom says. "And now I need to go to work, so Ben's watching Leap. You should get some rest." It's a thinly veiled order, but it's her mom who doesn't look well—her usually tidy hair is loose, and dark circles surround her eyes, making her blue one stand out. Last night wasn't kind to anyone.

"You need sleep too."

Her mom shakes her head. "I need to shave five hundred million off the budget, and nobody wants to give up their babies. So I've got my work cut out for me." She reaches out and squeezes Rylie's shoulder. "Go on, go relax. I'll rest after work."

"Deal." Relaxing is the last thing Rylie wants to do, but at least it's an excuse to head upstairs alone. Ben's pep talk in the car gave her an idea. She hurries up the steps with Castle on her heels, and opens the door to her grandpa's library. Custom bookshelves line the high walls, shelves her grandpa built to match the exposed beams on the ceiling. Right now stacks of boxes are everywhere—Ben has been turning it into his home office.

"Come on," Rylie whispers, but Castle just whines in the doorway, watching her with his head tilted. "Fine, be my lookout," she says, and then she starts searching the room, not quite sure what she's looking for. Ben must have already started unpacking, because the shelves are filled with textbooks, mostly dense tomes on psychology, and a surprising amount on history too. She's just started on another shelf when her phone beeps with a text from Nathan.

You feeling okay? Can I stop by tonight after work? Another text pops up: *I want to talk about yesterday.*

So do I, she texts, but what Sara said at the party, about

Rylie not knowing Nathan that well anymore, had planted a little pebble of doubt in her stomach. Now it feels like a fist-sized rock, lodged right below her sternum, right where her belay slipped once, dropping her ten feet to the ground. Trust is a precarious thing—once it breaks, it's hard to get back, which is why she wants to remember what happened last night. Nathan chose the trail. Nathan led them to the clearing.

Rylie shakes the thought away. Of course getting lost wasn't his fault. Only . . . Only, it happened before, years ago. Lily and Nathan led her down a trail and then vanished on her. She had to find her way back to Thea's cabin alone, and it took so long that she ended up with a sunburn that peeled for days. But they'd just been kids, playing around. Lily and Nathan both swore that they thought *she* had left *them*, and there was no reason not to believe them. They were her friends.

Call me when you get off work, Rylie texts. Maybe by that time she'll remember more of what happened. She shoves her phone into her pocket and starts scanning the shelves again. Just then there are footsteps, and Castle gives a little yip as Rylie spots a thin textbook: *Becoming a Hypnotherapist: Techniques for Addiction, Pain Relief, and Memory Regression*. It might do the trick. She grabs the book and heads out the door, running straight into Kai in the hallway.

"In a hurry?" Her stepbrother is dripping wet from the pool, his dark hair weighed down by water, the ink on his arm smeared. His gaze goes to the open office door behind her.

"I was looking for old *National Geographic*s," Rylie says before he can ask. It's always better to lead when on the defensive—both her parents taught her that. "Lourdes is driving all the way here, and I remembered she could use them. For her latest collage," Rylie adds. "Like that one she did of the Little Golden Books."

"Where she rearranged the images into disturbing pictures . . ." Kai looks between Rylie and the open door again, dripping water onto the carpet.

"Might want to get yourself a towel?" Rylie swerves past him and into her room. She settles onto the bed and opens the book, then finds the chapter on memory regression. She needs the bit on *self*-hypnosis first—better not show anyone her so-called mind-iceberg if she can help it.

The chapter is long and she scans it, lingering on the section about memory loss; there's a list of potential causes. Stress, hypothyroidism, vitamin B_{12} deficiency, tumors. But Dr. Singh thought her case was pretty clear-cut, and all she wants right now is information on how to actually *remember.* Then her brother's voice rings out from downstairs, something about the latest audio file on his Talkboy, and Rylie shoves away the textbook. Owen would use YouTube as a research hack. She grabs her earbuds and pulls out her phone for a quick search on self-hypnosis. Links from MindzEye, HipHyp, and Enlightandlove show up first, no surprise, and she clicks on the shortest video. A second later the screen is filled with a glowing infinity symbol, and ambient electronic music starts playing as a gentle voice says, "Please get into a comfortable position."

Rylie leans against a pillow, setting the phone down beside her. Her dad was into meditating for a while, until her mom made fun of him for it. Then he only did it when he was driving, which seemed like a bad idea, even then. *It doesn't have to make you sleepy, Little Lee,* he told her. *It's fine, I promise.*

"Now I want you to pick a spot on your hand to look at," the gentle voice commands, "and look at only that spot."

Rylie stares down at her bandages. Underneath, her skin is hot and itchy, but at least the sticky feeling is finally gone.

"Each time you hear my voice, you'll find yourself getting more and more relaxed, until your eyes decide to close," the voice goes on. "And when they do, you might try visualizing your favorite place, real or imagined."

Her favorite place. She shuts her eyes and imagines Denali, and then Owen's dream—a trip to the base camp at Everest—but her mind suddenly flashes to a beach. She's walking with her mom and dad, her hands in theirs, her mom's hand greasy with coconut oil and her dad smelling like smoke. They're swinging her between them, and she's taking great big leaps and then digging her bare feet into the brown sand. Jump and swing, jump and swing. The air smells salty, and waves are lapping against the shore, and her dad is singing David Bowie's "The Jean Genie," and all she wants to do is see him again, just once.

"Now hold that favorite place in your mind as you take three deep breaths."

Rylie breathes and tries to stay with the memory. The pillow feels hard under her neck.

"When you're ready, think of the event you wish to recall, and a feeling you might have experienced at that time. While you think of this feeling, your unconscious mind will take you back to when you felt it. You might see an image appear in front of you, like an image on a movie screen."

The feeling she remembers most about yesterday is confusion, but that's not what she was feeling on the hike, not at first. She was worried about finding her grandpa's journals, and about Owen keeping up, and she was worried about Nathan too, because of Lily, and then all of a sudden the memory comes sharply into focus and it's like being there again: the cabin a shadowy hunch as they walk away from it, the moonlight turning everything gray, Owen and Kai and Sara behind her on the narrow trail, Nathan ahead.

"Now tell me what images you see," the voice says. "You may choose to speak aloud or silently."

"We were hiking. We stopped for a drink." Rylie squeezes her eyes shut tighter. She had her Nikon out, and then . . . the memory fades away. "This isn't working," she says.

"What's not working?"

Rylie snaps her eyes open. Kai's standing in her bedroom doorway, jeans and a Kylo Ren shirt on, his hair still wet from the pool and his guitar hanging from a hand. Two new decals are on it: THE TRUTH IS OUT THERE and TRUST NO ONE, each phrase stamped below Gillian Anderson's face.

"All right if I come in?"

Before she can tell him no, he shuts the door behind him, strides over, and plucks the book from the bed, flipping to the cover. "Hey, I know this one. Memory regression, right? I've tried it before a couple of times."

She pulls out her earbuds. "Why?"

Kai grins. "Probably for the same reason you are." He's already tidied up the sketch on his arm—a mountain range this time—and it reminds her of last night's hike at Joshua Tree. "You should just ask Ben to regress you," he says.

She shakes her head. "Anything I tell him will get back to my mom, and I want to know what happened first. Don't mention it to them, okay?"

Kai smiles again, the glint in his eye looking anything but innocent. "Just say what you're really thinking, Kai."

His smile widens. "What gave me away?"

"It's that look. You use it on Ben to get what you want."

"Can you blame me? It's effective." Kai pulls the pen from behind his ear. "The thing is, I want to know what happened to you, Rylie. You tried to attack us when we found you."

She goes tense with the reminder. "I was confused."

"*Exactly*," he says, nodding. "Plus you don't remember leaving the trail, and Owen basically only has light perception, right? So he didn't see what happened to you."

"We've been over this, Kai," she says, but he keeps talking.

"Owen says you warned him about a snake, and by the time it was gone, you were too." Kai opens the book. "And now your mom keeps asking me about it, like she thinks I'm holding something back." He raises his eyebrows and lets his point sink in before flipping to a page and tapping the heading: *Memory Regression with a Partner.*

"So let's set the record straight, shall we?"

Rylie almost laughs. "Thanks but I'll pass. Ben told us that if you do it wrong—"

"You can implant false memories? Not going to happen." Kai angles the book at her. "Look, there's a script to follow." He taps the page again. "I'll put you under, and you'll remember."

He's making it sound simple. Easy. And since the self-hypnosis was a dead end, it's worth a try. "Keep to the script," she says. "Don't change a word."

Kai grins and the glint in his eye is back. "What, don't you trust me?"

CHAPTER 8

HER STEPBROTHER'S VOICE ISN'T AS soft as the recording, but somehow it's still lulling, and when he counts down slowly—*five, four, three, two, one*—an image comes to Rylie: a boulder, gray in the moonlight. The one she fell from.

She's lying on the ground next to it—rocks are digging into her arm from how she landed—and she scrambles to her feet, feeling dizzy. A few feet away is a coyote, watching her. Another is at the edge of the boulder. They seem . . . especially large. Their paws look dark, almost cloven.

She crouches down and grabs a loose rock. *Just in case.* Then she steps back. Another step. She feels cold and slow on her feet, and she still can't see the trail.

One of the coyotes growls but doesn't move. She tightens her grip on the rock. There's a searing pain at her temples—she must have hit her head. A burst of heat lightning flashes across the sky, lighting up the ground and the boulder she fell from. On its side is red graffiti: WE ENTER THE CIRCLE AT NIGHT AND ARE CONSUMED BY FIRE. Next to it is a drawing of something that looks like a star, or six long, razor-sharp petals surrounded by a circle. Above the circle is an arrow and the number sixteen, and it suddenly reminds her of something.

Her grandpa's cabin—the number that's etched into his door. So the arrow . . . might be pointing toward it?

She raises the rock as she takes another step back. The coyotes aren't following her. It's fine; she's fine. She turns, and a shadow flits past. At the edge of her vision, other shadows start to move, hunched things with too-big heads and shining eyes.

Oh God. She throws her hand over her mouth. Everywhere, all around her, are yellow-green eyes.

There's another burst of lightning, and then she's running, sprinting in the direction the arrow points. Overhead, more bright gashes tear across the sky. She gets a burst of speed, her necklace thudding against her collarbone, her breath ragged. It's just ahead—her grandpa's cabin. She hears a faint whistle, hears her name in the distance. Kai must be calling for her, Nathan too.

But she can't see them, and the cabin is closer.

She keeps running, passes a gaping hole in the yard, comes up to the door. Reaches for it.

And then, all of a sudden, she stops.

There's a humming sound in her ears. Something cold seeps inside her chest. A tight feeling, a heavy dread. Something terrible is coming. Something terrible is already here.

She slowly turns around. Behind her is a girl covered in blood.

It's me.

It's me.

———

"Rylie, stop! Wake up!"

She blinks, rubs at her eyes. Her face is wet, her heart pounding. Kai's hand is on her shoulder, and a gasping sound is coming from somewhere close.

"Deep breaths," Kai says, and she realizes that her chest is heaving and she can't get air. She leans forward, her whole body tense, desperate. It's like she's at a higher altitude, that's all; it's like she's trail running up Mount Laguna, keeping a fast pace. *I can do this; I can breathe. I can breathe.* She stares down at the bandages on her arms until her lungs start to work, and then she shrugs off Kai's hand.

"I'm fine now." But she's not; she feels like she did on the drive here when she thought she'd hit someone, and her shirt is drenched for some reason, just like her face. Her eyes narrow on the dog bowl Kai's holding. "You threw Castle's water on me?"

"You were doing this really freaky thing with your breath, and then when you started screaming—"

"You're kidding."

"Usually. Not now." Kai shoves the hypnosis book at her.

"Five percent of people are highly suggestible. You must go really deep, like you're asleep or something. Dad will kill me if he knows we tried this."

"That's why we're not telling him." But it's not Ben she wants to keep it from. It's her mom.

"You were talking about coyotes, how they were everywhere." Kai picks up his guitar, absently runs his pick over it. The strings are out of tune. "I'm no wildlife expert, but I'm pretty sure coyotes don't normally travel in packs. What do you think—"

"A panic attack," Rylie says, sounding it out. "I saw two coyotes, and I panicked and thought there were more."

It's one explanation. There's another one too. Dr. Singh told her that head injuries can cause visual hallucinations. But something else is bothering her about the hypnosis, something Kai wouldn't understand.

"And that graffiti on the boulder," Kai says. "'We enter the circle at night and—'"

"Hang on a minute." Rylie pushes past him and heads into the bathroom. The front of her shirt is wet and sticking to her skin. In the mirror, the bruise on her forehead looks dark and tender, and she clutches the granite counter to steady herself. She feels dizzy. She feels like she did last night. Flashes of the hypnosis come back: the coyotes, the cabin, the hole in the yard, what she saw when she turned around . . .

She stares at the mirror and squeezes the pressure point on her hand. Probably it was nothing. Probably it was just her imagination, all of it. But now she needs to go back to the cabin; she *has* to. She has to go for Lily. Her reflection blurs in the mirror, and she shuts her eyes until she feels steady again.

When she walks out of the bathroom, Kai is sketching on his forearm. "That regression was pretty wild," he says, and Rylie sinks down to the bed, her head still spinning. It's probably the painkillers—the pharmacist mentioned side effects. Once the dizziness passes, she'll drive out to the cabin. She'll see what was true and what wasn't.

"You all right?" Kai asks.

She nods at his forearm. "Another girlfriend?"

"Her name's Noor Inayat Khan. And no, not a girlfriend." He finishes drawing the eyes, and it's almost like they're looking out, watching her, and when Kai glances up at her too, it's like she's seeing double. "Sure you're good?" he asks.

She doesn't want to talk about how she's feeling. "Tell me who this Noor girl is," she says to distract him. "Wait, let me . . ." She pulls out her phone and searches the name, and the first thing that comes up is a Wikipedia link. Kai tries to grab her phone away, and she turns, shielding it.

"Okay, okay," he says, giving in. "She worked in occupied territory—"

"As a British spy during World War II until she was tortured and killed." Rylie finishes reading and lowers her phone. "And you drew her on your arm? That's . . . weird."

Kai shrugs. "I have a thing for history."

She glances between the photograph on her screen and his sketch. "It's a good portrait anyway."

"Let's drop it. We were talking about *you*."

"Ben never mentioned you were into art," she presses, but now Kai seems to relax slightly. "The music I knew about," she says, "because of that song and dance thing you roped me into at their wedding, but—"

He grins. "Hey, who doesn't like a rowdy Nat King Cole? It was *unforgettable*, right?" He groans at his own joke and then taps the pen against the bed in a quick rat, tat, tat. "You're a lot different from how I imagined you too, you know."

"How did you think I'd be?"

A wry smile is playing across his face. "The hiking and climbing were unexpected." His smile widens. "Being strait-laced wasn't."

"Is that right?"

"Well, I've met your mom."

It's not a jab—he says it easily, like Owen might. Like it's a shared joke between family members. And Kai and Rylie *are* family; that's what her mom and stepdad keep insisting, anyway, even though Kai was hardly around before, but right now she's glad he's here, keeping her mind off the things she doesn't want to think about.

"With you," she says, "I expected a miniature Ben."

Kai shrugs. "I'm a little like my dad," he says. Then his mouth scrunches up. "Hold up, what's a mini Ben to you?"

It's an easy enough question. "Perpetually upbeat, zero cynicism, open-book kind of guy. A good listener too."

"What? What'd you say?" Kai jokes. Then he tucks his hair behind his ears, studying her more intently. "You know, if I were a mini Ben, I'd be analyzing your hypnosis. I think we should talk about what you saw."

The room suddenly feels crowded. "What's the point? It got messed up. My imagination took over."

"I think we should talk about it anyway." Kai sounds concerned—almost protective—the same way she gets around Owen. "You pretty much hyperventilated earlier, and you look terrible right now, to be honest."

"Thanks." She doesn't keep the sarcasm from her voice.

"I'm just worried about you. And—"

"Don't be." She strides to the door, hoping he'll take the hint, hoping he doesn't notice when she holds the knob a little too tightly, steadying herself. "There's nothing to worry about, because the hypnosis didn't actually work right." She swings open the door and finds Owen standing just outside her room. "Hey, O," she says, going for casual. "Come in if you want."

He lingers in the doorway, looking hesitant. Almost afraid. "Is everything okay?" he asks. "I heard screaming."

CHAPTER 9

EVERY TIME RYLIE TRIES TO sleep, she sees the coyotes, their yellow-green eyes everywhere. The coyotes, the hole, the open door. Her head is aching and her mind keeps replaying the hypnosis and now she can't stop thinking about Lily and the hole she saw at the cabin. She has to go back to look, in case it means anything for Lily. But she's been trapped in her bed, and not just because of her mom and Ben. All day they kept knocking on her door to ask how she was feeling. She couldn't tell them about the hypnosis, because most of it didn't make any sense. She also couldn't tell them about being too dizzy to drive out to the cabin. Now moonlight is shining through the window as she finds her earbuds and pulls up the one playlist that might help her sleep off the dizziness.

The acoustic guitar starts up first, slow and mournful, then: "Out among the rock and sand, they say to be careful for snakes," she hears. "They say to watch for getting burned, and all the things you hate." Her dad's voice is steady, melodic. "But I say don't believe what you hear, because the desert's where I found you."

She whispers the words to the rest of the chorus. "And yes, it's dangerous, just like love, but it's also good and true."

Another song starts, and Rylie grabs her Nikon and turns it on. She selects the folder she's never moved off the memory card, the one that no one ever sees but her. The first shot always hits the hardest. It's the one she took of her dad, his hair wild with curls, his eyes crinkling at her little brother, a newborn in his arms. Owen was three when he died. Owen doesn't even remember him.

Owen. She slides off the bed, suddenly wanting to check on him. It's a habit. She used to tuck him in whenever their mom had to work late. As she walks down the hallway, she feels steadier on her feet—skipping her last dose of pain-killers must have worked for the dizziness. In front of her, the door to Owen's room is cracked and he's sleeping soundly, curled up on his side, the sheet pulled up to his tousled hair. There's a faint humming sound in the room as she steps inside. It's the radio; he likes to fall asleep to it or his Talkboy. Even with her earbuds still in, she can hear Mojave Mix talking about the second "commune killer" slaying, how it happened at a gas station off Highway 62. The same highway she drove to get to Twentynine Palms. A wave of dizziness hits her as the report continues.

"The seventeen-year-old suspect, Ethan Langhorne, was caught on video, and the public is being asked to come forward with any information, and to take careful measures—"

She turns down the volume. Her brother stirs but doesn't wake, and she leaves the room just as her phone beeps. It's a missed call from Lourdes—it didn't even ring. When Rylie taps on the voicemail, it won't play, so she sends a message: *I thought you'd be here by now. Where are you?*

Text dots appear right away, and Lor's response comes through:

Hey, so we had to turn around because I forgot my wallet, and then I kid you not we got a flat tire and my cell service cut out. Iggy's on his way to pick us up. It's late so I'll see you tomoooorrow!

Rylie tries calling, but the line goes straight to voicemail. She's about to try again when her phone beeps. This time it's Nathan.

Hope you don't mind if I drop by? Her phone beeps an instant later. *Actually, I'm already here. I didn't get a chance to call first.*

She wants to be annoyed but instead she's the opposite as she hurries down the stairs in the near-dark, slowing when the world starts to tip again. Then she pulls her sleeves over her bandages and swings the front door open. Nathan's in the yard, holding two lawn chairs and smiling. Seeing him in front of her makes it impossible not to smile back.

"I gave you a fifty-fifty chance of coming outside," he says, grinning now. He glances at the truck behind him. "Thea was my secret weapon. She wanted to see you too, but she fell asleep on the way over."

Rylie nods at the lawn chairs. "And you thought I wouldn't invite you in?"

"After last night," he says, turning back to her, "I wasn't sure."

"You're showing up late too. That's always a risk. The Sandman and all." She says it lightly, but a shadow crosses his face and he rubs at his hair.

"Sorry, I got held up at work, and then I had to change and—"

"I want to talk to you too." The truth just tumbles out; she's telling him exactly what's on her mind, like she always did before. This is the problem. It's a bad idea to be out here with him, especially after what she saw in the hypnosis, but she can't seem to make herself go back inside.

"I keep playing it over in my head," Nathan says, setting down the lawn chairs. "When you got lost?" She doesn't miss the question in his voice, like he's waiting for an explanation she doesn't have. "One minute you were there, and the next you weren't. Kind of like the last time I saw you."

He's talking about yesterday's hike, but he's also talking about four years ago, the last time she visited her grandpa's house. How she left without saying goodbye. A breeze hits her neck, and suddenly the air between them feels more intense.

"I remember it differently." She sits down in one of the chairs and pulls her knees up to her chest. It's like she's reverting to being thirteen all over again; all her old habits are coming back. Nathan's must be too, because he sits down right beside her. His arm grazes hers, and another chill shoots down her neck.

"I shouldn't have pressured you into hiking," he says. "It's my fault we went."

"It's nobody's fault. I'm fine. Really." *I'm fine.* She's been saying that a lot lately. If Ben could hear her now, he'd pick her apart. "I've had worse, anyway."

"I've seen you worse." Nathan's looking up at the sky now. "The tibia summer."

"The tibia was the easy part. Lily's the one who scarred me for life." It's out before she can stop herself, but the corner of Nathan's mouth turns up.

"She was all, 'Walk it out, walk it out,'" he says, mimicking his sister, and it's so unexpected that Rylie laughs, and then Nathan's laughing too. When they stop, the silence seems so much more quiet, and she doesn't feel the need to break it. *Sit with silence, Little Lee,* her dad used to say. *Let it sing to you.* She never really understood what that meant until now.

"Rylie?"

Nathan's dark eyes are on hers, and she can't look away. "Yeah?"

"When you were missing yesterday," he says, his voice just above a whisper, "I kept thinking that right when we'd gotten you back, we'd lost you again."

For one swift second, hope flares inside of her. It feels like everything they used to have is still *here*, still between them.

"And then I couldn't stop thinking about all the search parties last year, the ones that never ended the right way for Lily." Nathan pulls a small box from his pocket and taps out a toothpick. He puts it in his mouth and then takes it out a second later and twirls it between his fingertips, its cinnamon scent lingering. "I was worried the same thing had happened all over again."

Rylie tightens her arms around her knees. What she saw in the hypnosis almost slips out. "Are the police still looking for her? Did they talk to neighbors? Her friends?"

"Friends?" The tone of Nathan's voice is hard to read, and so are his eyes. They've changed: the tiny scar across his left eyebrow is still there, but underneath his dark lashes there's a gravity to his gaze.

"The police have been doing what they can, apparently," he says. "They claim she ran away—well, left home *willingly*, which is bullshit. Lily doesn't run from things. She runs *toward* them."

"Did she leave a note?"

Nathan shakes his head. He looks like he's going to say something more, but instead, he just keeps his mouth shut, his jaw tight.

"What do you think happened?" she asks, steeling herself.

Nathan sighs. "I actually didn't come here to talk about Lily." The toothpick is gone now and he starts twisting his leather bracelets. "I came to talk about you," he says, and when his eyes go to hers, it's like he's not looking at her but *into* her, into her very soul to measure what it's made of. Sitting next to him makes her feel like she can't stay hidden—it feels like she's rising up and outward, into the space between them. It feels like she's touching him even though she isn't, like a part of her has floated up into the air and brushed against his skin.

"Seeing you yesterday caught me off guard," Nathan says softly. "Thea told me you and your mom might come by, but it was still a shock. You seemed . . . different from before."

Different in a bad way.

That's what it sounds like he means, and the world narrows a little, hardening at the edges, and then Rylie is back on the lawn chair in her own skin. Nathan can't see into her soul, and he can't see what she's hiding either, but it's for his own good.

"Four years is a long time." She resists nudging him with her shoulder like she would've before. "I didn't think you'd be living here anymore. You always wanted to move away, see where Thea's from in Canada, see everything. Climb the seven summits." He would bring it up every summer, rattling off the list whenever he could. She still knows it by heart. "Everest, Denali, Kilimanjaro, Vinson, Elbrus . . ." She expects him to finish but he doesn't.

"I always was a dreamer," Nathan says. "I also wanted to invent a video game about saving the world, remember?" He rubs at his dark hair again, and when he pulls his hand away, his hair is mussed and spiky, just like it used to be. "Do you ever feel like no matter what you do, the life you want gets further and further away?"

"Sometimes," she says. Nathan did this when they were kids too. He'd talk like he could read her mind. "Sometimes it feels like I'm not in control of anything." Like last night, how she attacked her mom when they found her near the hiking trail. Like four years ago.

"I thought you'd get it." His voice is just above a whisper again. "On top of everything else, it feels like I'm losing Thea too, because of her memory." He looks away. "And—"

He doesn't finish, so she says it for him. "And Lily's still missing."

Nathan slowly nods, gives her a lopsided smile. "Why'd you stop talking to us, Rye? When we were younger."

She expected him to ask, but her stomach still tenses up anyway. "I guess when my grandpa cut off contact with us, it was just easier."

"Your grandpa cut off contact before he died?" Nathan's brows knit together. Maybe he thought it'd been the other way around.

"He and my mom had a fight, that last summer we were here. About my dad, about what happened to him. About Owen too."

"I'm sorry."

"So am I." It's hard to look him in the eye, but she does. "Mom told me we wouldn't be coming back, so I just . . . I decided not to want a reason to."

Nathan nods again, and then he does the worst thing possible—the reason she didn't want to tell him in the first place. He stands. "Hey, it's late, isn't it?"

He says it casually enough, and it's definitely getting late, but before they would have talked for hours, they would've laughed more. She packs up her chair, deciding how hard to hold on.

"On the hike yesterday, when I got lost, I thought of Lily too." It isn't the whole truth but it's part of it. She hands her chair over, and Nathan doesn't step away like she thought he might. He's standing close now and looking at her again. She should tell him what she saw in the hypnosis—she should tell him about the cabin, where she thinks Lily could be. Her lungs tense, and she almost spills everything she's holding back—the hole she saw, the blood—but something stops her. She needs to go see for herself first. See what's really there before telling Nathan. *Tonight*, she thinks. She'll drive out tonight. She'll go to the cabin as soon as he leaves.

"Nathan?" The truck door creaks open, and they quickly step away from each other as Thea gets out and heads their way. "Feeling okay, Little Lee? Nathan told me what happened."

It's still hard to hear the nickname, and Rylie's throat squeezes. "It really could've been worse."

"Yes, it could have," Thea tells her. "Be more careful," she adds, almost brusquely. She smooths Rylie's tangled braid like she used to, brushing the stray hair away. "And I have something for you but I forgot to bring it. I've been hanging on to it since your grandpa's funeral last year. I thought I'd see you there."

"You went to his funeral?" Rylie asks. She hates how small her voice sounds.

"Of course I did," Thea says. "Nathan did too." Her eyes

go watery. "Lily was already gone by then." The little huff she makes sounds like frustration. "Anyway, come by to get it soon, will you? Nathan would like that too."

Nathan lets out a cough or a laugh—Rylie's not sure which one—and then Thea looks between the two of them, her brows raising almost imperceptibly.

"Well, I'll start up the engine," she says, walking back to the truck and climbing in. "I'll just shut this . . ." She slams the door closed, too loudly, and this time Nathan definitely laughs. Some of the tension has left his shoulders, and he turns back to Rylie.

"Are you around this Wednesday?" he asks, and just as she's wondering why, he keeps talking. "There's a party at Sara's if you want to go. Her mom's got a double shift at the hospital, but it's not like she cares," he adds quickly, suddenly reminding her of the kid she knew before, the one who never broke the rules or let anyone down. The kid who never hid anything from anybody, unlike her. "Sara's parties usually involve pressing flowers, or, you know, origami or body paint."

"You had me at 'flowers,'" Rylie deadpans, because it feels good to see him less serious, and then his smile does something funny to her stomach.

"Wednesday it is," Nathan says, getting into his truck just as her phone beeps. It beeps a second time like it's mimicking her racing heart, and she glances down at two new messages from Lourdes.

Still waiting on Iggy to pick us up.

He swears he's coming.

Lor texts again—*Try me now before my phone dies*—as Nathan reverses out of the driveway, lifting a hand to wave. She waves too and then calls Lor as the truck pulls away. The call goes straight to voicemail. Rylie gets a tingle of unease, but at least Lor's not alone and Iggy's on his way.

She needs to go too. In the far corner of the house, her mom's bedroom light is off—she must be asleep. Rylie hurries inside for her car keys, hoping Castle won't bark and trying to process her conversation with Nathan. Inside, the shutters are drawn over the windows and there's hardly any light and she wishes they didn't have to live here, in this big husk of a house.

"Rylie?"

She stops halfway down the hall. Her mom is standing in the darkness and looking very much awake—she hasn't even changed out of her uniform yet.

"You're not going anywhere, are you?" She flicks on the hall light, and Rylie braces herself in the brightness. "Until you heal up, I want you staying close," her mom says, and then she steps forward and hugs her. "Plus with the news lately . . ."

"I know, Mom," Rylie says. She pulls away, and a wave of dizziness hits her again. There's no leaving for the cabin tonight, not now. She'll have to drive out first thing tomorrow. She owes that much to Nathan. And she owes Lily even more.

CHAPTER 10

In the morning, the skin around her scrapes is hot and red, but she's not dizzy anymore and Lor is safe with Iggy and Miles—she texted an update late last night. Rylie texts her back, and then she smears ointment over her arms, wraps them with fresh gauze, and heads downstairs and straight to the jeep, wanting to get to the cabin fast. A neighbor's minivan is practically inching down the street in front of her, and she gets a sudden, strange urge to slam into it, just as her phone rings—it's Lor calling.

"Finally," Rylie says, switching her to speaker. "Are you still at your cousin's dorm?"

"Iggy won't let me leave." Lor's voice sounds faint through the phone. "It's like he doesn't want me to see you." Lor's always blunt, but maybe she realizes how that sounds, because she keeps talking. "Not *you* you, just anyone. He's trying to convince me and Miles to drive back to San Diego. It's weird," she says. "The whole trip out here was weird. I'll tell you about it later. In person."

"When?" Rylie speeds through a yellow light. "You're still coming over, right?"

"Of course I am. I'll be there by dinner, I promise," she says. "But what about your text? You said you needed to talk. ASAP."

Rylie suddenly regrets her message, and she doesn't want Iggy or Miles overhearing either. "It can wait."

"Hang on, I'm taking you into the bathroom for privacy." A door creaks shut. "Right, what's up? And don't do that thing you usually do. Just tell me. Also please hurry because I'm choking on aftershave in here. I can taste it."

Rylie shoves sunglasses on and veers onto the highway toward the cabin. What she'd seen during the memory regression with Kai kept her up most of the night, especially after talking to Nathan. The bad feeling leaks into her chest again, and she's not sure if she's making too much of it. She needs to make sure she's making enough of it too.

"So you know how people use hypnosis to remember things?"

"I do now," Lor says.

"Okay, so yesterday I did one to remember the hike."

"Did it work?"

"Sort of," Rylie admits. "It actually reminded me of something else, too. Something that happened when I was a kid."

The phone goes muffled; then Lor's voice comes through. "And?"

Rylie lets out a breath and plunges ahead. "When I was about ten, I was playing near my grandpa's cabin, racing around in his yard." The memory isn't a bad one, or it wasn't in the moment at least, but looking back . . . "And then I fell."

"You fall all the time. You climb things and you fall."

"This was different. I fell into a hole in his yard that I didn't know was there. I dropped down fifteen feet and broke my ankle."

Lor makes a wincing sound through the phone. "What was it? A well? Oh, I know. One of those old mine shaft things?"

"No, it was a tunnel. There was a ladder down it, and a doorway at the bottom." Rylie clenches the steering wheel, and the cuts on her palms sting. "Turns out it was an outside entrance to a basement under my grandpa's cabin. He called it his safe room." There's irony in the name—she's just now seeing it. "Usually the opening was covered, but he forgot on that day. He made me swear not to tell anyone."

"Jesus," Lor says quietly.

Rylie skips the part about the blood. She skips the worst part too: how the basement door at the bottom of the hole was open, how her grandpa was inside the windowless room, bent over a table with a wire cutter and a radio. He must have heard her hit the ground, he must have heard her cry out, but instead of rushing to check on her, he set down whatever he was working on and made a note in his journal. Her ankle bone was sticking out and she was screaming, but he took the time to make a note. Then he opened a drawer and tucked everything away before striding over to her, the wire cutter still in his hand.

"Jesus," Lor murmurs again. "You remembered all that because of the hypnosis you did?"

"Not exactly." Rylie clenches the wheel harder, this time wanting to feel the sting on her palms. "Last night, Nathan talked to me about Lily. About how looking for me on the hike was like looking for her." Her mind flashes to the hypnosis: running toward the cabin, seeing the dark hole in the yard. "The Seguins live next to my grandpa's cabin. And Lily was last seen hiking on the trail right next to it. What if—" She can't say it aloud, and maybe Lor knows it, because she cuts in.

"Let me get this straight. You're telling me that your ex-boyfriend's sister—"

"Nathan wasn't ever—"

"Anyway, Lily's been missing for a year, and she was last seen near your grandfather's cabin." Lor exhales a sigh. "Where there's a hole she could have fallen into." Her voice has an edge to it now. "That no one knows about but you." She sighs again. "It's probably fine but—"

"I have to check it."

"Yeah." There's a clatter like she's dropped the phone. "Why do I hear that humming noise again—" Lor's words are lost; it's a bad connection.

"You there?" Rylie asks, and then the line goes dead. A second later her phone rings—it's an unknown number but maybe it's Lor calling back—and she picks up right away. "Hello?"

"I saw you," a man says. She doesn't recognize his voice.

"I think you have the wrong number."

"I saw you," the man repeats. "I saw what happened," he says, and Rylie instinctively cuts the call. Her mouth is suddenly dry. A wrong number, that's all it was. The view out the windshield is desert wilderness—no one's in sight. No one's watching her. She grips the wheel tighter, suddenly aware of how alone she is as she looks for the turnoff to the cabin. It reminds her of the night she drove out here, how empty the road felt until suddenly it wasn't. That thud, that lump under her tires, the stickiness on her hands. She pushes the thought from her head and then dials Lor.

"Hey, I tried to call back but it wouldn't go through," Lor says. "Are you almost there?"

"I'm here," Rylie tells her, just as the small cabin comes into view. She parks and gets out fast, before she can change her mind. The air is dry and cool as she jogs toward the back, her hiking boots crunching over the rock, the phone still on speaker. There are bees buzzing nearby, and the minty scent of desert sage. She squints into the sunlight at the yard and the arroyo trail beyond. It all looks harmless, even beautiful. No wonder developers build resorts out here. People want palms and pools and a pristine view that makes them forget about all the billions of people crowding in on the world— the stark opposite of the desert.

"So is it there?" Lor asks.

"Give me a minute." Rylie turns away from the trail and starts searching close to the cabin, between tufts of cholla and behind spiky Joshua trees. Something thorny gets at her ankles, stabbing her through her leggings as she slowly circles the yard. And then she finds it, but it's not the gaping hole she saw during the hypnosis. It's not a hole at all. She nudges it with her boot. The tunnel down to the basement is closed off, its cover shut. She crouches to run her fingers over the rough mound of dirt, the metal lip just visible, and tries to yank it up. It's either stuck or locked.

"The lid's down," Rylie says into the phone. "And if it's shut, then Lily couldn't have fallen in." Another thought comes to her, and her stomach twists. "Unless it shut after she fell."

"Can you get in another way?" Lor's voice sounds distant as Rylie heads around to the front. She still has the spare key—she kept it the other night. She's about to shove it into the lock when she stops, staring at the etchings on the door. Below the number sixteen is that circular flourish that she noticed before. She steps closer, running her finger over it. It's a circle surrounding a flower with six pointed petals— almost identical to the graffiti she saw during the hypnosis. It's suddenly hard to breathe.

"You still there?" Lor asks.

"Yeah." Rylie snaps a picture of the etching and then switches the call to video as she unlocks the cabin and opens the door, her eyes adjusting to the darkness inside. For a second it looks like the furniture has been moved, but as she opens the door wider, light seeps in and everything rights itself. The room looks the same as she left it on the night of Thea's party—the night of the hike.

"It's exactly how I expected," Lor says through the phone. "Kind of a rustic chic, huh?"

"Or rustic hick," Rylie says, hurrying down the hallway and nearly tripping over a hiking backpack on her way to the small bedroom. And there, crammed in the corner, is a mattress and a built-in shelf full of antique cameras, just like in the main room. Only here the shelf is a façade, another excessive touch of her grandfather's. Rylie reaches for the black Leica in the middle and holds her breath as she turns the lens.

There's a clicking sound, a lever lifting, and then the entire shelf creaks open. In front of her is a concrete stairwell: dark, dusty. When she raises her phone, Lor gasps with delight.

"Your grandfather was ahead of his time, wasn't he? Anyone with money has hidden rooms these days. Celebrities, politicians, even . . ." Lor's voice is breaking up again. "Hey, how did you know to get in this way? I mean, I know you fell down the other—"

"He carried me up the steps," Rylie cuts in. "After I fell that day." He took her to the base hospital too, exerting just enough effort to make it seem like he cared, but after that she watched him even more. Her grandpa always kept track of everyone at the house and cabin, but she kept track of him too. Maybe it would finally count for something. She flicks on her phone's flashlight and starts down the stairwell. It smells stale, and it's airless, and she wants to turn back. Instead, she moves faster.

"I'm getting motion sickness," Lor says.

"Almost there." Rylie hits the bottom step, and everything goes quiet. Her screen's black—the service must have dropped. She crouches down and runs her fingers along the rough concrete floor. At the edge of the last step, the key's tucked into a crack, right where it used to be. Finding it should feel like a victory but it doesn't—now she's out of excuses.

Now she has to go inside.

CHAPTER 11

THE PHONE LIGHT JERKS, STREAMING over the basement's concrete floor and throwing shadows. Rylie ignores the wave of goose bumps on her arms and heads straight for the back corner of the room, to the outside door there. When she reaches it, the door knob is cold to the touch. She steels herself as she heaves it open, its hinges creaking, and then she aims her phone light.

On the concrete floor in front of her is a rust-colored stain. Her breath goes shallow as she steps forward with the light, adrenaline coursing through her. Along the wall is the narrow metal ladder running to the surface, to the opening she fell through so long ago, her ankle shattering. But no one's here now—Lily didn't fall too, she didn't get trapped down here. Rylie checks the dark corners again, just to be sure. Then her light snags over something small and slender.

It's a bone.

Her heart skids as she bends down to inspect it. Not a bone—just a small rusty tool. She kicks it away and straightens, rubbing at the bandages on her arms and her itchy skin underneath. *Lily isn't here.* For a second it feels like a weight's been lifted from her shoulders, a weight she didn't even know was crushing her. Nathan must feel like this every day. Every day he probably wonders where his sister is, why she hasn't come home. Lily isn't here—but she's still missing. And so are her grandpa's journals, the daily accounts of what he saw and heard. If what Sara said was true, if Lily really *did* disappear on the trail near the cabin, then maybe finding the journals could help find her. Maybe her grandpa hid them down here.

Rylie turns back to the basement, her phone light casting it gray. The room's clean, tidy, efficient. Half of it is devoted to stacks of water bottles and canned goods, complete with a utility sink. The other side of the room has a wall of shelves and cabinets, and against another wall is a large worktable with drawers. Pinned above the table are maps and papers, and lying on top of it are neat coils of electronics, a stack of yellow legal pads.

She sets the phone light on the chair and opens the drawers first. There aren't any black Moleskines, nothing resembling the journals she remembers, so she aims the light at the table, at the stack of yellow legal pads. Her grandpa's handwriting is at the top.

Shutters shut and open so do queens. Shutters shut and shutters—

"This isn't . . ." Rylie scans down, reading quickly. Then, from somewhere in the cabin she hears a creaking sound.

She goes still, watching the basement door. It doesn't open. Everything is silent. She lets out a breath and glances back at the yellow paper.

Exactly as resembling, exactly resembling, exactly in resemblance exactly and resemblance.

The scrawl becomes illegible until the note at the bottom: Gertrude Stein wrote this when she vis . . . Rylie can't make out the rest, but at least she knows what she's looking at now. It's just a poem, not one of his journals.

She tosses the yellow pad back onto the table and keeps moving as another shudder of goose bumps crawls over her skin. Beside the table is a small bookshelf, and she drums her fingers over the top of it, the sound as fast as her fluttering pulse. The Moleskines aren't on the first row, or the second, or the third. She's turning away when her beam of light hits the wall, revealing faces.

Photographs.

It feels like someone's pressing on her ribs, clamping them down. On the wall are pictures of children and adults and teenagers, but mostly teenagers. And Lily Seguin. Lily is in the center, looking straight at her. Saying, *I'm right here. You found me after all.*

Rylie snatches Lily's picture off the wall. Then there's a thud overhead and she turns so fast, she knocks the chair over. The thudding's on the stairs now, and she grabs the first thing in sight—a wrench—and raises it, ready to swing.

The basement door opens wide, and a shadowy figure pauses in the doorway.

"Rylie?"

Kai. It's just Kai. But her heart is still going fast in her chest, and it's enough to make her angry. "How'd you get in? Did you *follow* me here?"

"You left the cabin door open," Kai says. "I was on the trail and saw your jeep."

"Why were you on the trail?"

"To find that boulder with the graffiti on it. The one you saw during the hypnosis," he tells her, but he's hardly looking at her. He's looking around the basement. "What *is* this place anyway?" He flicks on his phone light, and his eyes fall on the photographs. "What's that on the wall?"

She has no idea what it is, and maybe a part of her wants him to see it, because it's almost too much to take in alone. "I think my grandpa—" She can't say it, can't finish the thought.

"What about that?" he asks, nodding at her hands.

She glances down. She's still holding the wrench and the picture too. "It's Lily. Lily Seguin."

"The missing girl, right? Why do you have her picture?"

"I didn't. My grandpa did." Rylie turns back to the wall, to the photos there. They don't make sense. *Lily* doesn't make sense. "Why would he . . ." She feels her whisper die in her throat.

Kai steps closer, shining his phone light. And there they are, lit up again, all the faces. He stops asking questions, and somehow his silence makes it worse.

"It's strange, right?" She has to say it out loud—she has to make sense of the churning feeling in the pit of her stomach, the feeling that it's all wrong, that there's something terrible here, because *strange* isn't half of it. "That he'd have all this, locked away down here?"

Kai glances over his shoulder at her. His face is surprisingly neutral. "Your grandpa did contract work when he got out of the military, right? Security-type work? That's probably what this is."

"Maybe." She wants to believe it, but she doesn't, and maybe Kai doesn't believe it either. He's trying to give her an out, but she can't take it. She can't brush this off as normal. Her eyes start to sting as she stares down at the picture in her hand. The black hair, that cynical smile. Lily disappeared a year ago, right *before* her grandpa died—Thea said that in the driveway last night. So maybe he'd been trying to help find her. It'd be easy enough to call Nathan to ask, but then she'd have to explain *why* she was asking. Her grandpa's journals would also have answers. She sets down the photo and turns toward the cabinets near the worktable, then opens the closest one. Inside are more piles of wires and cords. She swings open the next one, and at first she doesn't understand what's in front of her, the rows and rows of thin clear boxes.

"Are those old cassette tapes?" Kai steps toward her. "They're smaller than eight-tracks, aren't they?"

"I don't know what an eight-track is, Kai," she says, picking up one of the containers. But he's right, there's a small tape inside. The thin plastic is light in her hand, and the label has a name on it in black permanent marker: s. PARKER. All the tapes have names on them. She's just turning away from the cabinet when she sees it, in big letters across one of the labels: ETHAN LANGHORNE.

Her breath stalls in her lungs. Black marker. Neat print. As clear as clear.

"What is it?" Kai asks.

"We need to call the police."

She grabs the tape, but Kai reaches out and pulls it from her hand. "It's that guy who killed someone," he says. "The guy from the commune." His voice drops to a whisper. "Should I play it?"

Rylie folds her arms across her chest. Her bandages feel hot. Her whole body feels hot. "Play it."

Kai shoves it into the recorder. The tape clicks on midsentence—it probably needs rewinding—but now that it's on, she doesn't want to stop it.

"No one believes me." A male voice, coming through the speakers. Maybe it's Ethan?

After a pause, Rylie hears another voice, a lower one: "I believe you, Ethan."

Her heart kicks into gear again. It's her grandpa. It's her grandpa talking to Ethan Langhorne.

"Sometimes," Ethan says, "sometimes I get angry." She hears him breathing through the speakers, and a chill passes over her.

"Sometimes"—he's louder now—"I want to make them believe. I want to make them afraid."

"What are you willing to do about it?"

This time, there's a longer pause on the tape. Then Ethan comes back on. "I want the money first. Then we'll talk."

The tape runs out.

For a minute there's only silence. Rylie feels numb, half-paralyzed, but she forces herself to reach forward and pull out the tape. "We have to tell someone. We have to tell the police. If this is really Ethan Langhorne . . ."

Kai nods. "I know." His mouth twists up. "It's just that . . ."

"What?"

"Nothing," he says, turning away.

"*What*, Kai?"

He shakes his head, like he's trying to figure out how much he should say. "It's just—your friend Lily."

"What about her?"

"Well, you want to know why your grandpa had her picture, right? If you tell the police about this tape, they'll take it all." He sweeps his arms out. "Everything down here. It'll probably just sit around in some storage locker. I mean, your grandpa died a year ago, so it's all pretty old, right?"

"Kai, I *have* to tell them." She holds up the tape; she's practically crushing it. "We can't keep this a secret."

"That's not what I'm saying." He shakes his head. "Listen, Rylie, what if there's something down here that will lead you to your friend? If you hand everything to the cops, they'll prioritize finding that Ethan guy over finding Lily. I've seen it happen before."

"They wouldn't." But even as she says it, she knows she's wrong.

"What if you give yourself, I don't know, a day or two to figure out what you're looking at?" Kai picks up the photo of Lily and hands it back to her. "I'll help if you want."

She lets out a breath, thinking it over. What's the harm in keeping it, just for a day or so? And if she's really going to comb through everything, she'll need help. She'll need someone unbiased, someone emotionally uninvolved. Lor would be good for that too—she should be leaving Iggy's dorm soon anyway. Between the three of them, maybe they really *could* go over everything, find out if there's anything more about Lily. And then she could turn it all over. Then she'd tell her mom and Nathan what they'd found too.

"Okay," she says. "Let's do it."

CHAPTER 12

AFTER LISTENING TO THE ETHAN Langhorne tape at the cabin, Rylie can't focus on anything else, not on Lourdes and definitely not on dinner. Ben made a production of it since Iggy and Miles came over too, and now they're all sitting at the massive cedar table, candles lit, the windows open to the glowing pool in the backyard. In front of them are bowls of Ben's homemade ramen, along with fried eggplant and skewers of red peppers and shiitake, all of it vegan for Iggy.

"Thought we'd never make it here," Lor says, her brown eyes wide, mascara slightly smudged. "Poor, broken Camilla. At least she's all fixed up now."

"Who's Camilla?" Ben asks.

"Her car," Iggy sighs, pushing up the sleeves of his jacket. He might be Lor's cousin, but they act nothing alike, and he keeps glancing at his watch like he's too busy to eat, and right now Rylie feels the same way. Next to him Miles has been busy charming everyone with his grin and enthusiasm over the ramen, as if his British accent wasn't enough to do the trick.

"Anyway, Camilla got a flat tire and *stranded* us in the

desert," Lor says, lowering her voice dramatically. "After it happened, our phones stopped working. And then we kept hearing the strangest noise."

"A humming sound?" Owen asks, leaning forward in his seat.

"It was probably a power line." Rylie's mom helps herself to another skewer as Rylie picks at hers, still thinking about what she found in the cabin.

"And *then*, since our cells weren't working," Lor goes on, "we flipped a coin to see who had to walk to a gas station for help."

Kai points his skewer at her. "You watch horror movies? Splitting up in a bad situation is never good."

Lor nods, her hair dangling across her bowl of ramen. "True, but splitting up is actually *very* good if the whole time you're with someone, he keeps jumping out at you and screaming, 'Serial killer, serial killer!'"

Miles gives a sheepish grin. "It was a rare opportunity I couldn't pass up."

Iggy looks over his glasses at Owen. "Should we really be talking about this?"

"Agreed," Rylie says, trying to speed things along. Dinner needs to end soon, so she can focus on the cabin, figure out how Ethan Langhorne was connected to her grandfather. And why.

"Don't worry." Her mom pats Owen's hand. "Owen's already been following the headlines."

"They're everywhere!" Owen says. "Did you know that people aren't supposed to go out alone after dark anymore?"

"It's called a voluntary curfew," Rylie says, glancing down at her phone. A curfew, because of the murders. Because of *Ethan*. Ever since finding the recording today, she's been checking for news updates too. But so far running searches on Ethan hasn't turned up much. He isn't on social media, and the photograph that the news keeps showing is a year old, from his junior prom at Black Rock High—bleached hair, acne, shy smile, a too-big sports coat. And that's where the trail ends. Apparently he was mostly absent from school since last year's prom, and his legal guardian has "declined to comment." Other than that there's no mention of family members or friends. No sports teams or after-school jobs. And no reason for him to have crossed paths with her grandfather.

"In fairness, Miles isn't the only one sensationalizing things right now." Ben gets up from the table and busies himself at the stove, then brings over more fried eggplant. "The media gets a kick out of scaring people."

"Still, I'd prefer that you all follow the curfew at night," Rylie's mom says. "And be careful any time, for that matter."

"Yeah, especially Rylie," Owen adds. The table goes quiet and Rylie starts thinking of the hike again, how she attacked her mom when they found her, and she pushes her bowl of ramen away.

"Well, Iggy said the exact same thing to me," Lor says,

probably trying to break the tension. She nudges her cousin. "He totally freaked out last night when I finally got a call through and told him we had a flat tire."

"Breaking down out here can be dangerous," Iggy warns.

"Says the guy who wants to work with bees for a living," Kai jokes.

"Well, I'm with Iggy," Rylie says. The little food she's eaten is sitting heavily in her stomach. "You can't rely on cell service in the desert."

"All right, enough about our trip here," Lor says to everyone cheerfully. "How's the move been so far? Besides Rye's hiking disaster, which she told me all about before dinner, among other things."

"Other things" being the cabin. Rylie exchanges a look with her. Earlier, she gave Lor a quick rundown while Miles and Iggy made small talk with Ben, and Lor swore secrecy.

"Yeah, what's it been like being back, Eve?" Kai asks. "You're the one who grew up here."

Rylie stiffens—she knows exactly what Kai is fishing for, but her mom only shrugs. Somehow she's making eating noodles look efficient and easy, like everything she does. "It's better than I expected, actually."

"But it must be a little hard for you, right?" Kai presses, drenching his ramen with chili oil. "I mean," he says, "Ben mentioned that you didn't really get along with your dad. Is it because of something he did?"

Rylie holds still. Her mom goes tense too—she's gripping her chopsticks like they're her service pistol—but then she smiles. "For me, it was more about what he *didn't* do that bothered me." Her blue eye looks dewier than her brown one as she squeezes Kai's hand, and Rylie sends him a glare.

"What didn't he—" Kai starts, but then a phone beeps and everyone checks their pockets. Rylie has a message from Dr. Singh's office, reminding her of her follow-up this week, but it's her mom who's already texting furiously.

"Just give me a minute," she says without glancing up. "It's work again."

It's also an exit. "Actually, we're about finished," Rylie says loudly, piling up the bowls.

"Miles and I have to run too," Iggy says. He stands and shakes hands with Ben. "Thanks so much for dinner. Best I've eaten since starting the term out here."

"Come over anytime," Ben says, and beams. "I swear not to serve anything with honey."

"Oh, the sweet, sweet beeees," Miles drawls out as Rylie and Lor walk them to the door. "Who knew such a small insect would require so much studying?"

"Speaking of . . . ," Iggy says, checking his watch. He quickly doles out his goodbyes and then hurries down the steps. Miles gives them both a cigarette-scented hug before hurrying after him.

"Well." Lor swings the door shut. "I told you Iggy was acting weird. Did you know he got into a fistfight recently? *Iggy*," she says, watching him through the window. "A fistfight." She shakes her head. "One of these things is not like the other."

Rylie nods, but it's hard to think about anything but Ethan Langhorne and what she found at the cabin. "Come on," she says, taking the stairs two at a time. Kai's already waiting for them at the top, just outside her room.

"Time to roll our sleeves up, right?" he asks, throwing them a meaningful look as they all head inside.

"I think we went too far tonight at dinner." Rylie shuts the door. "You two weren't exactly subtle."

"If we want to figure out what your grandpa was doing with Lily's picture, we need to dig," Kai says.

"Unless you want to just tell your mom what you found?" Lor asks softly.

Rylie tugs her sleeves over her bandages and shakes her head. "I don't even know what I found."

Lor nods, her face going thoughtful like it does when she's dreaming up stage choreography. Then her mouth gives a little twitch, which means she's decided on something. "In that case, let's go back to the cabin to investigate." She opens Rylie's closet with a flourish. "But I'm borrowing a pair of running shoes. These vintage oxfords will *not* hold up if we have another breakdown."

Her lightness is catching, and Rylie tries to match it. "Don't spoil your look. We actually brought everything back with us."

"Sister, may I?" Kai asks, and even though he's joking too, it still feels strange to hear him call her that. Before it has a chance to sink in, he upends the backpack they took from the cabin. The taped recordings come tumbling out, including the one with Ethan Langhorne's name on the label. There's also her grandpa's cassette player—smaller and less clunky than her dad's Talkboy, but just as ancient. Beside it are the maps, rolled up, and the photos from the wall in his basement.

"All that fit in there?" Lor asks. "It's like a small car where too many clowns come out."

Rylie pulls the pile toward her. Now that it's out in the open, she wants to snatch it all up and shove it back into the bag. But she can't, because of Lily.

"Let's divide and conquer, see what we got." Kai tugs away the maps. "How about I take these and—"

"I'll take the photos," Lor cuts in. "That leaves the old-school audio for you, Rye."

The pile is diminishing. Rylie tenses as Lor scoops away all the photographs and sinks to the floor while Kai shoves on his thick reading glasses, jet-black like his hair, and hunches over the maps at her desk. He even pulls out the notebook he keeps in his back pocket, flips to a blank page.

"I'm going to take digitals of these," Lor announces from where she's sitting with the pictures. "And then I'll—"

"Do a reverse image search, figure out who the others are," Kai says without looking up from the maps.

"Yes, sir." Lor mock-salutes him and then pulls out a pair of cherry-red headphones from her overnight bag. They match the red in the rainbow nail polish she's wearing. "And you'll need these, Rye," she says, tossing the headphones.

"Thanks." Rylie shoves a few of the tapes into her pockets

and grabs the old cassette player, then opens the door to the balcony. "I'm going to get some air."

"You're not doing the roof thing, are you?" Lor asks. "You almost fell that one time at my mom's house."

"I'll focus better." The cool breeze hits her face as she steps out, heading to the balcony's railing. Far below her, standing on a side street off Sundown, is a guy in a dark jacket. The light from her room must catch his eye, because he looks up, right at her. A second later he shouts for his dog and starts walking off. From up here, the dog almost looks like a coyote, and she shivers before climbing onto the ledge.

CHAPTER 13

ONCE SHE'S UP ON THE roof, Rylie swings her legs off the side and stares at the long drop. Vertigo doesn't bother her—a ledge gives a sharpness to the world, a clarity. Balanced, unbalanced. Solid object, thin air. She grips the slats, feeling strong, in control. Being up here, high up like this, makes it seem like the stars are closer, and the darkness too. She lifts a hand to adjust the headphones and then carefully pulls a tape from her pocket. There weren't any other Ethan Langhorne recordings in the pile so she chose the one labeled S. PARKER. When she shoves it into the old cassette player, there's a scratching sound, and then:

"Did you do what I told you?" her grandfather asks. Then a woman's voice trickles out—it's too slow, too loud.

"I don't know," the woman says. She sounds unsure of herself, and Rylie leans back against the roof, listening.

"Everything's blurring together. I can't keep track."

"Then you'll be caught," her grandpa says.

Rylie stops the tape. *You'll be caught.* In the Ethan Langhorne tape, there was talk of payment. *I want the money first,* Ethan said. She presses play again, and the wheels scratch.

"I can't control it anymore. I go on walks to calm down, but sometimes I can't remember anything when I get home. It feels like someone else is taking over."

"I told you what to do." Her grandpa again, short on patience, and then there's a long silence.

"I almost ran over my neighbor the other day," the woman says quietly. "She was walking her dog past my driveway, and I just thought, *I could tell everyone it was an accident.* I just, I *wanted* to do it. Strangers . . . seem ugly to me. Everyone seems ugly. Every living thing."

"Can I give you some advice?"

"I'm here, aren't I?" The woman's voice has hardened. "You're always so patronizing."

"You need to do what I ask. You need to keep quiet."

"I make my own choices."

"Do you?"

"That's not fair. I never meant to kill any—"

Rylie hits stop, then rewinds the tape and punches play again. She holds her breath as the woman's voice repeats itself: "I never meant to kill any—"

"There's a place you should go," her grandpa cuts in. "There are others like you there."

"Others like me?" All the anger's gone from her. Now she just sounds scared. "I don't want to be around others like me."

The tape ends abruptly, and Rylie yanks the headphones from her ears. Her arms are itching and she glances down. The gauze is full of bright red splotches—she must have scratched at her bandages without realizing it—and then the woman's words echo in her head: *I never meant to kill.*

The hike comes back to her again: how she attacked her mom, how she told her family they would die. She gets the sudden sensation of being watched, almost like Lily Seguin is on the roof with her somehow. Rylie shakes off the feeling and grabs her phone, finds the track she needs. She'll just listen for a minute, to clear her head, then she'll go back to the tapes. A second later there's the clang of a guitar and she shuts her eyes, shutting out everything but him.

"Out among the rock and sand," her dad sings, "they say to be careful for snakes. They say to watch for getting burned, and all the things you hate . . ."

Her phone pings and she glances down. It's her news app; there's an alert with the latest on Ethan Langhorne. She clicks the link.

> Authorities have recently confirmed that
> Ethan Langhorne is the son of Carl Gregory,
> a Black Rock resident who killed his wife
> and two young daughters. His son, Ethan
> Gregory, now known as Ethan Langhorne, was
> seven years old at the time. Ethan was the
> sole survivor of the tragedy.

The next article goes on to say that Carl Gregory later killed himself in prison. Rylie closes her eyes, suddenly nauseous. Ethan was about Owen's age when it happened. She doesn't want to read any more, but she can't help but look at the photos attached to the article. One of them is the day Carl Gregory was arrested. In the picture two police are flanking him, and he's got his arms behind his back, his head lowered. On his face and neck are thick, ropy scars.

"You still up there, or are you a pancake?" Lor's voice is loud through the window, and Rylie startles, then edges down the slats and onto the balcony. But the lights in her bedroom seem too harsh now, like hospital lights, especially when Lor starts spreading the photos from the cabin on the bed.

"To find out why Lily's picture was on your grandpa's wall, we need to find out why the others were there too," Lor says. "So that's what I've done." She gives Rylie a look. "Hey, perk up. I promise this isn't what you think it is. Forget about the Ethan Langhorne tape for a minute."

But it's not just the Ethan tape. Rylie feels the nausea creeping up her throat. *I never meant to kill.* That's what the S. Parker woman said on the recording. Rylie should tell Lor and Kai about it—it's just on the tip of her tongue—but something stops her. It won't hurt to listen to Lourdes first, hear her out.

"What did you find out?" Rylie asks, and Lor taps a manicured finger on a photo of a girl on the bed. The girl's about their age, with curly brown hair and an LA Galaxy hat on.

"Let's start with Mackenzie Soren." Lor tosses her phone onto Rylie's lap. "She's a senior at Mojave High, just north of here." An article's up on her phone screen: *Local teen goes missing on school field trip.* Rylie rereads the headline as Kai leans in. The article has a quote from Mackenzie's parents about how she's an honor student and a competitive swimmer, how she helps out at the Boys and Girls Club on the weekends and wants to major in environmental science. They've held fundraisers to try to help find her, they've hung signs on bridges and left flyers at gas stations, they've begged for someone, anyone, to come forward with information.

Lor gently takes the phone back. "So far she's still missing." She nods at another photo—this one of a man a little younger than Ben. "But not this guy." She flashes her phone at Rylie again, and the headline makes her stomach clench.

BELOVED MUSICIAN AND FATHER OF TWO FOUND DEAD NEAR CAR; POLICE SUSPECT FOUL PLAY.

"Jed Hendersen, thirty-nine years old, singer-songwriter and resident of Wonder Valley. It's rural. Close to Twenty-nine Palms."

Rylie slides off her bed and grabs Kai's notebook from her desk, then writes down both names.

Mackenzie Soren, 17, missing
Jed Hendersen, 39, dead

She grips the pen too tightly, and it digs into the scrapes on her hands. Lor points at another photo, this time of a white-haired man with a kind smile—he looks like the grandfather Rylie always wished for.

"Juan Ramon-Ortez. Sixty-two." Lor seems extra animated, like she's playing the part of the girl detective. "He went missing from his home near the Mojave National Preserve a couple of years ago. He had early-onset Alzheimer's, his family claims. He was friendly too. Always picking up hitchhikers on I-40."

"And what about the kids?" Kai asks, nodding toward them, and Rylie forces herself to look at the two photos, side by side. A dark-haired boy, his chin jutting out, brown eyes. A skinny-looking girl, smiling.

"I don't know." Lor's voice softens. "Nothing came up on them."

Rylie sets down the pen. Without names, she can't add them to her list. She doesn't *want* to add them.

Lor clears her throat; her eyes are watering now too. "The next is Emily Okada." She points to a photo near the end of the row. "A history professor who went missing on a camping trip to Black Rock Canyon, not far from here. It was her first vacation in years. Her son claimed that when he woke up in the morning, she was gone."

The list is getting longer—too long—especially when Rylie adds the twentysomething tourist couple who were last seen eating breakfast at Sierra Trails RV Park before their bodies were found in the desert, and the teenager who ran away from rehab in Palm Springs.

Mackenzie Soren, 17, missing
Jed Hendersen, 39, dead
Juan Ramon-Ortez, 62, missing
Emily Okada, 49, missing

Odele Kucharski, 26, dead
Robert Kucharski, 27, dead
Fern Childers Gallagher, 14, missing

Rylie stares down at the list and then quickly sifts through all the tapes. She reads the names on every label, but there aren't any matches. She's just checking a second time when Kai pushes back his chair and runs to the bathroom. A second later she hears a coughing sound, then the toilet flushing, the sink running. When he comes out, he gives an embarrassed smile.

"Sorry," he says. "Must have been the ramen. Anybody else feel sick?"

Rylie shakes her head. She does feel sick, but not because of the food. "Are you okay?"

"Now I am." Kai sits back down at the desk. "I guess chili oil's not my friend, but does that stop me? No. Let's pretend that didn't happen."

Lor screws up her face. "Um, I think we should take a break." She edges away from him, not bothering to be discreet. "Are you sure you don't have the flu, or—"

"No to both." Kai spins the desk chair around so that it's facing the bed. "Let's keep going," he says. "You missed one of the photos." He reaches forward and tugs a rumpled newspaper clipping from the pile. A young man with a buzz cut and an infectious grin stares up at them. "What about him?"

"He's the one who doesn't fit." Lor taps their list.

"Everything on here happened within the last five years or so," she says. "That clipping's from forever ago."

"Well, 1975 anyway," Kai says. He starts typing into his phone as Rylie picks up the news article. It's brief: a write-up of a ghastly murder that happened on base in Twenty-nine Palms. The victim was found bleeding in a field outside his barracks; the reporter actually used the word "mauled" to describe his condition. The reporter added that the deceased, only twenty years old, had just requested leave to see his family, because he hadn't been home since returning from Vietnam.

"Jesus," Rylie breathes, and Kai sets down his phone.

"I got nothing," he says. "The only thing on the internet about it is from some legends-and-lore blog. Apparently the case was never solved."

Rylie stares at the photo. "My grandpa was based here back then," she says. "After his number was pulled for the war, he stayed in the military."

"Right, so that's how this guy fits. He was probably a friend of your grandpa's." Lor says it confidently, like there's not even a question, and Rylie feels a nudge of uncertainty.

"We should add him to the list anyway."

Lor nods. "What about the tapes you listened to?" She turns to Kai, still keeping her distance. "Or the maps?"

Kai holds one out for them to see. "This one's of the area. Not just Joshua Tree and Twentynine Palms but the Mojave preserve too. A bunch of places are circled on it, Rye. Mostly around your grandfather's cabin."

"What do you think they're for?" Lor asks as Rylie tears her eyes away from the map and then stares down at all the names on the list. Missing, dead, missing, missing . . . She suddenly knows exactly what Kai thinks the map is for, because there's a hard set to his chin and she's thinking the same thing herself. She turns toward the window and opens it, wanting out. Outside, the cars along the street are traveling in slow, orderly lines like everything is normal, like the world hasn't shifted on its axis, like the list doesn't exist and Lily is home and her grandpa was a good person.

"Rylie?"

She turns, and the way she's feeling must be all over her face because Lor grabs her hand. "'Wisely and slow; they stumble that run fast,'" Lor quotes. It's Shakespeare, and she's saying it to make Rylie feel better—it's a running joke between them. "Come on, you're supposed to tell me that you want the SparkNotes instead," Lor teases.

"I just want to know what all of this is," Rylie says. "Why he collected all of this before he died."

Lor squeezes her hand. "Kai told me that your grandpa was ex-military, a contractor. And he must have been good at his job to afford a place like this. I bet he was hired to help these people."

"Exactly." Kai nods. "He was probably investigating. Or maybe he was just interested in local news, that sort of thing."

"And what if it was something else?" Rylie grits out. If

they aren't going to say it, she will. "What's the worst-case scenario?"

"I'm not sure." Kai's eyebrows stitch together. "But it reminds me of this story my mom told me once," he says. "For college, she moved to this small town in Australia, nice town, normal town. But sometime in the nineties, while she's there? The mayor gets beheaded. Turns out he'd been trafficking kids. The city council was in on it. It was this whole dark underbelly that most people didn't know about. I'm not saying that's what this is—"

"That's right," Lor cuts in. "We don't know what this is yet." She squeezes Rylie's hand again before letting go. "So what *do* we know about your grandfather?"

Rylie goes back to the window and stares out at the night sky. The stars blur together. "He was strict, but it wasn't like he ever hurt me or Owen. And he liked his privacy."

"Everyone does," Kai says. "It doesn't mean they have something to hide."

Rylie lets out a slow breath. How can she look at the surface of someone's life and decide what sort of person they were deep down? Ben would say that her degree of trust in others is a reflection of her trust in herself. Her dad would say that the difference between a flower and a weed is a judgment. And Owen would switch on his Talkboy and listen to what the world has to tell him.

As usual, Owen wins, and Rylie turns from the window. "If he was hiding something, we need to find out what it was."

"Then how about some good news?" Lor asks, raising her eyebrows dramatically. "Here." She lifts a photograph of a teenager—dirty-blond hair, baggy sweatshirt—and then grabs another, almost identical picture from the pile. "Allow me to present May and Amy Bishop." Lor hands over both pictures and her phone, and when Rylie sees the screen, she has to read the headline twice.

MISSING BISHOP TWINS RETURN SAFELY.
Last week two teens from Twentynine Palms
who were reported missing on a family out-
ing returned home, apparently unharmed.

She scans the article. The spread includes a photograph of the Bishop twins and their mother, all standing outside their home on the fringe of Twentynine Palms, a water tower in the background. Rylie holds the phone closer, staring at the screen. The photographer made a mistake: he forgot to crop out their mailbox in the corner of the photo, and their house number is right there, in plain view. Between that and the water tower, it won't be too hard to find the street, talk to them. Because if these girls came home, and their pictures were on her grandpa's wall, there could still be hope for Lily. There could still be hope for Nathan and Thea too.

Rylie pulls the final photo from her pocket. Shiny dark hair, chin-length on one side, shaved on the other, eyes full of sarcasm, eyes Rylie sometimes hated as a kid. She adds the last name to the list: *Lily Seguin, 19, missing*, and then runs a Google search. The first few results appear:

Local teen still missing, community fearful.
Missing teen an ROTC scholarship recipient.
Brother of missing girl begs for help.

Rylie's throat closes up. *Brother of missing girl . . .* She can't click on the link; she can't look at it. Because it's not just anyone, it's Nathan. *He's* the brother of the missing girl. She clicks out of the search engine. She doesn't want to see any more headlines; she doesn't even want to see Nathan right now. They're supposed to meet at Sara's party tomorrow night. How can she tell him what she found? How can she *not* tell him?

"I'm sorry that your friend's missing," Kai says quietly.

"She isn't really my friend. Not anymore." It's hard to get the words out. "I didn't stay in touch."

"Rye . . ." Lor trails off, for once at a loss. "Look, what about the journals you mentioned? The ones of your grandpa's. Did you ever find them?"

"Not yet." Rylie passes the notebook back to Kai, and his eyebrows furrow while he reads over the list. The wind picks up and comes through the open window, rattling the pages of the notebook, and there's the tap, tap, tap of his pen hitting his leg. He glances at Rylie and then back at the list.

Pity.

That's the look he gave her. Like he thinks she's afraid of the truth. Like she's clinging to the chance that this is a mistake, that her grandpa wasn't involved in Lily's disappearance, that a member of her *family* wasn't involved in any of this. The list, the photos, the recordings . . .

A white-hot anger rushes through her. She won't make excuses for her grandfather, no matter what. Kai should know that. "The girls who were found. The twins," she says. "They live around here. We could ask them if—"

"I like it," Lor cuts in. "And then we'll know your grandpa's role. My guess is that you'll start laughing instead of worrying. Well, maybe not laughing exactly, but you know what I mean."

The weight on Rylie's chest lifts a little. Lor could be right. Lor's usually right. The weight lifts a little more as she takes hold of the idea, the breeze from the window cooling her face.

"I feel like we're overlooking something," Kai says, standing.

"What's that?"

"You." His eyes go to Rylie's bandages. "Are you sure *you're* okay? We never really talked about the hypnosis. Your memory of the hike. Getting lost."

Out the window behind him, the moon is casting a silvery light across the desert, and Rylie glances down at her bandaged arms. Something *did* happen to her, but her name didn't end up on a list, her picture wasn't on the news, and she's right where she's supposed to be: at home.

"Compared to this, it's nothing," she says, but Kai doesn't back off. Instead, he keeps staring at her.

"What if it's not?"

CHAPTER 14

THE NEXT DAY, RYLIE FEELS like she hardly slept. She stayed up late falling down rabbit holes of internet research with Lor and Kai, and doesn't feel any wiser for it. At some point Lor and Kai both went to bed, and she brought out more of the recordings—but some had been damaged, and others didn't make any sense. She fell asleep before finishing the stack and was woken in the morning by Lor, who handed her a lukewarm coffee in her mom's US Marine Corps mug, and two photographs. Now the pictures of the twins who went missing and came home again are propped up on the end table, side by side. *Come talk to us,* they're saying. *Come see what we know.*

"I figured out their address with a little help from that article and a real estate website." Lor opens a drawer and throws a shirt and a pair of Columbia leggings at her. "Let's go. Early bird gets the worm."

"Ah, more Shakespeare," Rylie says, pulling her sleeves down over the bandages on her arms, just as there's a knock. She swings the bedroom door open to Kai, his hair messy like he also just rolled out of bed, and his guitar and red

Volcom hat in hand. He's wearing the same thing he had on last night: jeans and a rumpled *X-Files* T-shirt, completely out of place next to Lor's vintage dress, and Rylie looks between them. "I thought we were going for discreet."

Kai smirks. "Not backing out, are you?"

"Wouldn't give you the satisfaction, Brother." She grabs the hiking bag with the recordings—they're too important to leave behind—and then hurries down the steps so that Owen doesn't hear them and ask to come too. Her mom is already at work, so Rylie leaves a quick note for Ben, and then they're out the door.

"Who needs breakfast when you can eat from the tree of knowledge?" Lor says as they get into the jeep, and Kai starts strumming his guitar, channeling his inner bard.

"Tree of knowledge, tree of knowledge," he sings, "feed me full, oh tree of knowledge."

"Feed me, *treeeeee*," Lor belts out at the top of her lungs, ending the song, and Rylie grins, feeling the tightness in her chest ease even more. The morning is comfortably overcast. It's a good day for a desert climb—no bright sun, no squinting on the rock. Maybe after the recon trip they can take a hike with Owen.

"Okay, so we show up and tell the twins we saw them in the news," Rylie says, shoving the key into the ignition. "We ask if they knew my grandfather, but without telling them who we are. And then what?"

"Then we all feel better." Lor buckles up and then checks her nail polish. "There's got to be a reasonable explanation for what you found in the cabin. I'd bet my college savings on it. Which is actually quite substantial."

"And I'll raise you a firstborn child," Kai jokes back, but when Rylie catches his eye in the rearview mirror, he glances away like he's nervous.

"Hey, what's that on your windshield?" Lor points at something black pinned under one of the wipers, and Rylie unrolls her window and snatches the paper. It's pressed into the shape of an animal—a bird, or maybe a bat. Rylie unfolds it and finds a note written with silver ink inside.

I hope you're feeling better. Let me know if you want to go hiking again. I've got a book with some good trail recommendations.
    —Sara

P.S. This is a California condor. They almost went extinct.

Lor leans forward. "Did she just mention the hike you nearly died on and then give you a *vulture*?" she asks. "It's a joke, right?"

"Not sure. She's actually pretty nice." Rylie speeds out of the neighborhood. "I'd call her talkative, but not necessarily a people person."

"Sounds like my cousin," Lor says as Rylie turns onto the highway so fast, the tires screech. After the odd note from Sara, it doesn't feel as satisfying as it usually does.

Overhead, the sky looks coarse and cloudy now, like dark gray quartz.

"Might be hard to find the turnoff." Kai nods at the thin fog coming down from the mountains, turning the wide expanse of desert around them gray and shadowy too. "Maybe you should slow down."

"This is slow." Rylie flicks on the headlights. The fog is a relief from the usual brightness. "I'm glad you found the address, Lor."

"It won't help if we can't *see* it in all this," Lor says grimly, her voice way more subdued than it was a few minutes ago. "I didn't even know the desert had fog."

"It's rare, but it happens." Kai's knee is bouncing against the back of Rylie's seat. "Usually only in winter. But it's uncommon regardless."

Rylie glances at him in the rearview mirror, raising a brow. "It's your first time here but you're an expert?"

"Along with every other man in the world," Lor says knowingly.

"Oh, is that how this is going to be?" Kai asks, his rebuttal halfhearted. "Outnumbered, outmaneuvered." It sounds like he's trying to joke, but he definitely looks nervous, the kind of nervous that you can catch, that gets you on an inhale and goes straight to your sternum, where it starts to spread, just like it's spreading through Rylie now.

"I know what you're thinking," Lor says, elbowing her hard enough to make her squirm. "You wish you were going alone."

"I wish there wasn't a reason to go."

"Me too," Kai says. "That list we made last night . . ." He doesn't finish his thought, and they all go quiet, watching scraggly mountains and twisted spires appear through the fog, then the tip of a water tower. Rylie doesn't dodge a pothole fast enough, and the jeep bounces just as Google Maps tells her to turn. The house in the newspaper article was on a gravel road, with a metal fence to its side—and then gravel is clunking against the side of the jeep as the house comes into view. It matches the photo exactly. A tidy-looking home with a kennel stretching all the way to the back, near a small wooden hut. A beehive.

She glances at Kai in the rearview mirror. By the look on his face, he's seen the hive too. "How allergic are you?" she asks.

"They're in their little honey house," he says, staring at the beehive. He takes off his hat and rubs at his hair. "That means they're pretty much contained, right? Shouldn't be a problem."

"Same for the dogs," Lor says as Rylie parks at the edge of the dirt driveway. Dogs start appearing at the kennel's chain-link fence, one after the other, eyeing her as she gets out of the jeep. Lor's faster, already heading toward the house. There's a sign on it. PRIVATE PROPERTY: TRESPASSERS WILL BE SHOT. Rylie can't help but think of Ethan Langhorne. She locks the jeep and then hurries after Lor, with Kai right beside her.

"I used to think suburbia was scary," Lor stage-whispers as she knocks. "But this has it beat."

Rylie knocks too. Still no answer. "We should check around back."

"Not a chance." Kai points to the PRIVATE PROPERTY sign. "If anyone's getting shot, it'll be me. Plus, the *bees.*"

"How about you and Lourdes wait in the jeep, and I'll go around back."

"And then never forgive ourselves when you're shot instead?" Lor pounds on the front door again. "Anybody home?"

There's a footstep, a shuffling sound. Rylie has a sense that someone's peering through the peephole. Then comes the double click of two dead bolts. A college-aged girl in a New Mexico State sweatshirt and fingerless gloves opens the door, her blond hair lank, unwashed. Her face is strikingly familiar.

"You're one of the Bishop twins," Rylie says, her stomach suddenly taut with nerves. "Aren't you?"

"Don't worry, we're not selling Tupperware or anything," Lor jokes, and the girl's eyes narrow. "It's just that we saw this article about you on the news and—"

"I need to go."

"This'll just take a minute." Rylie pulls the photo from her pocket. "We could go inside or—"

"Right here is fine."

"Okay, sure." Rylie notices that the girl's wearing a pair of black Ahnu hiking boots, and feels bolder. "We were hoping you could clear something up for us. You and your twin—"

"You mean May?" The Bishop girl glances over her shoulder. "She's not here." She goes to shut the door, and Rylie steps forward, catching it.

"I don't want to talk about May," the girl says. "That's what I told the others."

"The others?" Rylie asks, and the girl starts to close the door again. "Wait, you don't have to answer. You don't have to talk about your sister either," Rylie says, holding up the photo of her grandpa that she brought. "Could you just tell me if—"

"Who's there?" someone calls from inside the house. A woman steps into view, holding a glass of murky-looking water. "Go take your insulin, Amy," she says, and the girl nods and then retreats back into the house as her mother turns to them. "Are you selling something?" she asks, not unkindly. "I don't have money, and we already donated to St. Jude's this year. That's our charity."

"Actually, we're wondering if you know this man." Rylie holds up her grandpa's picture again, and the woman goes still.

"Did he send you?" she asks quietly. There's a faint hum in the air, coming from somewhere close. The glass of water sloshes in her hand, and droplets hit Rylie's legs.

"We thought he might have helped you when your daughters went missing," Lor says. "Our friend is—"

"Did he *send* you," the woman repeats, an edge in her voice this time.

Rylie shakes her head. "He died last year."

The glass drops from the woman's hands. It breaks when it hits the floor, shards scattering. Rylie bends to pick them up at the same time that the woman steps forward, her shoe crunching down, narrowly missing Rylie's fingers.

"Leave."

The humming noise gets louder. Rylie straightens, a piece of glass in her hand. "We just—"

"You're doing it," the woman whispers. She's staring wide-eyed at Rylie, at the shard of glass she's holding, and Rylie forces herself to drop it. There's a scrabbling sound, and then Amy Bishop appears in the hallway again. This time she's holding three large dogs on chains, and they're tugging at their leashes and snapping.

"Get off our porch or I'll call the cops," Amy says.

"We've overstayed our welcome," Kai says at the same time that Lor clutches Rylie's arm and yanks her out the door. It shuts in their faces, and the bolts lock in quick succession.

"I wasn't expecting milk and cookies or anything," Lor says in a low voice, staring at the door, "but that was a little uncalled for. Maybe there's someone else we can talk to?"

"They were terrified," Rylie says, but the humming noise is even louder now, and it's hard to think.

"Hey, car keys!" Kai suddenly shouts beside them.

Rylie turns, following his gaze. The kennel door is wide

open and more dogs are in the yard, but there's something in the air too, something buzzing and dark. Bees, it's a swarm of bees—and then Kai and Lor start running, the dogs trailing them. A dog snaps at Kai's legs as Rylie races to unlock the jeep. Lor reaches the front just as Rylie slings the back door open and pushes Kai in first. She jumps in behind him and then slams the door shut.

"Did they bite you?" Lor's eyes are wide as she turns from the front, watching Kai pat himself down. "Are you okay?"

"It's not the dogs," Kai gasps. "It's the bees. Are they on me?" He keeps patting down his body, his arms, his legs, but there's no buzzing sound, no sound of wings.

"I don't see any, Kai," Rylie says quickly.

"They don't sting unless provoked," Lor adds, half-breathless. "That's what Iggy told me anyway, and he would know," she goes on, talking too fast.

Rylie climbs over the console to the driver's seat. "We need to go," she says, but when she glances at her stepbrother in the rearview mirror, he's gone pale, almost rigid. "Kai?"

He grasps at his neck. "My EpiPen," he rasps. "I need it." Red, swollen blotches are spreading across his skin. "Pocket," he whispers. His hands are shaking as he fumbles for it. He drops the EpiPen on the floor, and Rylie grabs it just as his eyes roll back in his head.

"Rylie!" Lor shouts, and Rylie stares down at the EpiPen in her hand, her heart racing. It can't be that hard to work. Thigh, they always do the thigh in the movies.

"*Hurry.*" Lor's voice sounds far away as Rylie pops off the top. Kai is wheezing beside her, his breath sounding dangerously shallow. Her breath feels shallow too as she tightens her grip on the EpiPen and then plunges it into Kai's leg, but he's already gone completely slack.

"Kai?" Rylie shakes his arm. "Kai!"

"Is he breathing?" Lor asks, a hitch in her voice, and Rylie feels like she can barely move. She reaches out and puts her hand on his ribs. They're still. Her own lungs seize, and she's just about to start shaking him when his eyes open.

"I'm not dead," Kai says gruffly. He slowly sits up, and then he *smiles*, he actually smiles.

"Well, you tried your best," Rylie says, suddenly angry. She turns and grips the wheel so that he can't see her hands shaking as she starts up the engine. "I'm taking you to the hospital."

"Don't bother." Kai rubs at his thigh. "Nothing like a dose of epinephrine to get the blood flowing."

"Not funny," Lor says, looking unusually flustered.

"Let's get out of here." Rylie reverses fast out of the driveway, shifts gears, and presses on the gas.

"I bet they intentionally opened that kennel," Lor says. "And maybe they aggravated the beehive too?" She nudges Rylie. "We should take Kai to the hospital and then call the cops."

"No to both." Kai props his feet up on the console. "We were on *their* property. The police will want to know why," he says. "And I don't need a doctor. Rylie stabbed me with a needle, so I'm good. Plus I have a backup, in case she needs to do it again." He picks his guitar up from the floor, then starts repeatedly plucking a high string on it. It sounds like the tune from *Psycho*.

"If I had to guess, I'd say you kind of enjoyed it, Rye. At least it worked." Lor holds up the EpiPen and turns to Kai. "Have you ever used this thing before?"

"Yeah, on a camping trip." He stops with the *Psycho* tune. "It makes you feel strange, kind of hyped-up in a bad way. But once it's out of my system, it's gone, so it's not like I'm sick or anything."

Rylie glances at Kai in the rearview mirror. He *does* look fine, but a minute ago he was in anaphylactic shock, and all because of her. Going to the twins' house had been her idea. She's the one who needs information about her grandfather. Just thinking about him makes her feel like she's had a dose of epinephrine too.

"So now that my airways have opened up again," Kai says, "we really do need to find that other twin. Give her a ring."

Rylie pulls out onto the highway. "That's assuming she'll even talk to us."

"And, unfortunately, there's got to be, like, a thousand May Bishops in the world," Lor points out, but Kai's already typing into his phone. A second later he gives a hoot.

"*But* only one May Bishop with a food blog called *Twin Plates*," he says, and grins. He looks down at his screen for another second and then hands the phone to Lor, who's fixing her mascara in the mirror. "Actually, you read. I'm feeling too jittery to focus."

"Because you need a *doctor*," Rylie says.

"Because I'm excited about our *lead*." Kai taps on the back of Lor's seat. "What's the website say? Got any contact info for her?"

Lor quickly scrolls. "It looks like the site's pretty inactive—though, wow, their post on gourmet glamping had a ton of comments." She scrolls some more. "But the contact page only has a generic email address. It probably goes to both of them."

"Try the 'About' page?" Rylie asks, and Lor taps the screen.

"Let's see, May and Amy Bishop nurtured a love for food from an early age, and . . . *Oh*." Lor glances up. "No wonder Amy didn't want to talk about her sister. We probably should've dug through more articles last night."

"What does it say?" Rylie asks quietly, part of her already knowing what's coming.

"This says that 'due to ongoing complications from last year's ordeal—'"

"How they went missing?" Kai interrupts, and Lor shrugs.

"That'd be my guess. Anyway, it says that May lapsed into another coma and that prayers are appreciated, along with donations to Feeding America or Desert Heights, where she's in care in the ICU."

Intensive care. May Bishop is in intensive care. Rylie floors the gas. They didn't do their homework. They harassed the Bishops—first by casually asking Amy about a traumatic event, and then by bringing up her sister, who, as it turns out, is seriously *ill*. What did they think they were doing? And on top of that, Kai almost got hurt, and they didn't actually learn anything useful, not about the Bishops, and not about her grandpa—except that the Bishops are scared of him. She glances down at her phone and hits the map app. The police station is close, minutes away—there are no excuses. She can give the cops the list from last night. She already memorized it: *Mackenzie Soren, Jed Hendersen, Juan Ramon-Ortez, Emily Okada, Odele and Robert Kucharski, Fern Childers Gallagher.* She can hand over the tape of Ethan Langhorne too—the recordings are already in the jeep, in the backpack. The police can decide what to do with her grandpa's photographs, his maps, all of it. Everything she found in his cabin. It will be the cops' problem, their responsibility, their lead. They're the ones who will need to talk to Nathan and Thea—they're *trained* for that.

"So if May Bishop's out, where are we heading next?" Kai asks, leaning forward and reaching for her phone. When he grabs it, Rylie spots the ink on his arm: *We enter the circle at night and are consumed by fire.* She narrows her eyes, remembering the hypnosis, another thing they tried to do that went sideways. Her resolve hardens and she keeps her course into town.

"Hey, are you sure about this?" Kai switches off her app, but she already knows the way, and a minute later she's turning into the parking lot. "Seriously, Rye," he says, "you need to think about Lil—"

"I *am*," she cuts in. "That's why we're here."

CHAPTER 15

WHEN RYLIE PARKS IN FRONT of the police station, Lor raises her eyebrows. "Want us to come in with you?" she asks.

Rylie shakes her head and leaves the jeep running, then grabs the hiking backpack from the floor near Lor's feet. Everything they found came from the cabin, her *family's* cabin, and handing it over feels like something she needs to do alone. "That's okay. I think it would just make it weird."

"Even weirder, you mean," Kai says. Before he can gear up for another argument, Rylie gets out with the bag. Kai's the one who convinced her to wait on going to the police in the first place, and he was wrong. She takes a breath of cool air and then walks up to the small substation and swings open the door with a gauzy fist.

Inside, it's eerily quiet: there's an empty seating area near a wall of brochures and framed photographs; a vacant counter, with a phone and a computer on a desk behind it; and a frosted glass wall hiding offices at the back. The glass looks dark, like all the lights are off.

"Hello?" she calls out.

"Sorry," a voice says as a bathroom door opens. Rylie's heart falls when she sees who's coming out.

"Sara?" Seeing her here doesn't make sense, but it's definitely Sara Mazur. She's in another long flowy skirt and bangles, her short hair showing off her moon-shaped earrings.

"Hi," Sara says, looking as surprised as Rylie is. "Everything okay?" For a second it seems like they might even hug, but instead, Sara steps past her and heads behind the counter. "How are you feeling?" Sara asks. She's talking about the hike, but right now Rylie's feeling blindsided more than anything else.

"Do you *work* here?"

"Just for the school break." Sara nods at the framed photos on the wall. "My uncle's the chief. They've had a lot of staff turnaround lately, and it's been so busy that he hasn't had time to hire anyone." She shrugs, fiddles with one of her earrings. "He wanted my mom to come work here, but she'd never leave nursing, so I got volunteered instead."

Rylie clutches the hiking backpack, trying to figure out how to pivot. "It doesn't look busy," she says, and it's the truth. The station looks empty, like no one's working at all.

"All the officers are out on cases," Sara says. "Anyway, I'm glad to see you out after the hike." Her gaze goes to Rylie's bandages. "Is that why you're here?" she asks, her voice sounding strange.

"No, it's just that . . ." But Rylie can't make herself say it. She can't say that she's here because of Lily. She can't tell

Sara any of it without telling Nathan first. It'd feel too much like a betrayal, and now she wants to leave, she wants to pretend like she never walked in at all. It's nothing personal against Sara, but she might mention it to Nathan, and then what would she say?

"Actually, it's not really for me, and—"

"You know what? I shouldn't have asked," Sara interrupts. She picks her cell phone up from the desk and sends a quick text, then pushes a piece of paper across the counter. "If you fill this out, I can leave a message for you, have an officer call you back?"

Rylie stares down at the form. "How long would that take?" she asks. "For them to get back to me."

"Honestly, I'm not sure." Sara starts stacking forms behind the counter, her bangles jingling again. "Do you follow the news? I usually don't, but I guess there was another Ethan Langhorne slaying last night. It happened at a rest stop," she says, and then there's the sudden loud crunch of a stapler from behind the desk. "They found this creepy *veil* at the scene, so the news is calling him the beekeeper now too. They think someone's helping him," she adds, as her pale eyes glance up briefly. "Plus there's been this random uptick in violence lately," Sara goes on, "and—"

"Should you really be telling me all this?" Rylie asks. She holds the backpack closer, and it smells faintly of mold. "I mean, isn't it official police business or something?"

"They don't tell me anything official. The story already broke." Sara punches the stapler again and then glances back at the frosted glass wall. "Listen, my uncle's back in first thing tomorrow. Drop by during his lunch break," she offers. "Oh, and I'm having a party tonight. You should come."

Before Rylie can tell her that she was already planning to, the phone on the counter rings shrilly, and Sara puts a hand on it. "It's just the desk line but I'd better take it," she says. "We've been getting these strange prank phone calls lately," she explains, and Rylie's reminded of the call she got on the way to the cabin yesterday. *I saw you,* the man said. *I saw what happened.* It had to have been a wrong number.

"Twentynine Palms Patrol, perimeter substation." Sara sounds different—older, more professional, but she's fiddling with a piece of origami paper with her free hand like always. She pauses, her hand going still. Then: "Hello? Could you speak up, please?"

Rylie feels a tug of curiosity. Even with the receiver against Sara's ear, Rylie can hear the sound of raspy breathing, or maybe something like static. Then a loud whisper comes over the line. It sounds like *"Helloooo."*

"Can I help you?" Sara asks, but now there's a tremor in her voice, and her eyes flick to Rylie's just before the line goes dead.

CHAPTER 16

WHEN THEY PULL UP TO her grandpa's house, the January sky is already dark, even though it's just after five p.m. The police station was a fairly quick stop, all things considered, but when Rylie came out, her jeep was missing from the parking lot. Then she got a text from Lor about driving to the hospital because they *looked up EpiPens and Kai def needs to see a doctor!!!* So Rylie walked the few blocks to Desert Heights, where Kai had already been admitted. A few hours later, after Rylie and Lor had taken endless turns roaming the hallways for vending machines, Kai came out looking gloomy, until she showed him the hiking backpack. He instantly perked up, throwing an arm around her, and then talking about their "next moves" all the way to the house.

"So you're going back to the police tomorrow at noon, Rye?" Lor asks as they pull into the driveway.

"It's like a high noon," Kai says meaningfully, and Rylie turns off the engine but doesn't get out.

"I can't believe Sara Mazur works there." Rylie stares through the windshield at the house, at its sprawling gabled roof full of shadows, but she's still thinking of the police station. "It just makes everything feel so much worse."

"Because you're worried about Sara telling Nathan," Lor says.

Rylie nods. "If you were me, what would you say?"

"To the cops?" Kai asks.

"And maybe Nathan too. Or my mom."

Lor squeezes her hand. "No one's expecting you to have all the answers, Rye."

"But it would help," Rylie says as Kai leans forward.

"Okay, so we know your grandpa was documenting things, right?" he starts. "That interview with Ethan—"

"It wasn't really an interview." She listened to most of the other recordings, and they weren't formal like that. "What we know is that he recorded conversations with people. Maybe secretly."

Kai nods. "Because he was collecting information."

"Or for blackmail," she counters.

Kai and Lor both stare at her for a second. "That's taking it a step darker," Lor finally says, but Rylie *has* to take it there.

"The recording with Ethan talked about payment. It talked about hurting people."

"Maybe your grandpa was trying to help him," Kai says. Now he's looking at the house like he's afraid to meet her eye.

"Or my grandpa was trying to hire Ethan, or even manipulate him," she presses. "Lily's disappearance, everything we found in the cabin, it all took place *before* my grandpa died."

"There's another angle too," Lor says softly.

"What?"

"How did he die?" Lor asks, her voice barely above a whisper. "What if he was onto something and got too close? What if you need to be careful too?"

Rylie tamps down the sudden unease in her stomach. "It was natural. He was in his seventies; he had leukemia. He refused treatment for it." She knows they're getting the wrong image. Even through all of that, her grandpa was strong; he stayed in shape from his military years. And he'd always, *always* been smart. The air in the jeep is starting to feel too stale, and she gets out quickly, suddenly wanting to talk to her mom.

"Come on," she says, her throat strangely tight. And then, just as she's almost to the house, the front door swings open, light falling across the yard.

"Dinner is served," Owen calls out from the doorway. "It's paella!" His grin has a gap from a missing tooth, and Ben is beaming right behind him, wearing his chef's apron over a San Diego Padres jersey. The whole place smells like tomato and garlic, and her mom's nowhere to be seen.

"You two are saints," Lor says as she steps inside. "I'm *starving*. We spent nearly all day at the hospital—"

"Doing community service work," Kai cuts in smoothly, clearly not wanting to bring up the EpiPen. "For their college applications," he adds.

"*And* for the common good, I hope." Ben rubs his hands together. "I, however, spent all day trying to perfect my anniversary dinner for Eve," he says. "Gotta celebrate the day we met in style."

"We're ready for taste-testers." Owen pulls Rylie and Lor into the kitchen. "Mom isn't home from work yet, so there's plenty for everyone." The enormous steel pan in the center of the table has garlic-scented steam seeping from it, and with the spread of side dishes, it really does look like a feast.

"You outdid yourself, Ben," Rylie says, and he takes a mock-bow.

" 'Give them great meals of beef and iron and steel, they will eat like wolves,' " Lor quotes, genuine awe in her voice.

"Or ravenous kennel dogs," Kai adds, pulling out a seat. "Too soon?"

"Too soon." Rylie veers into the bathroom to wash her hands. She closes the door and lets out a breath, staring at her reflection in the vaulted mirror. The bruise on her forehead is yellowish now, already starting to fade. And by this time tomorrow she'll be through the worst part, the *telling* part, and eventually it will be okay. Eventually there'll be order again—her dad used to remind her of that. *Even in chaos, the universe has order.* She swallows, hard, and turns on the faucet, but when she grabs the bar of soap, there are dark lines under her fingernails, almost like dried blood. Maybe she scratched under her bandages without realizing it? She aggressively washes her hands before heading back into the brightly lit kitchen, where everyone's already sitting down to eat.

Owen launches into a play-by-play of all the dishes: bread, fried plantains, roasted red peppers, pimientos de Padrón—food Ben learned to cook during a study abroad in Spain. Rylie eats mechanically, her mind on the Bishop twins and the disaster that was. She really needs to get it together—go through everything from the cabin, all the tapes, all the maps—so she knows what to say to the police tomorrow. But they'll want to know where she got the recordings *from*. Her stomach gives a violent twist, and she sets down her fork.

"Guess what? A car accident happened right in front of us today," Owen says, a little too excitedly. "It was so loud."

"It was terrible." Ben shakes his head. "Apparently a cyclist had collapsed on the side of the road or something, and a truck swerved, and . . ." He trails off. "Well, you get the picture. It was not good," he says, heaping more paella into Kai's bowl.

"But you said they'd be fine," Owen points out, and Ben makes a strained *mmm-hmm* sound in his throat as he turns to Rylie.

"And what about you, Rye? How have you been feeling?" he asks, just as the doorbell rings.

Rylie stands, eager to escape the concerned look on Ben's face. "I'll get it," she says, quickly heading down the hallway.

She flicks on the porchlight and swings the door open to Iggy and Miles, who stuffs a piece of gum into his mouth and then flashes a minty grin.

"Hello, 'ello," Miles says cheerily. Beside him, Iggy's doing his best to peer around her.

"Is my cousin still here?" Iggy asks, skipping the greeting. "I need to talk to her."

"Come on in." Rylie opens the door wider, but Iggy doesn't move from the porch. "She's—"

"Right here," Lor says, her hair brushing across Rylie's arm as she steps out to give Iggy a hug. "What's up? Here for dinner again?"

Iggy shakes his head. "I've been thinking about something." He pushes up the sleeves of his black jacket and then scrapes his shoes against the porch mat. He's sweating a little, and his eyebrows are furrowed as if he's still deep in thought. Lor sometimes calls him Mr. Telenovela, but he reminds Rylie of her dad, how the workings of the universe filled his mind so that he couldn't focus on the life in front of him. When he finally came down to earth, he'd be humming a melody, he'd say that a song was whispering to him from the silence. Her mom jokingly called him a hippie physicist, and Iggy looks the same, with his shaggy hair and glasses and that faraway gaze in his eye. But when he finally raises his head and looks at Rylie, the faraway gaze hardens into something else.

"Your hike," Iggy says abruptly. "I've been thinking about

your hike, ever since dinner last night. You don't remember anything."

It isn't clear whether it's a question or not. "No, but I—"

"Nothing," Iggy cuts in. He's staring at her bandages now. "That's not good." He glances over at Lor. "I need to talk to you, Lourdes. Maybe then you'll listen to me and go home."

"Go home?" Lor's laugh is breezy. "Still trying to get me out of here, Cousin?"

"It's not just you," Miles says, lighting a cigarette. "He's been pushing me out the door too. Got a bee in his bonnet."

Lor laughs again, but it's a pissed-off sort of laugh. "Look, I don't know what your problem is, but you need to relax." She stares Iggy down. "And I've got an audition tomorrow *anyway*, so I'm leaving in the morning. That fast enough for you?"

"Hey, how's your degree going, Iggy?" Rylie asks. Someone needs to rein in the tension, and since it's her porch, it might as well be her. "Lor says you've been working with bees."

"What else would I do?" Iggy snaps, looking her way again. "Their populations are declining," he says. "Ninety percent of plants depend on pollinators. Thirty-five percent of the global food supply exists because of them." He hisses air through his teeth. "People think food just grows magically or something, just appears out of nothing, right? They think it's always going to be around?"

"Ignacio—" Miles starts, but he just shakes his head and makes a show of waving smoke out of his face.

"Bees are *bioindicators*," Iggy says tightly. "That means they sense the slightest disturbances in their environments. They have elaborate communication dances, telling each other where to land. When to fly away to safety."

"Get to the point," Lor cuts in, and Rylie looks between them. For a long minute the cousins just stare at each other, neither one of them speaking, and then Iggy sighs. Miles holds out his cigarette, and Iggy takes a drag from it and then stubs it out, sighing again.

"I just need to talk to you, Lourdes," he says. Then he glances at Rylie. "You mind?"

She shakes off the sting. "Not at all." It's clear that whatever he wants to say is meant for Lor and Miles, and she needs to listen to the rest of the recordings anyway.

"I'll meet up with you later, then, Rye," Lor says. "We're going to that party tonight, right? At that Sara girl's place?"

That party. The one Nathan's going to. She almost forgot. "Yeah, just text me when you're done."

"I'll follow you," Lor tells Iggy. She sets off toward her car, Miles flashing an apologetic smile at Rylie before heading after Lor. And then it's just Iggy on the porch—scraping his shoes against the mat without leaving—so Rylie keeps the door open.

"Iggy, you need something?"

He finally stops fidgeting and looks up. "Do you feel like hurting people?"

"What?" She must not have heard him right.

"Do you do things you can't remember?"

He must be talking about the hike again. "That was a one-off."

"I doubt it." Iggy stares at her, no longer a trace of her dad in him. Her dad never looked this cold. "This place isn't good for you." He steps forward. "*You're* no good here, Rylie."

The community mourns the loss of May Elena
Bishop, 19, who unexpectedly passed away at
Desert Heights Hospital last night while in
a coma. She is survived by her mother and
her twin sister, Amy Elaine. The family has
requested a private ceremony.

CHAPTER 17

A COUPLE OF HOURS LATER, Rylie still feels shaken as she heads down the hallway, looking for Kai. Earlier Iggy had got her worrying about the hike again and how she attacked her mom afterward too—but right now she needs to focus on what she found in the cabin. Debriefing with Kai would help her get her story straight for the cops tomorrow. She feels a headache coming on, and the bandages on her arms are too hot, too constricting.

"Kai surface yet?" Ben asks, calling out from his office as she walks by. The computer screen is reflecting off his glasses, and it looks like he has two sets of eyes. "That boy's been sleeping since dinner." He goes back to typing his thesis, and she's off the hook from telling him that Kai isn't sleeping—she doesn't think he's even in the house at all—and he hasn't been answering his phone either. It feels like Kai's intentionally avoiding her. She already texted him twice about wanting the maps from the cabin back; she has to go over everything so that she misses nothing. *Then* she'll start worrying about the hike again. She flicks on the light in her room and checks her phone, but the only text is from Lor:

Forgot to mention that I took some of the You Know What. Will call after Iggy decides to chill.

Rylie pushes the phone away. This whole time she's been trying to figure out what was wrong with her grandpa and Ethan Langhorne, but Iggy acted like there's something wrong with *her*. A tight anxiety starts spreading under her ribs, spreading faster when she dumps out the hiking backpack and sifts through the pile of You Know What on her carpet. There's no Ethan Langhorne tape in the pile; Lor must have it. The anxiety in her chest flares to anger, and Rylie chooses an unlabeled tape instead and shoves it into the cassette player, nearly hard enough to break it.

A second later, the speakers go loud with voices, so many voices. Then there's a rush of water, ice clinking, a faint shout for a refill. It's a restaurant, then. Not an interrogation room.

"I think I did it." When the voice comes through, it's low and hushed.

"You think?" It's her grandpa. He's talking clearly, like he doesn't care about being overheard.

"I'm not sure. There was blood. . . . It might have been mine." Another whisper. "I cleaned it up the way you showed me."

"Did anyone see you?"

"I . . ." The other man's voice is shaking now. "I don't

know." He sounds young, way too young, and Rylie's heart skips a beat. It's Ethan Langhorne. It's another tape with Ethan.

"I don't want to do it again," Ethan's saying. "I can't—"

"Find a way to cope. Your generation . . ."

Her grandfather doesn't bother to hide the disgust in his voice. For a second Rylie almost feels sorry for Ethan, before she remembers who he is. Then there's some sort of scuffle, a drink spilling, the recorder hitting the floor, heavy footsteps. There's nearly a full minute of noise—it must be the end of the conversation—but another jostling sound comes, and then:

"You know that girl you live by? Lily?"

Rylie stiffens, then hits rewind, and then there's no mistake:

"You know that girl you live by? Lily? Lily Seguin."

She stares incredulously down at the recorder, watching the wheels of the tape turn. Her heart stutters in her chest like it's forgotten how to work.

"Stay away from her," her grandpa says. "It's too risky."

"I think she saw me. I think she knows."

Knows *what*? Rylie keeps staring at the recorder, the wheels still spinning on the tape. She feels like she's listening in on something she shouldn't, like she's Owen's age again, sticking her ear against the door to her grandpa's room, wondering about the sounds inside.

"I think someone else saw me too. One of the other kids here. Bas. I think he knows."

Silence. "It would be unfortunate if that were true," her grandpa finally says.

"It's just—"

"If you won't handle it, I will."

Rylie stops the tape. She feels like her lungs are being crushed, and for one brief second she feels like crushing the tape too, pulling out the awful black ribbon just so she won't have to listen to it again. *If you won't handle it, I will.*

A kid suspected of multiple counts of murder was talking about *Lily*. And her grandfather implied that Lily's life was at risk. Rylie grips the recorder. Her pulse is going fast like it does when she's about to reach the top of a route and she's almost there and doesn't want to fall. It's fear, but it's also that rush of adrenaline she always craves, something close to excitement. Maybe there *is* something wrong with her, just like Iggy said. She lets out a slow breath and then hits play, and Ethan's voice fills the bedroom again.

"Fine, I'll do it," Ethan says. There's a loud thud like he's slammed his fist. "But I'm sick of hiding."

"They'll lock you up."

"Not for long."

A chair screeches. "We've been over this before," her grandpa says. "You need to go to—"

"Datura?" Ethan sneers. "Already did."

"You go every time."

"She thinks I'm some kind of chosen one. That's why she lets me in."

So Datura was a woman's name? Rylie makes a mental

note as Ethan lets out a bitter laugh. "The assholes don't know that my dad set the stage for me."

His dad. She shuts her eyes, remembering the news story she read. Ethan's dad was a monster. He murdered his entire family, everyone but Ethan.

"So you think it's hereditary?" her grandpa asks.

Ethan laughs again. "I think it's bullshit."

A loud click startles her—it's the end of the tape.

"Hey, Rylie?"

At the sound of her name, she shoves the tape deck under a blanket and turns to see Kai. If he knocked, she didn't hear it, but he's already pushing her door open. "Can I come in?"

"Actually—"

"Palindromes," Kai says, stepping forward. He's got his red Volcom hat on, and his face is in shadow. "It's a palindrome."

After what she just heard, it's hard to think about anything except for Ethan. "Where have you been?" she asks. "And what's a palindrome?"

"The graffiti you saw during the hypnosis." Kai bares his forearm, angling the ink toward her to read, but she already saw it earlier. " 'We enter the circle at night and are consumed by fire,' " he says.

She shakes her head. "No, what's a *palindrome*."

"Oh, right." Kai turns and shuts the door behind him. "It's a phrase that reads the same backward or forward. Like 'I did, did I?' "

"But you can't reverse 'We enter the circle—' "

"Latin. It's a palindrome in Latin. I looked it up." He pulls his notebook from his back pocket and steps closer. *"In girum imus nocte et consumimur igni,"* he reads. " 'We enter the circle at night and are consumed by fire.' Remember how you saw it on the boulder?"

"It was just graffiti, Kai."

His eyes look too bright. "I think it might be some sort of message. A code or something." He tugs out the pen from behind his ear. "Can you draw that design that was next to it? The one you saw on the boulder?"

He's talking about the circle, and then her heart quickens as she remembers the cabin. "I can do better than a drawing," she says. "I've got a photo. The same shape was on the cabin door."

Kai's eyes go to hers, and she's ready for him to say "I told you so," but he doesn't. "Show me," he says instead, and she finds the picture on her phone and holds it up.

"There." She points at the screen. "It's small, but it's the same design."

Kai enlarges it. It's the six sharp petals again, a circle drawn around them. He keeps staring at it, almost as if he's entranced. Then he opens his notebook to a new sheet of paper and sketches the image. When he stops, she notices that his hand is shaking.

"Hey, what's with you?"

Kai looks up. "What do you mean?"

"I've got plenty at stake, but why do you care so much?" she asks. "Why are you helping me?"

"Aren't we, like, stepsiblings now?"

"Seriously, Kai."

He pulls off his hat, then rubs his head. "It's just . . ." He glances down at the sketch again, his dark hair falling in front of his eyes. "I saw them once before. This exact shape."

"Where?"

His pen goes still. His whole body goes still. "On this camping trip I went on with my mom. It was just the two of us. And then . . ." He trails off as her phone beeps with a text: *I'm outside. Should I come to the door?*

It's Nathan. Rylie's stomach feels heavy, like it's full of what she just heard about Lily on the recording, like she somehow ingested it.

"Hang on, Kai." She stands so fast, her head spins. "I have to take care of something. It'll just take a minute." She hurries downstairs and straight out the door. In the driveway is Nathan's truck, engine on and headlights shining, and he's standing in front of the hood. The collared red shirt that he's wearing makes his skin look tanner than usual, and his hair is dark and wet like he just showered.

"We got off early from work," he says as he walks toward her, "which basically never happens."

Rylie's stomach knots tighter. She heads into the dark yard and meets him halfway, and he shoves his hands into his pockets and grins. "I like that we're falling back into old habits," he says. "But without the slap bracelets. Or the Skittles. We ate so many of them, I can still taste the rainbow."

"It's the Jolly Ranchers that did me in," she says, smiling, and then she thinks of the recording she just heard, and it's like decking it—falling and hitting solid rock, the crash so hard that it rips the breath from you. She should call off everything with him until tomorrow.

"I can't go to the party with you, Nathan."

"That's why I stopped over, actually. I can't go either."

The lurch of disappointment in her chest catches her off guard. "I guess it works out, then."

"Not really, not for me." Nathan gives her a little half smile. "You should know that, Rye."

It's the way he says her name that does it. Suddenly she's remembering the day he kissed her, that last summer when she came to visit. They were on top of Trashcan Rock, and it was windy, and her hair was blowing across her face, and it only lasted a few seconds, but when it was over, it felt like the whole world had somehow changed.

"Thea's having an off day," Nathan says quietly, "and I don't want to leave her alone tonight."

"Then you shouldn't."

"But I don't want to leave you either."

Her chest does another lurch. "Nathan—"

"How about coming over? I want to show you something. It's a surprise," he says, but he says it playfully—so much like the old Nathan—and she wants to say yes. She wants them to be like they used to be.

But Lily.

"The thing is, there's that voluntary curfew, and I haven't seen Owen much lately and—"

"It's okay!" Owen shouts, and Rylie turns. He's standing under the porchlight, Ben right beside him, both of them with matching grins. "I don't mind," Owen goes on. "We can hang out tomorrow, Rye. Dad said I could help him in his office."

"We're actually on our way upstairs right now," Ben says, way too earnestly. "You two enjoy yourselves." Then he winks and swings the door shut.

"I guess that's a green light?" Nathan asks good-naturedly, and Rylie feels like she's split down the center. "We can drive together. So we won't be violating the curfew."

"It's just . . ." The edge of her bandage is coming loose on one hand. "I'm supposed to change all of this." She's grasping for excuses now.

"Change away. I'll wait. *And* I'll throw in some Skittles." Nathan's brown eyes are on hers again, and they're eyes that she somehow knows and doesn't know. The younger Nathan she knew is blurring into the older Nathan that she doesn't, and it's making things way too confusing. Way too tempting.

"Come on, Rye." He reaches out for her hand, gently, and runs his finger along the edge of the gauze, right where it meets her skin. "Please come over and play?" he asks, and then she has to hold in a laugh.

"Doesn't that kind of question have an expiry date?"

"Only if you want it to." Now Nathan looks like he's holding back laughter too, and she can practically feel the warmth from his body radiating off him. If she goes to his house, maybe she'll find a way to talk to him about Lily.

"And hey," Nathan says, a smile still playing on his face, "if you won't come for me, come for Thea. She made me swear to keep you close."

CHAPTER 18

RYLIE KNOWS SHE'S MADE A mistake the second Nathan opens the door. The house is dark and silent, the opposite of how it was during the party.

"I'll go tell Thea we're here," he says, and she follows him upstairs out of habit. But she realizes that maybe she shouldn't have when she gets to the top. "Hold on a minute. She might be asleep." He knocks softly on Thea's door and then goes inside.

Across the hallway, Lily's door is open, moonlight from the window bathing the room. The comforter is crumpled in the middle of the bed as if someone's been sitting on it. Probably Thea, missing Lily.

Rylie takes a deep breath. Deep breaths slow the heart rate before a climb, deceive the mind into calming down. Right now they're not helping. Every corner of this house is a reminder of Lily. Rylie shouldn't have come here—she's not ready to talk to Nathan about her. If she says the wrong thing, or implies the wrong thing, she could do even more damage, and she doesn't even know the full truth yet. . . . Her phone beeps, breaking the silence in the hallway. It's a text from Lourdes: *Iggy's acting weird again. I probably won't make the party. If I'm not at your place by midnight, come extract me from his dorm.*

Call me if you need to. I'm skipping the party too, Rylie texts back. Then she turns away from Lily's room, and her eyes snag on the open door next to it. Nathan's. Even in the dark she can tell that all his old posters are gone, except for the world map that Thea gave him for his eleventh birthday, the map where he marked the seven summits. Next to it is a cluttered desk. An unexpected legion of potted plants is near his window, some of them leaking water onto the carpet. Draped over his unmade bed is a pair of fatigues, and piles of clothes and papers are scattered around on the floor.

"I've got no excuses," Nathan says from behind her, flicking on the light. "Lucky no one sees it but me."

Rylie steps back, away from the door. "Sorry, I was just—"

"You don't have to apologize. But for the record, I usually *don't* bring people back to my room." There's a playful gleam in his eyes that gets her in the chest.

"Must be a new policy," she says. "I seem to remember a certain someone showing off his new cleats up here when we were kids."

"I brought you up here to show you a set of cleats? I'm sure you were riveted."

"Well, they did have fluorescent laces. Plus I got to see Ewoks and your baseball cards."

"All hand-me-downs from Lily. Blame her." Nathan's smiling, but Rylie looks away, the guilt suddenly back.

She turns toward a photograph of Nathan and Lily on the wall—it must be recent. They're both in blue T-shirts that say ENIGMA across the front of them.

"Why the matching shirts?"

"So we could find each other in a crowd." Nathan's smile falters a little, the scar on his eyebrow creasing more deeply. "Enigma's this tour group Lily worked for. She took tourists out into the desert, told them about the local history, the ecology. Sometimes they'd hold ayahuasca ceremonies, all legal."

"What's that?"

"It's a tea made from a South American vine. It's called the Little Death, because your consciousness is supposed to break away from your body when you drink it, show you insights about the world." Nathan shrugs. "That's how Lily explained it to me, anyway. It's a sacred plant, but as far as I could tell, there was nothing holy about working for that tour group. They're just another company trying to make money off something they shouldn't."

Enigma. Rylie makes a mental note. Maybe Lily ran into Ethan Langhorne while working there. But that doesn't explain how her grandfather met Ethan. "Did Lily go hiking a lot?"

Nathan takes the frame off the wall. "Before she went missing, she'd meet up with friends at all hours, but she never said what she was doing, where she was going." He stares at the photo. "Not that she ever told me much. You know Lily." There's something loaded in his words, but

Rylie doesn't know how to ask about it without telling him everything, and she doesn't *know* everything yet.

"Almost forgot." Nathan puts the frame back on the wall and turns. "Thea wants you to have this." He picks up a cardboard box from the floor with her name written on the side and sets it on his mattress. "It's just some old stuff of your grandfather's, I think."

"I'll check it out later," Rylie says quickly, but Nathan has already started rummaging through it, and it's hard to look away. At the top is a photograph of her grandpa as a young Marine, his arm flung across the shoulders of another guy in fatigues. Thea's standing beside them in a nursing uniform, her hair black instead of white. They're all outside the Joshua Tree cabin—maybe back when her grandpa first moved into it, back when he and Thea first became neighbors. The Shakespeare quote Lor always throws around pops into Rylie's head: *Love all, trust a few, do wrong to none.* If you mix up the order, the world becomes a monstrous place.

"How well did Thea know him, in the end?" The question's out before she can stop it, and Nathan looks up.

"Your grandpa? He kept to himself mostly. He . . ."

"He what?"

"Nothing. He worked a lot; you know that. He got into religion too."

"That doesn't sound like him. The religious part."

"People change, Rye."

"Not that much."

Nathan holds her gaze for a moment too long. "You might be right. Just look at us."

Us. Her heart feels unsteady and she busies herself with the box. Below the framed photo is a book by Gertrude Stein. Stein again—her poem was at her grandpa's cabin, written on a yellow legal pad. Next to the poetry book is a whittling knife and a half-finished sculpture made of dark wood. Its odd, misshapen form suddenly makes her want to shove away the entire box. She settles for looking at the map on his wall.

"You had that up before." Red pins are scattered across it—there's a cluster right in their part of California. "You used it for all the places you wanted to see one day, all the mountains you wanted to hike."

Nathan nods. "Now I use it for my markers."

"Markers?"

"For the places Lily might be," he says, and then Rylie feels her chest constrict even more as the map takes on a darker meaning. The pins in it must have been painful to place, like sticking them into your skin every time you pressed one down.

"Nathan, I—"

"I'm going to find her," he says. There's a resolve to his gaze—it's in the way he holds his shoulders too. He turns toward his computer. "I've got algorithms set up online, and I spend a lot of time on message boards. I read everything I can." He pulls books out from underneath the pile of twisted sheets on his bed. A few cinnamon toothpick boxes tumble onto the carpet. "Like *Lost Person Behavior*, by this search and rescue expert? It's all about looking at previous cases, to figure out what might have happened. People don't just vanish, Rye."

He tosses another book aside, Sun Tzu's *The Art of War*, and then picks it back up. "The source of strength is unity, not size. That's what I remember about this one. I'm not sure it applies to search parties, but I'm hoping it does." His eyes lift to Rylie's, and the way he's looking at her splits her right down the middle again. "I talk to armchair detectives too. Did you know that was a thing? Websleuths, Reddit. They've found people too. They've found others."

Nathan doesn't say if the people they found were alive, and he's looking at the map now the same way he looks at Rylie, like he's hoping the ink and borders and markers will somehow shape into a truth he can understand. Rylie's throat clamps tight. She fiddles with her pendant, the jade figure eight cool in her hand, her skin feeling flushed against it.

"We don't have to talk about—"

"It's okay." Nathan shrugs again. "It's kind of nice, actually. I never bring it up with Thea."

"Why not?"

He looks away from the map. "Her memory. Some days she even forgets that Lily's gone."

"It's hard sometimes, right?" She didn't mean to say it aloud, but now it's hanging between them. "Loving people. Because deep down you're afraid you could lose them."

"You know what's harder? Thinking it's your fault if they go."

Rylie reaches for his hand. The tension in Nathan's jaw is the opposite of her fingers on his: light, barely touching. A tingle shoots up her arm, and the warmth comes back, everywhere.

"I'm always thinking of Lily, even when I don't want to," Nathan says softly. For a moment they're both still, neither of them moving, and then he shifts and his hand is gone. "Hey, I brought you here for a surprise. That's what I promised you, anyway." He manages a smile, and she follows his lead.

"You know I'm not big on surprises."

"Let me try to change your mind." His smile brightens. "Just wait here a minute."

He leaves the room, and Rylie's gaze drifts back to the cardboard box. The Gertrude Stein book is on top, and she opens it. Inside there's an inscription: *To Ryan, from Thea. My theory is that Stein took a Union Pacific train to the Kelso Depot, through the Mojave.*

So Thea thought the poetry had been inspired by the desert here? Rylie flips the page. The first poem is called "If I Told Him, A Completed Portrait of Picasso," and red pen is slashed across it, probably the work of Thea or Rylie's grandpa. The words "Shutters shut and open so do queens" are underlined. There's more red ink under "exact resemblance to exact resemblance."

Rylie turns to the next page. Here, only one passage is underlined: *If they were not pigeons what were they.*

She flips to the next page, and the next, and for a while there isn't any red pen at all. Then, toward the back of the book, there's more underlining: *What is the current that presents a long line.* Rylie reads it again, trying to make sense of something that feels just out of reach. There's more underlining: *a dark place is not a dark place.* And at the very end of the poem: *A line distinguishes it.*

"Rye?"

It's Nathan, calling from the bottom of the stairs. She shuts the book and then takes the box down with her. Nathan has lit the fireplace, and he's standing near it, holding something behind his back. "Okay, close your eyes," he says as she sets down the cardboard box. "Please."

"Is this some sort of trust game?"

"Everything's a trust game."

"True." She closes her eyes and then feels him slip something heavy over her head. A helmet? Whatever it is smells faintly of cinnamon.

"Now hold these," he says, pulling something over each of her hands. They're gloves. A second later there's a glowing light just beyond her eyelids, and she peeks, blinking at what's in front of her.

It's a virtual canyon. A high cliff face is overlooking the bluest sky, and birds are flying past and the sound of wind is rushing through the headset. She laughs.

"So you looked," Nathan teases, and she turns toward

him, but of course she can't see him. Instead, her view shifts, moving past the rock ledge where her hands are perched. Her hands are the deep tan color of Nathan's skin, with aqua climbing gloves and two Fitbit-sized bracelets that are flickering with light.

"Since you're still hurt and can't climb, I figured you might like this instead."

"It's unreal," she says.

"Literally."

"Virtually." She smiles and lifts her arm, and the hand on the screen lifts too. The sound of jagged breathing fills her ears, and the red cliff wall she's hanging from has little beetles crawling over it. To her side is an outcropping of rock that's blinking—maybe she's supposed to grab it. "I never play games."

"Good to know," Nathan says, and the way he says it makes her wonder if they're talking about the same thing.

"First time for everything, right?" she teases, to keep him guessing too. There's a sheer drop down to the desert floor underneath her, and she reaches for the hold. Her virtual hand catches it, the bracelet on her arm flickering to show that her strength's diminishing. A grunting sound comes out of the speakers, and she grins. "This is nothing like real rock climbing, but it's the next-best thing."

"It's Oculus Rift. The original version. Bought it with my signing bonus."

The virtual view is almost dizzying, and another bird flies past, so close that it startles her, and then the howl of a coyote comes through the speakers. She stops herself from ripping off the helmet.

"You have to keep moving or your energy runs out," Nathan tells her, "and you lose your grip and fall."

Climbing, falling. They're easier to think about than strange coyotes, or the night she got lost on the hike, or the pictures from her grandpa's cabin, everything she's hiding from Nathan about his sister. Rylie wants to clear her head.

"It's good to fall sometimes," she says, "so you know how your body's going to react, so you can climb more freely without being scared. It's all about getting back on the wall and not being afraid to start over."

"Starting over isn't too bad," Nathan says, and for the second time Rylie wonders if they're talking about the same thing. Curious, she lets her virtual hands run out of strength. The bracelets around her wrists go red, the sound of panting gets louder, and then the screen goes black as she falls, but she's laughing when she never would in real life, and it feels good, like a release. She pulls the headset off. Nathan's watching her from the couch and grinning too.

"Come over more often. I think you need more practice?"

"Or a better coach." She's quick to the couch, trying to don him with the headset, but he catches her wrist in his. The nearness of the fire feels warm on her skin, and so does his touch. She lets him pull her gloves off.

"Close your eyes," she says. "It's only fair." And she's surprised when he does, surprised at what her heart does when she looks at him. There's the tug of something like gravity between them, a downward swoop of her stomach like she's falling again. For a second it feels like the only place in the world is right here, right next to him on Thea's couch, but then she sees it. The glimpse of black hair behind him.

It's a photograph of Lily. In it, Lily has her sleeves rolled up, and she's standing out back, near Thea's succulent garden, a pair of shears in one hand and a thick green aloe leaf in the other. Rylie can almost see her tilt her sunglasses down; she can almost hear Lily talking: *Find me. You're wasting time.*

Wasting time, and sitting way too close to her brother. "Here." Rylie pushes the headset onto Nathan's head.

"Want me to show you how it's done?" he teases as he stands, and then a moment later he turns away, starts playing Oculus Rift. At the window behind him is a view of the yard, a lone outside light splaying across Thea's rocky garden. The aloe vera leaves are brown now, or maybe it's just the way they look in the orangey light. Rylie forces herself to stare back at the photograph.

Lily has a bitter smile. *There are others like me*, she's saying. *Other photos in your grandpa's cabin. I know you've seen them. I know you're trying to forget.*

Rylie suddenly feels like hurling the frame. She can't forget any of it. Every time she looks at Nathan, it comes back to her. Every time she thinks of Thea. No matter how much she tries *not* to think of it, it all comes back anyway, like there's an invisible thread between her and Lily, tying them together because of their past. It's like they're connected by an X-point. Rylie's dad told her about them once when he was writing a physics lesson, how X-points are places where the Earth's magnetic field connects to the Sun's magnetic field, creating an instantaneous portal from one to the other. Being around Nathan connects Rylie to Lily. And Lily is connected to her grandpa. Somehow.

Rylie stands. She needs to ask what she came to ask. "Hey, Nathan? Did my grandpa help with the search at all? For Lily."

He pulls off the headset and turns toward her, the scar on his eyebrow creasing again. "A lot of people helped, Rye."

"But did you hire him?"

"Like, pay him?" Nathan shakes his head. "Why?"

And just like that, her stomach feels like it has an X-point to the bottom of the ocean. "No reason. Never mind." Lying to Nathan makes her want to take the helmet back and shove it over her face. Nathan's the most honest person she's ever known, next to Ben. They both have the same respect for the truth, for laying it all on the table, which has never come that easy for her. Maybe it's because she was raised by a mom with a security clearance. Maybe it's because of her dad too—he even wrote a song about it, the one called "Only Human." *Spare the truth to spare the feelings; sometimes lying is the only real thing.* But what if you don't know the truth, or don't know all of it?

Nathan's phone beeps, and she feels a rush of relief as he

looks away to check it. "It's Sara. She said she canceled the party." Then Journey's "Don't Stop Believin'" starts blaring through his phone.

"Hang on, now she's calling," Nathan says. He steps into the kitchen and opens the fridge. "You want a drink?" he asks loudly, his phone still ringing. "Unfortunately, we no longer have juice boxes."

Juice boxes. Lily loved them, even when they got older, because she had a thing for chewing on the straws. "I'm good, thanks," Rylie says, glancing back at the picture as Nathan picks up. Lily's still staring out from the frame with that look of hers, the superior one Rylie couldn't stand, because it used to remind her of her grandpa. And now Lily's gone and he could have had something to do with it. Rylie can't stay here one minute longer, or else her heart might break. She picks up the cardboard box from Thea and turns back to Nathan, ready with an excuse to leave. He's got the phone propped up against his ear as he pours a glass of juice.

"Really?" he says into the phone. "That's messed up."

Rylie feels herself go still. What is Sara telling him?

"Shit," he says in a low voice. The glass is on the counter beside him now, sitting untouched. "Why?" he asks quietly. Then he glances over his shoulder, looking right at her, his face expressionless. Sara must have told him. She must have mentioned the visit to the police station.

Rylie steps forward. She feels like crushing the box she's holding. Either that or dropping it and running.

"Interesting," Nathan says, his voice still quiet, hushed. Then he nods. "Okay."

He sets his phone down and stares at the juice for a moment. When he looks up, he seems distracted. "Sara just told me something strange. . . ." He trails off, and Rylie braces herself.

"What's going on?"

"They got a letter at the police station," he says. "From Ethan Langhorne."

If you think it's just me, then you deserve what's coming to you.

CHAPTER 19

RYLIE SITS UP IN BED, her skin slick with sweat. The windows are dark and the room is cold, colder than it was at midnight when Lor finally came back, exhausted from both the talk with her cousin and the vodka Miles gave her to get *through* the talk with Iggy. Now Lor is still sleeping—she's a shadowy lump on the other side of the bed—and Rylie reaches for her phone to check the time. It's too early, just after five in the morning. Beside her, Lor rustles and turns over, her black hair in her face before she pushes it aside and groans. "Was that you all night, Rye?"

"Was what me all night?"

"I think you were talking in your sleep. Or maybe I dreamed it?" Lor yawns and then grabs her own phone, the screen casting a bluish tint over her face. "I'm so freaking tired but I need to leave soon," she says. "I can't believe my cousin sabotaged half my trip."

Rylie tenses. "So what did Iggy say to you?" she asks, and Lor buries her head under a pillow instead of answering. "Come on, tell me. You swore to fill me in." Rylie tosses another pillow onto her but she stays buried. "I'm not some delicate flower, Lor."

"No, you're like a flower that grows between slabs of cement," Lor says, her voice muffled, and Rylie tosses more pillows until Lor peeks out from beneath the pile. "Right, so it was honestly more of a *general* doom-and-gloom message," she admits, "and then Iggy strongly advised me to leave Twentynine Palms and, you know, not to trust anyone."

Rylie slides off the bed and stands. "'Anyone' as in me."

"You know what his problem is?" Lor gets up too, gathering up her clothes and stuffing them into her bag. "He thinks that because I'm younger, my judgments aren't valid." She walks to the bathroom and grabs a towel, turning back. "What are you saying to the cops today?"

Rylie steps past her and starts changing her gauze in the bathroom, slathering ointment over her cuts. "I've got till noon to figure that out."

Lor sighs. "What if the Ethan Langhorne tape is evidence or something? Are you telling them you kept it for two days?"

"It's not like I'm trying to help him." That has to matter, but maybe the police wouldn't see it that way. The note Ethan left them yesterday suggested that he wasn't working alone. *If you think it's just me, then you deserve what's coming to you.* Maybe the police would see her as a suspect; Sara told her they were looking for an accomplice. Rylie finishes wrapping her gauze. It feels too tight and Lor is staring at her now.

"What?"

"Look, just talk to your mom about it," Lor says. "Weren't you going to anyway?"

"She got held up at work yesterday," Rylie says, but it's a bad excuse and they both know it.

"Want me to come with you?" Lor asks softly.

"No. Shower. I'm a weed that grows between slabs of concrete, remember?" Rylie forces a smile as she picks up her grandpa's cassette player from the room and then hurries down the wide staircase. In the hallway, a faint smell of coffee is in the air, and the shutters are raised in the kitchen. The windows are open to the dark desert sky—the sun won't be up for another couple of hours, but she's suddenly wide awake in the cool air, revved up by what she needs to say.

"Mom?" she calls out, and then she hears a thud in the garage.

She opens the door and finds a light on and a pair of camouflaged legs under the jeep. A second later her mom rolls out from underneath, a wrench in her hand. Her face is swollen, like she's been crying.

"Owen said it was shaking when you accelerated." She sits up on the creeper. "Gotta keep your dad's jeep alive, right? And keep you safe."

Rylie loosens her grip on the cassette player. "Thanks," she says quietly.

Her mom sets down the wrench. "Sorry I got back late last night. Things should die down once I get this budget in order." She wipes her face with her sleeve, getting grease on her chin. It matches the dark creases under her eyes that still haven't gone away. "You're up early. How are you feeling? Remember anything more about the hike yet?"

Right now the hike's the furthest thing from Rylie's mind. "I actually wanted to talk to you about something else."

Her mom gets up from the creeper. "Then let's talk while I get ready." She heads back into the house and flicks on the kitchen lights, then grabs the rest of her uniform that's draped over one of the stools. "Ben said you were invited to Nathan's yesterday?" she asks as Rylie sets the cassette player on the counter.

"That's—"

"You're just getting to know him again, Rye. You're not thinking of . . ."

Rylie's cheeks go hot. Today of all days she does *not* want to be having this conversation. "Why would you even ask that, Mom?" But she already knows why: this is her mother, always thinking of security, logistics, the way machines operate.

"I just know how much he used to mean to you," her mom says, zipping up her laptop case. She reaches for her half-empty mug of coffee and then glances at Rylie and stops. "You know, you look a lot like your dad when you make that face."

Rylie goes still. Her mom must be thinking about him today. She always did when she worked on the jeep. "When would he look like this?"

"When he was plotting. Usually it was a surprise that he wasn't sure I'd like."

Rylie's dad loved surprises, even the small ones. Her mom, not so much, just like her. Her mom won't like this either. "Can you stay home today? Just for the morning."

"I wish I could, Rye," she says, twisting her hair into a bun. "Work's a mess. I need to go over the numbers again before my next meeting. There've been some issues, and—"

Rylie has heard it all before. All of her mom's jobs have been like this. She has to put out fires that no one is supposed to know about. "And you can't go into detail."

"A lot of it isn't actually classified this time," her mom says, but she's wearing that face she makes when she's deciding how much to sugarcoat. "The cuts are mostly coming from old defense projects that should have been decommissioned decades ago."

"What's 'decommissioned' mean?"

They both turn. Owen's also up earlier than usual, standing in the kitchen in his pajamas. So much for Rylie talking to their mom alone. "It means 'getting the axe,'" Rylie says.

"*What's* getting the axe, Mom?" he asks, switching on his Talkboy.

She leans forward conspiratorially. "Well, there's this one project that's so old, it's Depression era. Can you believe that? It's got the same birthday as you do, Leap. I noticed the February 29 start date when I was reading the brief on it."

"A leap year? So it's *not* that old, then." Owen's joke gets a laugh from their mom, and Rylie pulls the cassette player closer. He needs to go back upstairs—she can't play the tape in front of him.

"Well, the software's been updated over the years," her mom goes on in a faux-secretive voice, really playing it up for Owen, "but its only function is a daily pulse, sent out by a radio tower in the middle of the desert," she says. "Supposedly it's measuring the earth's electromagnetic field."

"You lost me at 'electromagnetic,'" Ben says, swooping into the kitchen and ruffling Owen's hair. "Is that one of the projects you've been asked to shut down, Eve?"

She nods and glances at her watch. "I'm talking it over with my boss this morning, but I won't know for sure until tomorrow." She reaches for her keys. "We've got a meeting with the base commander *and* about every civilian defense contractor imaginable, so everyone forgive me if I'm a ghost till then."

"At least you're not a spook," Ben teases, kissing her on the cheek. "Who wants an early breakfast? I was going to go running, but if everyone's up, let's eat." He dons his Padres apron. "Waffles on me," he offers. "Or anything you want. Rylie, got a craving?"

She shakes her head. "I'm not that hungry yet." The talk with her mom isn't exactly going to plan. If her mom can't be late for work today, maybe Rylie can pull Ben aside after breakfast, tell him instead. "Whatever Owen wants."

"Or Lourdes," Owen says, just as Lor appears in the doorway in one of her vintage dresses, this one emerald green, her hair damp and loose. She's got an open notebook in her hands—probably a script.

"None for me, thanks," Lor murmurs without looking up. "I've got that audition. Gotta hit the road soon."

"Poor road," Ben says, earning a laugh from Owen, but Lor doesn't hear him. She heads toward Rylie and grabs her elbow.

"I need to show you something," she whispers. *"Now."*

CHAPTER 20

WHEN RYLIE SEES WHAT LOR is holding, she pulls her friend upstairs. "You found them, didn't you?" The hallway is dark and empty, but she keeps her voice low anyway. "You found my grandpa's journals."

Lor nods toward the library. "The door was open, and I saw the shelves and just thought . . ." She stops in the doorway. "Should we wake up Kai?" she asks, and Rylie shakes her head as they step into the shadows together. The room has been cleaned up, reorganized. The cardboard boxes are gone, the desk is clear, and Ben has finished putting his textbooks away.

"I looked in here before," Rylie whispers, quietly shutting the door behind them. It's still dark at the windows, so it's hard to see, but she doesn't turn on a light. "I didn't find anything."

"You can thank me later." Lor walks to the corner of the room, and there, on a bottom shelf, is a whole row of black leather journals that match the one she's holding. Ben must have rearranged the shelves while he was unpacking—the

Moleskines weren't here the day Rylie grabbed the hypnosis book.

"Rye . . ." Lor glances down at the Moleskine in her hands. "I don't know if you actually want to read this." She tilts the journal toward her anyway, and Rylie takes it.

Finally, something solid to hang on to. Something that might have answers. She needs the month that Lily went missing, but there aren't any dates, just her grandpa's writing closely packed in. She can almost hear his voice as she reads it.

> It happened again. There are people here who shouldn't be here. I saw them. I saw Bobby Harcourt from Mississippi—Big B, everyone called him—and he said the exact words I wanted to say to him. He said: "I thought you were dead." But he's the one who got shot in the head. He's the one who died.

Shot in the head? The one who died? Rylie's stomach twists tight, and then she makes the connection. It's Vietnam. He's writing about the war. She flips to the middle of the journal, scans some more:

> Just got to this shitty wasteland. Chase the numbness with a beer, piss it away, do it again. Not even thirty and washed out, brain bleached,

soul gone. Might as well bury me now. The only person besides Reggie who treats me like I'm human here is this nurse I met. She was over in Vietnam too. Maybe that's why she puts up with me.

This time he must be talking about Twentynine Palms. It was his first duty station after returning to the States; she knows that much. His very first post, and then he came back before he retired, and never left. But this, this must be him just arriving. She wants to keep reading, but the entry isn't going to be about Lily or Ethan Langhorne. It's decades away from that. She skips to the last page to see where the journal leaves off.

I feel the same way here in 29 Palms that I did in Vietnam. It's worse than paranoia. It's the darkness coming back, messing with my head. It's people too. That hitchhiker I picked up at the gas station after Black Rock, I saw her again. She didn't remember. She didn't remember getting hurt, didn't remember the blood or how we ran away after. She didn't even ask about my scars. I need to get out of here before it happens again. Go do something else. Flip burgers. Go to school. But even if I left, I wouldn't be leaving it behind. Not after everything I've done.

Rylie slams the journal shut, and the loud clap of the leather stuns her, just like the words. *Blood. Scars. Everything I've done.* She wants to read more, but there's no time. "We need the recent ones," she says. "We need to find the one on Lily. From last year."

"Easy. The dates are on the spines," Lor says, tugging out two Moleskines littered with yellow sticky notes. The journal she hands over is stiff; its cover is firm as Rylie opens it. The first entry is from April of last year, a month shy of Lily's disappearance. This journal is orderly and precise, full of dates and times. It's just like the one she remembers reading as a kid, the day her grandpa caught her and slammed its cover on her fingers. She scans the page:

6:05, coffee. 6:53, went for walk, saw vultures.
9:43, conversation with Thea, discussed the leak.
10:12, tried to call Eve.

Eve. Rylie's heart skips. He's talking about her mom.

No answer, left first message of the day.

First message? That implies there were others. And didn't her mom change her number after their fight so he couldn't get ahold of her?

10:35, read newspaper, nothing in obituaries. 11:06,
drove to grocery store for pallet. 13:02, call from

doctor. 14:17, saw black jacket. 14:31, took supplies to cabin. 15:10, called Eve again.

Rylie pauses, her grip tight on the journal. It's the last entry of that day. She flips to the next page.

6:15, coffee, reinforced shelf. 6:48, went for walk, three hikers on northwest fork. 7:17, black jacket watching.

Black jacket. That's twice now, in just a few pages.

11:02, smelled smoke on way home. Wildfire. Heard explosions.

The wildfire line is highlighted in bright yellow, and there's a sticky note next to it. Rylie picks it up, trying to read the scrawl:

No wildfires reported on this day.
No significant fire destruction in this
region for the past two years.

She stares at the note. It contradicts the entry. Her grandpa must have been analyzing his own journals, testing his memory or its accuracy. She skips to the day of Lily's disappearance. Her lungs hardly take in air as she reads:

7:02, coffee, cleaned rifles. 7:48, saw black
jacket at intersection when driving to pharmacy.
7:49, witnessed a three-vehicle pileup.

Not what she's looking for. There's nothing else for that day, no mention of Lily or even Ethan Langhorne. But a few lines have been erased and rewritten, as if her grandpa altered them. The final line of the entry is highlighted, and there's another sticky note beside it:

No police record of car accident.
No hospitalization records.

The sticky note reminds Rylie too much of going to the hospital after the night hike, but there's something else about it that makes her stomach feel like she's rappelling, going too fast off the side of a cliff. She holds the two notes next to each other. The handwriting matches, but it's so different from the handwriting in the journal. . . .

Another sticky note is on the carpet at her feet—it must have fallen out. She bends closer to read it.

Signs of PTSD, among others. Misdiagnosis?
Recommend psychiatrist, not neurologist.
Follow up with Eve to confirm.

The sticky note swims in front of her. And then it hits all at once and she puts a hand on the shelf to steady herself.

"Are you getting all this?" Lor says quietly, setting down the journal she's holding, and Rylie nods. She has to know; she has to know *for sure*.

She steps toward Ben's desk. Pencils and pens and highlighters in a San Diego Padres mug. A pad of yellow sticky notes. Her hands go to fists. It's not proof, not yet. Ben's computer is on the desk too—probably password protected. They need to be quick; he can't find them up here now.

"Can you make sure no one's coming?" Rylie whispers, and Lor's brown eyes widen a little as she nods and moves to the door. Rylie turns back to the desk. Next to the monitor is a stack of paper. It's a draft of her stepdad's thesis, printed out, title page on top:

A DANGEROUS PRECIPICE
Erasing the Stigma of Mental Illness:
Identity, Memory, and Societal Beliefs

Rylie turns the page, trying to hurry. The next part is some sort of foreword, parts of it crossed out with pen:

Inside every scholar is a flame, burning strongly enough to singe the heart and mind, irreparably changing everything. We spend our lives trying to understand the flame and then trying to articulate it. We want it to spread to others so that they might see the light as well.

She keeps scanning, the paper shaking slightly in her hand.

My own curiosity, and this thesis, was
~~greatly~~ sparked by my wife's father, a man
from whom she was estranged for some time,
largely due to his behavior toward her
children. When she asked whether I could
help him, I initially declined, ~~but the~~
~~match had already been struck, the flame~~
~~sparking to life.~~ The two-year relation-
ship that developed with her father was a
fraught one, but it was also illuminating,
for both of us.

So it's true. *Ben* was the one who went through the journals. She hears footsteps somewhere close, and Lor puts
a finger to her lips, then shakes her head a moment later.
Clear. Rylie looks back down at the thesis. The knot in her
stomach is a taut figure eight now, but she needs to keep
reading.

When we first met, he described himself as
a Vietnam veteran with a head injury that
warranted the annual attention of a neurologist [see footnote 3]. Besides living
with pain from the injury, he also experienced a host of other symptoms ~~that he~~

~~refused to seek additional treatment for,~~
most notably: memory loss and a predilection for violence—both of which he docu-
mented in detail over the course of his
life ~~and which make his case so unusual,~~
~~and compelling. This rare documentation is~~
~~a reservoir of insight for anyone in the~~
~~field . . .~~

Rylie's hands tighten over the page, her bandages digging into her skin. *Memory loss. A predilection for violence.* Her
own memory loss on the hike was a fluke; it wouldn't happen again. She keeps scanning.

. . . Initially, he seemed eager to par-
ticipate in memory regression. ~~After our~~
~~first session, he confided to me that the~~
~~landscape itself was "alive" and that it~~
~~was constantly "watching him." To ac-~~
~~count for his experiences of missing time,~~
~~he claimed to have been in contact with~~
~~what he called "unwanted visitors."~~ However, over time, he became increasingly
less communicative during the regres-
sions. He kept insisting that he was not
a "weak man" and that his head injury ~~and~~
~~the subsequent symptoms he experienced~~ had
nothing to do with the "reality we faced."

Even to the end, he could not break out of
the bonds of self-stigma. So-called weak-
ness, in his mind, was only acceptable
when applied to humanity as a whole, to a
world "under threat."

We were at a dangerous precipice, he
told me, and this, at least, we could
agree upon. If we cannot stop stigmatizing
ourselves, then how will the world ever
change?

She clenches the page. *A dangerous precipice*. That was her grandpa's exact warning to her, that last summer when they came to visit. They never came back, not once; her mom had supposedly cut off contact. But all along she was talking to him on the phone, introducing him to Ben. And lying about everything. Rylie doesn't want to believe it, but it's right in front of her; she's holding the truth in her hands.

Ben knew her grandpa. Ben tried to treat *her grandpa*.

And her mom let him. And they kept it a secret the whole time. And if they kept *that* a secret, then maybe there were other secrets. Maybe Ben and her mom knew about Lily's disappearance last year too. Maybe they intentionally kept quiet about it.

Rylie blinks, trying to clear the accusations swirling in her head—she feels dizzy with them. She hears Castle barking from downstairs as Lor turns from the door. "Hurry,"

Lor whispers, and then a thought sears through Rylie and she flips back to an earlier section.

```
He described himself as a Vietnam veteran
with a head injury that warranted the an-
nual attention of a neurologist [see foot-
note 3].
```

It doesn't take long for Rylie to find the footnote. She stares at it numbly. The specialist that her grandpa saw was Dr. Reginald Singh. The same neurologist that Rylie was referred to, that her mom *asked* her to see after the hike. Rylie feels like she's been gut-punched. Her grandpa was Dr. Singh's patient too, and her mom didn't bother to tell her that. Her follow-up with him is tomorrow morning. There's no way she's going now.

"Rylie," Lor hisses, and then Rylie hears more footsteps, right outside the hallway. "Rye, we need to—"

Just then the door bursts open. Rylie holds her breath until she sees that it's Owen, just Owen. "Hey," she says quickly.

"What are you doing in here?" he asks, but he doesn't give her a chance to answer. "Dad has to work on his thesis today," he goes on, "and Kai's still sleeping and Mom has to go to base so she says you're supposed to watch me. But Dad's still cooking us breakfast if we want. Omelets or honey-almond polenta or pancakes?"

The thought of food makes Rylie's stomach turn, and she doesn't want *anything* from Ben. She sets down the thesis as quietly as she can.

"Actually, I've got a better idea," she says, steering Owen toward the door. They need to leave before anyone else finds them in here. "Why don't you and I go to the bakery instead, pick up some breakfast for everyone, O? That way Ben can get straight to work on his thesis." She keeps the bitterness from her voice, but Lor gives her a look anyway.

"I'll stay here longer, Rye," Lor offers.

"You can't," Rylie says. "You've got an audition."

"I never get the good parts anyway." Lor shrugs but won't meet her eye. "They only want cute and doe-eyed or hot-blooded Latina from me. I want to be the villain."

"So go prove them wrong."

"Another time. Barista Barry will fill in for me at the café tonight too. So I'm staying."

"You're not." Rylie delivers Lor's glare right back at her. "I'm fine, I promise." And she *is*. Lor has already done enough, and Rylie doesn't need help from her mom or Ben either, not now. The bakery is an excuse to get out without any questions. She's done here, done with all of it. On the way home she can drop everything off at the police station, let them deal with it.

She pulls Owen close. "Come on, Spaghetti O. We'll go to your favorite place. Italy Mine, right?" She turns to Lor, flashes her best smile. "And *you*, my friend, are going to kill that audition."

Lor stares at her for a second and then gives her a shampoo-scented hug. "If Camilla can get there without breaking down."

"I'll walk you out." Owen links his arm through Lor's.

"I'll catch up in a minute," Rylie says, and Lor blows a kiss over her shoulder as she heads toward the dark stairwell with Owen. A moment later Rylie's alone with the thesis and the journals. She can't leave yet, not without checking one more entry. She peers out the door—no one's in sight—and then she hustles back to the shelf and runs her fingers along the spines. Last year's journals are grouped together, and there, toward the end of the row, is the journal from four years ago. She listens for footsteps before opening it up. Then she flicks through the pages until she finds the day that makes her heart go sickeningly fast in her chest.

6:55, coffee. 8:13, Drove with Ari. The kids and Lily came too. Couldn't find it. Kept driving on Highway 62.

The page is shaking so much, she can hardly read. Find *what* on Highway 62? What was he trying to find that day? If only they'd never gone. She shuts her eyes, remembering the backseat of the hot car, how Lily begged to come with them. How the windows were rolled down. How they stopped for McDonald's ice cream cones on the way. The taste of the vanilla mingling with the smell of her dad's cigarettes. Warm air hitting her face from the open windows. How impatient her grandpa was.

8:56. Collision at Yucca Mesa.

She stares down at the page. The vanilla ice cream was all over the floor, and there was glass in it. Owen was crying in his car seat and Lily was rubbing her head but Rylie couldn't see her dad or her grandpa—they weren't in the front anymore. She unbuckled her belt and opened the car door. The pavement was glittering with glass. More glass in the wildflowers along the highway. Owen was still crying in the car, saying his eyes hurt, and her grandpa was just ahead, bent over in the sunlight. He was crouching over something in the road.

8:59. Tried to revive Ari.

Tried to revive. Rylie tears out the page, balls it up in her hand. The paper feels too light, too soft. She shoves it into her pocket and hurries from the room.

CHAPTER 21

A FEW MINUTES LATER, AFTER watching Lor drive off, Rylie makes a hard turn out of the neighborhood in the jeep, Owen and Castle beside her. Then they're on the dark highway, heading into a predawn sky. Power lines clip by fast, faster. Her mom lied; Ben lied too. The jeep climbs to eighty, ninety, and then she finally remembers where she is, who she's with. She can't scare Owen.

Rylie lets her foot off the gas, unclamps her fingers from the wheel. "You're quiet, O."

Owen turns toward her, his curly hair wild, that creased look between his eyes that he gets when he's thinking. "Did you have a nightmare last night?"

"No, why?" Rylie unravels her bandages as she drives, to focus on something besides her mom and Ben. Her scrapes need to air out anyway—most of the redness is gone now, but her scabs have pus at the edges, even with all the ointment she put on them.

"I heard you. Our beds are against the same wall." Owen pulls Castle onto his lap. "You shouted out in your sleep. At first I thought it was Kai again, but it wasn't this time."

"This time? Does Kai usually yell in his sleep?"

Owen's face scrunches up like he's not sure what to say.

"What?" Rylie asks.

"You kept telling someone to die. You kept saying that you wanted them all to die." He hugs Castle against his chest. "It reminded me of that night we went hiking."

Memory loss. A predilection for violence.

"That won't happen again, O," she says softly. It's hard not to drive faster now. The wind rushes against the jeep until they reach town and she swerves into the bakery's parking lot. Owen and Castle hop out after she parks, but Rylie stays in the jeep, digging into the pressure point on her hand. The sun's not even up yet, and the morning already feels like an avalanche. All the secrets have left her shaken, they've dislodged something hard inside her, and now the hurt is tumbling over her, burying her in rubble.

She glances at Owen on the curb. Being out of the house with him will lighten her mood—and then she'll go to the police station early. She won't even wait till noon. The hiking backpack with all the tapes is wedged on top of the console, and she runs her hand across it, the avalanche rushing inside her again, and then she gets out into the cool morning air and walks over to where Owen's waiting. Together they head past a few dark shops and tie Castle up next to a glowing Italy Mine, the only store open in the complex this early. As they walk in, the scent of butter and coffee hits them, and a tall woman waiting near the counter turns their way.

"We've got a problem, O," Rylie says.

His grip tightens on her hand. "What?"

"There are hundreds of different pastries here. We're going to have to make some hard choices."

Owen grins as they get in line. The tall woman in front of them keeps staring, maybe at Owen's cane, because there's no one else behind them. Rylie glares at her, but now the woman is staring pointedly at Rylie's arms. She forgot to rewrap her bandages.

"What happened?" the woman asks. Her turquoise earrings sway as she reaches for Rylie's arm. "How did you get them? The scratches."

Rylie steps back. "I can't remember."

"How's your impulse control?" she murmurs. She's studying her the same way Iggy did yesterday. "And what about the pain?"

"What pain?" Owen echoes, squeezing Rylie's hand again. "Are you hurt, Rye?"

"I'm fine," she says quickly.

"You can't just ignore it." The woman suddenly looks older, her face lined with worry, and Rylie gets the faintest hint of recognition. Not because of the woman's face but because . . . because it feels like someone has talked to her this way before. Asked her these same questions.

"Who *are* you?"

"I'm a survivor," the woman says, as if that should explain everything. She pulls up the sleeve of her dark jacket. Near her elbow is a long, jagged scar, and Rylie's heart starts going fast.

"Can you give me a minute?" Rylie wants Owen out of earshot. "I'm just going to order, and once my brother's in the car—"

"Then we'll talk." The woman nods. "I'll meet you outside. Under the awning." The bakery door chimes as she pushes it open, and she turns, lingering. "Just hurry. Once it happens, it doesn't stop. I can't control it."

"What can't she control?" Owen asks as the woman turns and strides off.

"Hey, we're up, O," Rylie says as an answer. Her appetite's gone, but Owen's isn't, thankfully, and he helps her fill a large box with croissants, baklava in every flavor, fried dough balls called lokma, cinnamon buns and bear claws, chocolate eclairs, and a small box of tea called Minerva's Creosote Cleanse, along with a hot chamomile tea because it's meant to be calming. Then she takes Owen's hand, grabs Castle on the way out, and gets them both settled into the jeep, windows down to the almost-dawn sky. The odd warning keeps running through her mind. *Once it happens, it doesn't stop. I can't control it.*

Owen opens the box. "Don't you want to eat too, Rye?"

"Of course," she says, picking up her tea. "I won't be long, okay?" She glances down at her bandages and then over at the awning near the shops. The streetlamps are on; she'll be able to watch the jeep the whole time. But when she strides over, the only person in sight is a guy smoking near a bench in the dark. She looks up and down the shop fronts, then checks the parking lot and the bakery again.

The woman's gone.

Rylie hurries back to the jeep, her tea lukewarm now and bitter-tasting. Owen is sitting in the passenger seat where she left him, carefully unraveling a cinnamon roll. He takes a bite of the center first, just like their dad used to, and her heart pangs. The woman stood her up, and then she stood up Owen and their breakfast date. It's contagious—people saying one thing and doing another. She gets into the jeep and glances at the hiking backpack before checking the time. It's not even seven a.m. yet, but the police station will be open.

"I need to make one last stop before we head home, O."

"Why did that woman say those things to you?" Owen asks, his mouth full of cinnamon roll. "Her voice sounded funny, like she was worried."

"I don't think she was feeling well." It's a lie—Rylie doesn't know what to think, and now the bad feeling is back in her chest. She leans over to check Owen's belt, then snaps in her own before starting up the jeep. There's definitely no one under the awning, and the guy who was smoking is gone now too. Rylie pulls out onto the road, too fast, and a second later she's blinded by headlights in her rearview mirror. She changes lanes, heading toward the police station. The car behind her changes lanes too. A headache starts at her temples as the headlights get closer in the mirror.

"Minor detour," she says, quickly veering onto a quiet back road full of subdivisions, with patches of undeveloped land just beyond. Owen's munching on a bear claw now and giving pieces of it to Castle. He licks his fingers and then pulls out his Talkboy.

"So did you have fun at Nathan's yesterday?" he asks.

"Why wouldn't I?"

Owen grins. "Do you like him?"

"Of course I like him," Rylie says. "We were good friends once."

"But do you *like* like him?"

"Are you recording this?" she teases back.

Owen laughs, just as there's a sharp glint of headlights—the car is behind them again and driving way too close. Her mom would slow to make a point, and Ben would wave, but Rylie hits the gas, her tires screeching as she makes another sharp turn onto a small road. Then they're jostling down a one-way dirt track, away from the asshole driver, but it's the wrong direction. The only thing around them is desert scrub, and in the distance are the shadows of foothills.

Owen clings to the bakery box and grins. "I like off-roading."

"Me too," she says lightly, but she's already regretting her decision. She needs to find a spot to turn around.

"Kai let me record him yesterday," Owen says. He bites into his bear claw, scattering cinnamon and sugar clumps all over his shirt. "It's really sad about his mom. It happened way after her and Ben got divorced, though." He swallows noisily as Rylie glances at her side mirror.

"What about his mom?"

Far behind them is a beam of light. The car's slowing near the dirt road that she's made the unfortunate mistake of taking them down.

And then the car turns too.

Rylie grips the wheel as her mind starts running through all sorts of scenarios: drugs, human trafficking, a random weirdo. The desert around them is still dark with the morning twilight, and ahead of them there's the thinnest line of red on the horizon. It should be beautiful, but it's not—the redness is almost unsettling. A bead of sweat works its way down her back.

"I'm thirsty, Rye," Owen says. "We should have gotten milk."

Milk's the last thing she wants right now, with the dark road in front of them and a strange car behind them, out in the middle of nowhere.

"Pull up Google Maps," she says. "Find out how far we are from home."

Owen voice-commands her phone and then taps her elbow. "It's not working. No service."

Rylie looks at the screen. The land around Twentynine Palms is a wide-open blank on the map, no roads filled in, nothing at all.

"Do we have any water?" Owen asks, rubbing Castle's ears.

"Just what we got Castle earlier." She glances at the rearview mirror. The car's still behind them, and they're on a single-lane road. Turning around now isn't an option. She just has to hope the road meets up with some kind of highway soon.

"But he already drank it," Owen says. He starts rummaging around on the floorboards like he thinks a bottle of water might materialize if he puts in the effort. She hands the last of her tea to him and he takes a drink and then switches on his Talkboy. "Rylie's driving too fast down Highway 62," he says into it.

She almost smiles. He's trying to cheer her up. "I *was* driving fast down Highway 62. We're currently stuck on some side road."

"Rylie's driving too fast down some side road," Owen repeats into the Talkboy, "because her brother's desperate for water."

She laughs now; she can't help herself. "Stop narrating, O."

"Okaaaay," he drawls out, working on the loose tooth in his mouth, "how about a question, then?"

She's still watching the car behind them, but there's no reason to get Owen worried too. "Shoot."

"What's your best memory out here?"

"My best memory . . ." She trails off, her gaze on the car behind them and then on a billboard ahead. The billboard's a good sign. A highway must be close.

"Rylie?"

"Probably just being here all together. Mom, Dad, me, and you." For a minute she lets herself forget about the car, forget about being lost, because it's one of her favorite memories. "The four of us stayed in the cabin because Grandpa had guests at his house. It was Christmastime, and instead of getting a tree, we decorated the Joshua trees in the yard with red ribbons and hung bells from the cabin's ceiling. Dad also brought out his menorah. The cabin's so small that whenever we took a step, the bells started ringing and the candle flames would dance. But you were so little then."

"I remember it," Owen says, nodding hard. "I remember the bells and the smoke. And I remember the humming sound. I can hear it now, too."

"The humming?" Rylie draws a blank, and then it comes back to her: the night they drove out here, Owen mentioned a humming sound—it was the night she thought she'd hit someone. "You mean, the way the desert sounds?"

"Yeah," Owen says, his voice suddenly uneasy. He reaches for her hand, just as the road angles. She takes the turn too fast, and the jeeps skids and then rights itself. Owen's hand is still on hers, and Castle is panting loudly, and it's hard to focus on driving because her headache is back. She floors the gas, wanting to get away from the car, the headlights still in her rearview mirror. Just ahead, a large blue van comes into view, lettering across its side. It's an Enigma Tours van, parked near the side of the road.

Rylie eases her grip on the wheel as they near it. Even *if* the car is following them, they'll be okay. The sun is just starting to rise, it's a white sliver on the horizon now, and they're not alone, they're not stranded—there are people inside the van. But they're—

"Rylie," Owen breathes, his head pressed oddly against the window. "Do you hear that?"

She blinks as they speed past the van and the people inside, the people who look like they're screaming. *What's wrong with them?* Castle's ears are pricked and he's growling, and then everything feels off. Suddenly the tour van is just a speck in the rearview mirror, and the car is gone. The sun is gone too and there's a blaring noise.

In the split second that she realizes that the jeep's idling halfway off the road, she's blinded by headlights rushing toward them, barreling down. A horn blasts again. Rylie slams the gas, and the jeep jerks forward. Then comes a heavy jolt as a semitruck shoots past, ripping off the passenger-side mirror and flinging it across the road. She pulls over, half in shock, her breath heaving. The wheel feels sticky and wet under her hands. There's blood on her shirt, and her heart speeds up, until she realizes where it's from— the cuts on her palms are bleeding. The scabs have torn off. Nothing is making sense. She was somehow in the wrong lane—the jeep was idling in the wrong lane, and she has no idea how it got there. She doesn't remember any of it, and now the sun is gone from the sky.

What time is it? The clock's blinking on the dashboard— it needs to be reset.

"Are you buckled, Owen?" she asks slowly. Her tongue

is dry and thick in her mouth, and she feels like she might throw up.

"Yes," Owen says, but he sounds far away. He's not buckled at all, and neither is she.

There's a loud snap as he pushes his belt in. The sound helps her focus, and she sits up straighter in her seat, trying to ignore the panic working its way up her spine. Castle's on the floor of the jeep, shaking. Her phone beeps, then again, and she glances at it. Six p.m. It's six p.m.

They left the bakery this morning.

A chill runs through her, even though she's sweating. Owen holds the phone up to his ear and voice-commands it to play messages. "Dad texted," he says after a minute, and for one wild second she thinks *Dad* instead of Ben. "He wants to know where we are. And Kai called too. And there's a text from an unknown number." He clicks on it. "Someone from the police station?"

The police station. Sara Mazur had told her to be there by lunch, but the day came and went, and she can't go now—not like this. She presses on her temples, tries to think. "Text Ben and Mom," she says. "Tell them we're almost home."

"Okay. My neck feels funny." He lets out a yawn. "Did I fall asleep after the bakery, Rye? Is that why it's so late?"

"You fell asleep," she repeats. It's better than telling him the truth: that she has no idea what happened, how so much time has passed. "Yes, you fell asleep."

"I remember a wasp in the car," Owen says, his voice still

sounding dreamy. "Or maybe it was a bee? I must've fallen asleep afterward."

"A bee," she repeats. The dread inside her is all-consuming, tightening over her lungs. It's happening again, the gap in her memory. It wasn't just a one-off. Ben's thesis flashes into her head, everything he wrote about her grandpa. The memory loss; the missing time. How it happened his *entire life*.

Rylie swallows. Her throat feels dry, almost raw. She doesn't trust herself to drive now, but she needs to get Owen home. She needs to get *herself* home. It feels like her world has bottomed out. It feels like the dream she used to have after her dad died, where she was standing outside on a bright, calm day and suddenly huge cracks appeared in the streets, concrete and earth splitting in two, people and homes falling into the darkness while she screamed again and again for her dad, who never came. After that nightmare, she'd wake up screaming and find herself out of bed and in a different part of the house. But this . . . this is different.

Rylie turns the key, and the ignition sputters, doesn't catch. She squints, trying to replay the last few moments in her head. She needs to know what happened. To her, to Owen. He's her responsibility. She turns the key again, and the engine flares.

Her brother is rubbing at his eyes, still looking sleepy but otherwise fine. He's okay; he's got to be. The hiking backpack is on the floor and the bakery box is on the dashboard, and so is Owen's Talkboy, its light glowing red. She reaches for it. It's recording—it's been *on*. It's been on *the whole time*. Rylie feels the tightness in her chest lift, just a fraction. The tiniest thread to hang on is still a rope, and a rope can save you when you're falling.

"Owen?" she asks, willing her voice steady. "Could I borrow your recorder?"

CHAPTER 22

THE PORCHLIGHT IS ON AT her grandpa's house on Sundown, and they're so late that Rylie half expects to hear sirens. She herds Owen and Castle inside, her head still reeling. Water—they need water. She hurries to the kitchen, washes the blood from her hands and then splashes her face in the sink as Owen grabs juice from the fridge. His hair is sweaty around his ears, but other than that he looks normal, perfectly fine. Really fine, not pretend-fine.

"That you, Rylie?" Kai rounds the corner with his guitar. "Your mom called the house because you weren't answering your phone," he says. "Ben was freaking out. He thought that . . ." He shrugs. "Doesn't matter. I covered for you. I told him that you and Leap were fine. That I'd talked to you."

Did he? She has no idea—the entire afternoon is a blank. She pours a glass of water and gulps down the coldness. It feels like there's dust in her throat, and her hair smells too, like the highway exhaust is clinging to it.

"I figured you were, you know . . ." Kai lowers his voice. "I figured that you were at the police station?"

The police station. Kai thought she'd been following the plan instead of getting lost on a back road and forgetting an entire day, then almost getting run over by a semitruck.

"Did you go?" Kai asks, and she fumbles for an excuse. Her head's too foggy—her mind-iceberg feels like it's sinking down to the bottom of the ocean, into darkness.

"We went to the new climbing gym," Owen pipes up, spinning on a stool. "A lot of people were there."

Rylie turns, staring at him. Where did he learn to lie like that?

"And then we went on a tour bus—"

"Really?" Kai sounds doubtful, and Rylie makes her move.

"Yeah, it was one of those Enigma tours," she adds. Her mind flashes to seeing the blue van on the side of the road. Something was wrong with it. . . . "We didn't have service."

"Fair enough," Kai says, doubt still in his voice. "Anyway, your mom got held up at work again. She said she'd talk to you tonight, whatever that means. Oh, and Ben went to get her an anniversary gift," he goes on. "Hey, you look pale. Are you sure you're good?"

Rylie nods and pushes the bakery box at him. "We got you chocolate eclairs."

But when he opens the lid, the pastries look like they've been deflated, and grease has pooled into the cardboard.

"Huh," Kai says. They both stare for a second. In the corner is the box of tea, and Kai picks it up. "This is what the hippie girl sells. Sara, right?"

Sara. Another memory comes: drinking Sara's tea before the night hike, drinking her tea before the drive today. Was it just a coincidence? The Talkboy feels heavy in her pocket, and her headache flares up again, pulsing between her temples. She turns away from Kai and stares out the back windows. The swimming pool looks inviting; green and blue lights are shimmering underneath its surface. She has a sudden urge to jump into the cold water, sink down into it, and stay there forever.

"So, now's probably not the best time," Kai says, "but I need to ask you something. About the maps we found at your grandpa's cabin."

The ache in her head gets worse. "Let's talk later," she says, and then she can't meet his gaze, so she looks down at his forearms instead. He's sketched another girl, and she clings to it—it's something else to think about. "Who is she?" she asks. "Girlfriend?" she adds, trying for a joke, trying to feel normal again.

Kai shakes his head. "Her name is Violette Szabo." He pulls his sleeve down. "Are you sure you're good?"

"Are *you* good?" She doesn't want to talk about herself. She shuts her eyes against the headache to focus on Kai instead. "Yesterday, when we were talking about the graffiti, you told me you saw something similar before. On a camping trip with your mom? And then—"

"Rylie, you look like you're about to faint."

"I'm fine," she says, but after what happened today she's *not* fine, not at all. The truth must be all over her face because Kai glances at Owen. "If you need a break or something, I can watch him."

"I don't need a babysitter," Owen protests, wiping juice from his mouth. "We're at home."

"I know, but I just thought you might save me from myself." Kai picks up his guitar. "It's just been me and the Gibson and one bad song after another all day," he says, strumming fast and off-key. "Oh, save me, Brother. Save me, pleeeease," he croons, making Owen laugh.

"Hey!" Owen shouts in his overly excited voice. "Why don't we make Dad and Mom a cake for their anniversary?" He hops off the stool. "We'll throw them a party tomorrow!" He turns toward the pantry, Kai and his guitar right behind him, and Rylie takes the chance to slip away.

"Back in a minute," she calls out, heading upstairs and to the bathroom. She blasts the shower, the sink. Then she sets her brother's Talkboy on the counter and presses play. The wheels start spinning. There's a long drag of silence, and then . . .

Screaming.

Rylie snaps it off, her heart thudding in her chest. She fast-forwards the tape and presses play.

The sound of her own scream fills the bathroom again.

"Rylie?" It's Owen—he's on the stairs. "Are you up here?" he asks, but the shrill noise is still coming from the speakers and then a sudden, swift anger overtakes her and she slams the Talkboy into the sink, hard enough for the sound to stop.

"Rye?" Owen is just outside the bathroom door now. "Are you okay?"

She stares down, her breath ragged. The Talkboy is in pieces and there's blood in the sink too. She's bleeding— the cuts on her palms are throbbing. She's opened them deeper. Bits of black plastic are scattered in the sink with the water and the blood, and all the anger is gone now, leaving her hollow. The Talkboy was her dad's, then Owen's. She'll never make it up to him.

"I'm fine, O." She hurriedly picks up each piece, shoves them into her pockets. She has to glue it together; she has to fix it somehow.

"Kai votes vanilla, and I vote chocolate with strawberries." Owen's voice sounds strange through the door. "What do you want? You're the tiebreaker."

Nothing; she wants nothing.

"Chocolate with strawberries," she says. It will take longer to make, and she needs all the time she can get. "Go ahead and start without me."

"Rye?" Owen's still outside, but she can't open the door, not with the Talkboy broken and her heart not too far behind. "Whatever happened today, it doesn't matter," he says. "I'm not scared."

Her chest goes tight—the bad feeling is back. "You're not scared of *what*, Owen?"

"Of you," he says simply, only it's the most complicated thing she's ever heard. The silence afterward swells around her until his voice breaks through. "I love you, Rye."

And then her heart feels like it's following everything else that went before it to the bottom of the ocean. There's that silence again, awful and heavy.

"Owen," she says. "Why would you be afraid of me?"

He doesn't answer at first. Then he slips a thin tape underneath the door. "Because of this."

The tape is unlabeled, but right away she knows what it is. It's the Ethan Langhorne recording she was supposed to give to the cops today. Owen must have found it in the hiking backpack when she left him alone at the bakery. "I listened to both sides," he adds, almost apologetically.

Both sides. Rylie kneels to grab the Ethan tape, then peers under the door. No double shadows, no feet. Owen has left; he's already heading back downstairs. She leaves the bathroom and hurries into her room, going straight for the old cassette player she took from the cabin. Then she slides the tape in—onto the side she hasn't heard yet, the side she *forgot* about—and she presses play. A second later the speakers go loud with Ethan's voice.

"I told you about it before," Ethan says. In the background there's the sound of footsteps, wind hitting the recorder.

Her grandpa's response is measured and calm. "And we talked about it before."

More garbled words and wind, and then: "She's out of control," Ethan says. "I think she killed—" Another gust of wind carries his voice away as Rylie tenses up, listening. *I think she killed.* That's what he said, but the rest of it . . .

Her pulse is thudding as she rewinds the tape and then plays it again, but whatever he's saying is obscured by the wind.

"It's hard to believe," her grandpa finally cuts in.

Ethan laughs. "It was her, all right. It was Rylie."

She stops the tape. Her heart's speeding faster now, pounding so hard, it hurts. Ethan Langhorne just said her name. *Rylie. It was Rylie.* She replays the tape again, but no matter how many times she listens, the words don't change. They echo back to her in his voice, again and again: *She's out of control. I think she killed.* Then that bitter laugh. *It was Rylie.* She tries to swallow, but she can't.

I think she killed.

She's out of control.

Ethan Langhorne was talking about *her.*

CHAPTER 23

RELAX. RYLIE SQUEEZES THE PRESSURE point on her hand as Kai picks up the book on hypnosis. The memory regression will work, she'll get answers about the drive with Owen, and then she can crawl her way up from this sinkhole she's in, figure out what the hell is happening. The Talkboy hasn't been much help. After gluing it together, she tried listening to the audio tape inside of it again, but the cassette was so damaged, it didn't play. Unlike the Ethan Langhorne tape that Owen had pushed under the bathroom door. *That* had been clear enough to be terrifying, and now it feels like there's a cinch knot under her ribs, pulling tighter with every breath.

"You're supposed to close your eyes," Kai says, tapping her knee with the book. "Hypnosis works best with sensory deprivation. You should be relaxed too."

"I'm trying." She crosses her legs on the bed as he sits on the carpet across from her and props the phone up beside him. Lor is on the phone screen, drinking coffee with a shot of Baileys to celebrate her audition—apparently she somehow channeled her inner darkness—and Rylie bites down on her lip. She doesn't want to ruin things for Lor, but she has to warn them.

"There's one more thing." She makes sure Lor is looking at her before she glances over at Kai too, his eyes shaded by his Volcom hat. "If this regression works? If it reveals . . . anything, anything at all, just promise me that you won't go to the cops until we figure out what happened to Lily."

"The police?" Lor asks. "I thought you went earlier today."

Rylie shakes her head. There's no way she can go now. Not after hearing the other side of the unlabeled tape, what Ethan Langhorne said about *her* on it.

"Just promise me."

Lor looks confused as she smooths her dress, but then she lifts her chin and stares back at the phone. "You know you can trust me, Rye."

"Let's do this," Kai says. He puts on his black-rimmed glasses and opens the textbook. "Okay, imagine yourself in a serene place. Somewhere you feel completely safe and re-laxed."

Rylie shuts her eyes. A serene place, a safe place . . . not the desert, then.

Just like last time, her mind flashes to the ocean. To brown sand between her fingers, a beach house. The one coastal vacation that she went on with her dad and mom before Owen was born. Every night she ran down to the cold dark water, let it wash over her feet while her mom made a bonfire and her dad smoked a single Lucky Strike and played the guitar until the fire died. At sunup every morning her mom went for a jog on the beach, and once Rylie tried to follow her, but she wasn't fast enough, and then her mom turned back and grabbed her hand, sprinted out into the frothy water until the waves were too strong and they both fell down laughing, the water the same color as her mom's blue eye, her brown eye the color of the sand, her lips cold when she picked Rylie up and kissed her.

"Okay," Kai says, "in ten seconds you're going to feel completely relaxed. I'm going to count down now. Ten, nine . . ."

Rylie's almost drifting into sleep—but then Kai asks her about the drive with Owen, and suddenly she's there again, in the jeep, holding the wheel.

"You've just been to the bakery," Kai says. "Can you tell me what happens next?"

The jeep smells like honey and bread, and Owen is thirsty and she's driving too fast. The car is in the rearview mirror, and she doesn't know how to get home. Everywhere around them is desert, wild and dark, and in the distance are the shadows of mountains she wants to be climbing, instead of being stuck in the jeep, lost on back roads.

"Rylie?" Kai's voice sounds far away. "What happens next? Tell me."

"We're driving past a billboard. 'Wash thy sins, not only thy face.' That's what it says. Then we pass a blue van. People are inside it; I can see them in the beam of my head-lights. And they . . ."

The memory pulls her in deeper, as if she's living it all over again. The people in the Enigma van look scared—they look terrified, like they're trying to get out and can't—and she takes her foot off the pedal, ready to turn around to help. But before she can, a headache rises up, thuds between her temples. She blinks, trying to focus on the road. The headache's so bad, she feels dizzy with it.

"Hey, O, I just have to—" she murmurs, pulling over to the side of the road. She squeezes her eyes shut, hoping the pain will go away.

"Rylie?" Owen asks beside her, but she keeps her eyes closed.

"Just a minute." The pain is intense, digging down into the middle of her skull, and she tries to breathe through it. She just needs a minute. She'll feel better in a minute. . . .

Rylie lifts her head from the wheel. She feels sweaty and groggy, like she fell asleep, but the jeep's engine is off now. Castle's on her lap and he's whining, trembling even.

"It's okay," she tells him, trying to get her bearings. They're still parked on the side of the road. On the dashboard is the bakery box, and a bee's crawling over it, its wings flicking, flicking, its stinger slightly curled. She looks at Owen, but his body is turned away from her, his head resting against the half-opened window, his headphones on. He must have fallen asleep too. On impulse she grabs her Nikon and snaps a quick photo of him, then sets the camera down. They should get going. She turns the key, and the engine sputters as Castle starts to whine even more. She turns the key a second time, and the engine still doesn't catch, and then there's a pattering sound outside. Near the front of the jeep is a single coyote. Rylie tries the ignition again but gets nothing. She checks her phone but there's no service, and the ignition still won't work.

"Hey, Owen," she says, trying to keep the alarm from her voice. He doesn't move. "Owen?" After a second he stirs, the Talkboy clattering to the floor as he sits up, rubbing at his head.

"Rylie?" he murmurs, but there's something wrong with his face—it's bleeding, there's blood all over his nose and mouth. Her heart spikes and she leans in for a better look. It's just a nosebleed, that's all.

"You're bleeding, O," she tells him, quickly wiping his face with the corner of her shirt. "It's probably from the dry air," she adds. And then, just beyond the window, there's movement.

The coyote is creeping closer. She hears more pattering, this time from behind them. When she glances over her shoulder, she stiffens. More coyotes are in the shadows, surrounding the back of the jeep. She can smell something feral and dank coming through the open window, and it's suddenly cold, freezing cold.

"Owen," she whispers.

He doesn't hear her—he's hunched forward in his seat, grabbing at his Talkboy. "What's that sound?" he asks.

"What is it, Rylie?" he cries out, and the coyotes move closer—they're right outside his door now. A scream works its way into her throat.

The coyotes are not coyotes.

They are hunched and pale, teeth and flesh. They're reaching toward Owen. They're reaching toward the open window.

This can't be happening. She tries the engine again, but it doesn't start, and it's so cold in the jeep that she can hardly move, can hardly turn the key.

All of a sudden there's a roaring noise, and a second later a truck speeds past. It screeches into a one-eighty, flinging rock and sand as it comes to a stop. Inside are a few kids her age, with an older woman at the wheel.

Help. Rylie tries to shout, but it feels like she's talking through sludge, like she's being smothered by ice. "Help us!"

The truck's engine revs, and then it's barreling straight at her, straight for the jeep, and all she can think is that she's dreaming, she must be, but she's not waking up, she's not—

"Stop!" A sweaty hand clamps over her mouth, and she bites down hard. Someone gasps, and then the hand is gone.

Rylie blinks, tasting salt. Kai is in front of her, shaking out his hand. "You were screaming," he says, "and I'm sorry but I just—"

"You put your hand over my mouth." Rylie looks around, disoriented. She's in her bedroom; she's just in her bedroom. Her legs are numb, full of pinpricks. Kai's still rubbing his hand—it's red where she bit him and nothing makes sense, until it does, and she's furious. "You must have led the questions."

Kai's eyebrows furrow. "What?"

"The coyotes. You must have planted a false memory again."

"*Again?* I stuck to the script in the textbook. I didn't—"

"Lor, did he lead the questions?" Rylie glances at the phone, but the screen's dark.

"She had to go back to work." Kai looks at her strangely. "Rylie, why did you *bite* me? What else did you see?"

She stands, needing air, needing height. She needs the roof; she needs to catch her breath. "It was just a dream. A fantasy." A wave of dizziness hits her, and she steadies herself on the mattress. Maybe the roof isn't such a good idea.

"You said you saw a truck. You said you saw a woman in a truck. She was yelling at you, trying to help you." Kai grabs her elbow. "What did she look like?" he asks. "What was after you?" He's holding her too tight, too hard.

"It wasn't real," she says, pulling away. It couldn't have been real.

"What if it was?" Kai looks like he's going to grab her arm again, so she sidesteps him. "Think about it," he says. "Your friend disappeared out here, and now you've gotten lost *twice* in the last few days, chased by something that terrifies you so much, your conscious mind has to bury it."

He doesn't know the half of it. The flip side of the Ethan Langhorne tape—everything Ethan said about her. Everything he claimed she'd done.

"Listen," Kai says. "What if it's all somehow linked to Lily, to finding out what happened to her? To finding out where she is?" His voice hitches. "Just for a second pretend like what you saw might be important. Pretend this isn't just about *you*."

"I *know* this isn't just about me, Kai." Rylie blinks back a sudden sting at her eyes.

Kai sighs, then pulls his hat off. "You're right. I shouldn't have said that. What's important is what happened to you. How it fits in."

"It doesn't," Rylie says. "Coyotes don't hunt people." She feels a chill as she says it. "They don't travel in packs that size," she presses. "They don't . . . They're not big animals, not like what I saw. What I *imagined* I saw."

Kai leans forward. "What about the billboard, then? 'Wash thy sins, not only thy face'? Do you think you imagined that?" He punches something into his phone. "It's another palindrome, Rye. From the Byzantine Greeks. Ever heard of it before?"

"No," she admits.

He nods. "And you told me during the regression that the truck you saw had spray paint on its windows." He pulls his pen from behind his ear and starts sketching on his palm. His hand is still red from where she bit down, and she shifts uncomfortably, remembering the salty taste in her mouth.

He finishes the sketch—it's the circle surrounding the sharp petals again.

"I did some research yesterday," he says, tapping on his palm with the pen, "and it's got a name. It's a hexfoil."

"A what?"

"A shape that's used to ward off evil."

Evil. A tingle gets at her neck. "And my grandpa has one carved into his cabin door."

"My point is, you didn't just *imagine* them. Seeing them again is proof that the hypnosis worked."

"Why?" She stares down at the sketch on his hand. "I've done my research too, Kai. Hypnosis puts you in a dream state. Sometimes it helps you recall a memory, and sometimes it's just your imagination, your subconscious randomly plucking images from your brain. That's all."

"Maybe." Kai rubs the ink from his palm. "But remember the map from your grandpa's cabin?" he asks. "I went to some of the areas that were circled on it."

For a second she feels a pulse of anger, like he should have asked her first. "And?"

"I found hexfoils in each place, etched into trees or buildings," he says, and at first she thinks he's lying, but he can't be, he has no reason to. "It was like . . ." He rubs at his hair again, making it even wilder. "It was like someone knew something bad was happening near each place and tried to ward it off."

Another tingle crawls down her neck. "You saw hexfoils at *every* spot on the map?"

"No." Kai meets her gaze. "I couldn't get to all the places. I want you to go with me next time. To—"

A sudden knock, loud. "Rylie? Kai?"

The door swings open just as Rylie stuffs the hypnosis book under her pillow. Owen's standing in the doorway next to Ben, and she digs her nails into her palms, tamping down a fresh rush of anger at the sight of her stepdad. At least the anger is keeping back the other emotions—the ones that are so close to flooding her.

"We, er . . ." Ben clears his throat. "Your mom wanted me to check in on you. She's sorry she's late again," he says. "You two all right in here?"

"Not really," Rylie says, and Kai almost spoils it by doing a double take. "It's just that Kai's been helping me with college applications, and I hate doing personal essays."

Kai nods, catching on. "Yeah, we're hard at work. You know us."

"I'm impressed. You're really turning over a new leaf, Kai," Ben says, and Rylie glances sharply at her stepbrother, but his face is blank, as if the remark hasn't fazed him at all. "We'll let you get back to it," Ben says cheerfully. "Ready to ice that cake, Leap? You can lick the spoon after."

"Yeah!" her brother shouts, just as Ben goes to shut the door. "Actually, how about I leave this open?" Ben asks. "It feels a little stuffy in here."

"Well, that was awkward," Kai mutters once they're gone. He glances at the open door and then back at Rylie, his eyebrows raised.

She steels herself. "What?"

"What if you asked Ben to do the hypnosis for you? Then you'd know for sure that they weren't false memories. He'd help you, Rye. He did the same for me, even after . . ." He trails off.

"I'm not asking him for help." Rylie crosses to the door and shuts it. "I found out that he's been lying to me. My mom has been too."

If she expected surprise from Kai, he doesn't show it. "Lying about what?"

"Ben knew my grandfather." The betrayal cuts into her again. "Ben used him as a case study for his thesis." She folds her arms across her chest, ready to field any excuses, but Kai just stays quiet. "This whole time I thought Ben had never even been out here before," she says. "What a joke."

Kai's jaw tightens. Then he picks up his guitar and strums a few chords. It's the happy, frenetic tune he always plays for Owen—the opposite of how she's feeling. "I'm sure they had their reasons," he says, but that's all he says. His strumming slows. He doesn't try to downplay it like she thought he might, and the longer he stays quiet, the more she thinks about all the lying she's been guilty of too—she's constantly lying—and she collapses onto her bed. The ceiling goes blurry.

"I need to tell Nathan about what we found in the cabin." Even saying it aloud makes her tense up, like she's on a slippery hold and about to fall. "I just don't know how to."

Kai stops playing his guitar. "It's okay. We'll figure everything out."

We'll figure everything out. She shrugs, suddenly unable to talk. Kai already saw her scream today—she won't cry in front of him too. Instead, she turns onto her side, looking at the smudged ink on his palm. The sketch of the hexfoil, a shape meant to ward off evil. A flash of memory comes to her. Hexfoils drawn in desert dirt. Hexfoils drawn outside her grandfather's cabin. She swallows, hard.

"My grandpa, he told me this story about the desert once," she says quietly. "He said that not everything looked the way it seemed, not even the coyotes. He said they hunted people." The tightness in her throat has moved to her insides—it's closing over her lungs. "I think he was trying to scare me into listening to his rules. Maybe that's why I saw coyotes in the hypnosis. It was just a childhood fear, coming back to me."

"Rylie—" Kai rubs at his temples. "What if it wasn't?" He grabs the hypnosis book from under the pillow and pushes it toward her, his eyes oddly shiny. "What if your memory was real?"

It couldn't be. "Then we have a lot more to worry about." She pulls out her phone, still thinking of the hypnosis. It was a lie. Ben and her mom lied, and her grandpa too. But so has she.

She pulls up the message thread with Nathan, all of today's texts that she hasn't answered yet. Then she punches in what she needs to. It's short and simple and to the point, and she hits send before she can erase the message. She doesn't expect him to answer right away, but he's already typing a reply.

I get off in a few hours. That too late to meet?

She hopes it's not too late. *I'll come to yours*, she texts back.

And then she notices a message from Lor.

Did you see the latest on Ethan Langhorne?!

After an Enigma Tours van driver was
fatally stabbed near a gas station in
Twentynine Palms mere hours ago, the
public has been left wondering whether the
alleged "commune killer" has struck again.
Authorities say that at this time there's
no direct evidence linking the 17-year-old
to the murder of the Enigma Tours employee,
but surveillance footage shows a male youth
driving away in a sedan shortly after the
incident occurred.

CHAPTER 24

THE HOUSE LOOKS DARK. NATHAN should be awake, but Rylie doesn't want to knock in case Thea's asleep. She leaves her jacket in the jeep and is about to text him when she sees movement near the front door—Nathan's stepping outside and into the shadows. "I didn't have you pegged for it," he calls out, throwing her off guard. When he gets closer, she notices the laughter in his eyes. "Defying a curfew?"

"A voluntary one," she says, matching the lightness in his voice, but her stomach feels tense and she can't seem to look away from him. He's in jeans and a black sweater the shade of his hair, and when he smiles it's hard to breathe.

"Semantics," Nathan says, and he seems so relaxed that she wants to hook her arm through his, lean her head against his shoulder and spill out everything, just like she used to. "I'm glad it didn't stop you from coming," he says, and despite everything, she's glad to be here too.

"You give me a fifty-fifty chance again?"

"Not even." He shakes his head. "After you didn't answer my texts today, I thought . . ."

"The Sandman got me." It's out of her mouth and making

him smile again before she catches herself. There's a reason she's here. She steps forward, puts the right inflection in her voice. "I came over because I need to tell you something, Nathan."

"I have something to tell you too. Maybe it's the same thing?" It's the way his brown eyes stay on hers that gives him away, and then it's hard to breathe again. It feels like he's about to confess something. Something good instead of bad.

"I should go first," she rushes out.

"You always do." Nathan's smile turns into a full-on grin. He doesn't get it. He has no idea what's coming, what she's kept from him. "Want to go in?" he asks, nodding at the door. The curtains flutter—Thea's at the window. "It's late but it's okay. Thea won't mind."

But Thea looks like she *does* mind. Thea, who has always been so welcoming. Rylie rubs the bandages on her arms. She's been covering up her skin, and she's been covering up other things too. The guilt's probably radiating off her— maybe everyone can see it except Nathan, because he only ever looks for the goodness in people.

"Actually, out here works, if you've still got those chairs?"

"I thought you'd ask for the roof. Better view from there."

"Is the roof on offer?" It isn't going to make talking any easier, but it will help her think clearly. It will help her say what she needs to.

"Whatever you want is on offer." Nathan strides over to the back of his truck, and then he turns, his eyes on hers, a playful challenge in them. "Coming?" He hops into the bed of his truck and then up to the roof of the house. She follows quickly, her steps lighter than his, and beats him to the top.

"See? You're always first." Nathan stands next to her on the ridge. He's a little too close and her stomach dips again. She looks away—at anything but him. The aloe vera in the yard, the rocky ground stretching into the dark expanse of Joshua Tree, all the protected land. The moon and the smear of starlight overhead, the same color as the gauze on her arms.

"I didn't text you back all day because I was avoiding you." She needs to tell him the truth. All of it. She sits down on the ridge—they could be here a while.

A slat creaks as Nathan sits down too, knees bent, his boots finding traction on the slope beneath them. He taps out one of his cinnamon toothpicks, offers her one like it's a cigarette. "That doesn't sound good."

Rylie takes the toothpick, rolls it between her fingers, then meets his eye. "It's not that I didn't want to see you. I'm worried about the other way around. That you won't want to see me, after . . ."

"After?"

Her cheeks go warm. "I need to be more open with you." She shakes her head—that didn't sound right either—her carefully planned speech is getting jumbled. She shivers, rubs at her bare shoulders. She shouldn't have left her jacket in the jeep. "Can I start over?"

"I was hoping we could do that, Rye," Nathan says, and

for a moment that's *all* she wants. To do everything over. Now, four years ago, everything.

"I was having the worst day at work earlier," he continues. "They make us do these simulations, to practice apprehending criminals and . . ." Nathan stops, then stares up at the sky like he's avoiding her gaze. "Anyway, it's intense, and on top of that I heard some bad news. You being here has already made the day a thousand times better," he says, and her lungs clamp tight. "Though, it's past midnight, so I guess it's actually a new day."

Her entire body is aware that he's next to her, his elbow grazing her arm. Nathan's list comes to mind, his dream of the seven summits, the dream he gave up on. She silently repeats it, so she doesn't think of how close he is. *Everest, Denali, Kilimanjaro, Vinson, Elbrus* . . . Her phone beeps twice, and she ignores it as he turns toward her.

"So why were you worried I didn't want to see you?" he asks, his eyes searching her face. He's so close, she can see the little divot of that scar across his eyebrow, the one Lily gave him by poking a stick into the wheel of his bike and making him crash. "You know you can talk to me about anything, right?"

"Just like we used to." The words escape before she can stop them, and Rylie snaps the toothpick in her hand.

This is about Lily. Not some pretend nostalgic feelings they have for each other, feelings that will vanish the instant she tells Nathan the truth. Maybe it won't be a conscious thing on his part, but deep down he'll resent her, or worse.

She doesn't know exactly how her grandpa was involved with Lily, but all signs point to nothing good. And the recording, the one of Ethan Langhorne . . .

Nathan nudges her shoulder, and suddenly she's back on the roof with him instead of lost in her thoughts, the slats cool underneath her skin, his sweater warm against her arm. Her phone beeps again, and she pulls it out of her pocket. It's her mom. *Finally off work but you're not home. I was hoping we could talk. Where are you? Are you okay?*

She hasn't been okay for a while now. "I should probably answer this," Rylie says, angling her shoulder so Nathan won't be able to see the screen. *Sorry, at Nathan's. Back soon.* She almost sends the text as is but then erases the sorry part. Her mom's reply is fast: *Are you alone or is Kai with you?*

Kai must be out too or her mom wouldn't have asked. She thinks about ignoring the question but sends a quick answer anyway. Her mom's text is as practical as ever: *Please don't rush into anything. I'll try to wait up.*

Rylie shakes her head. She's definitely not rushing into things with Nathan. She's dragged it out with him long enough.

"Done," she says, slipping the phone into her pocket. Nathan's twisting his leather bracelets and looking at her with that smile of his, and her stomach floods with warmth. She digs her nails into the gauze over her palms and tries to focus. *Everest, Denali, Kilimanjaro, Vinson, Elbrus.* It was actually Lily's list first. The dream of the seven summits started with her. Everything started with her.

"What I'm about to tell you, I should have said a while ago."

"It's okay," Nathan says. And then he brushes back the hair in her eyes—not slowly, not like he's trying to be romantic, but the way he might have done when they were younger. It's hard to believe that he's here, next to her, after all these years, and that he'll be gone again soon. She wants to stretch it out, just a little. Stay in this moment a little longer, before she has to tell him a truth that will hurt.

"All right, I'll tell you something first," Nathan says when she stays quiet. "I've been thinking about you for a long time. Ever since you came back, but before that too."

She turns toward him just as he leans her way. They're facing each other now, their knees bumping together, the open air surrounding them. One wrong move, and they'll both slip and fall. She can feel his nearness everywhere across her skin. From here, this close, she can see the way his nose is slightly crooked in the middle and how soft his lips look. A warmth spreads through her even though the night air is cold, and she's wide awake, alert. The first time she went climbing, it felt like this, like the world had let her in on a secret. That's what it feels like now, being this close. She wants to be here with him and not thinking about anything else.

"Rylie," Nathan says. She lets her fingertips touch his hand, and then they're both somehow closer.

This isn't real either.

If he knew everything . . .

She shifts, scooting away. It was only an inch, but Nathan's looking at her curiously, almost cautiously now. "You all right? This isn't about Sara's mom, is it?"

Rylie's caught off guard again. "What about Sara's mom?"

He swears under his breath. "I just thought maybe you'd heard, and it'd hit too close to home."

"What happened?"

Now Nathan's the one who doesn't want to talk; she can tell he's damming up the words inside. "Sara's mom passed away this morning," he finally says. "It was sudden. A brain aneurysm, they think. And the worst part was . . ." He trails off, and Rylie doesn't know how it can get any worse. "The worst part was that it happened while she was driving. She hit a school bus."

Rylie feels hot and cold all at once. "God . . ."

"Only one kid was injured, but the driver was killed, and I know Sara. . . . It'll weigh on her; everything will. Her mom, how sudden it was, how it happened." Nathan's voice is almost a whisper now. "Maybe you could talk to her?"

Rylie nods, feeling numb. "Of course." The news about Sara's mom is an excuse to back out of what she needs to say to him, but if she keeps stalling, it will just get harder to tell him. Three whole days. She's kept the cabin from him for three days. Three days is seventy-two hours, it's thousands of minutes, and she has no idea how much time is too long to keep a secret, too much to eventually forgive.

"Nathan, my grandpa had a photograph of Lily," she blurts out. "It was in his cabin. I found it a couple of days ago."

He straightens. "What kind of photograph?" His voice is the slightest bit tenser.

"It was . . ." She shakes her head. Already this isn't going well. "It was a headshot, a school photo, I think. But . . ." She lets out another breath and then plunges ahead. "He also talked about her. With his . . . friends, I guess. There's a recording." Rylie presses her nails into her bandages. "I should have told you sooner. It's just that—"

"What did he say?"

"I think he followed her places. And I'm worried—" Her throat closes up. "I'm worried he could have hurt her. The day she disappeared. I'm worried it was his fault."

Nathan stares at her. For a long moment he doesn't say anything; he just clenches and unclenches his left fist. "You thought I'd hold it against you?"

"I don't see how you couldn't. I would," she says. Feeling sorry for herself isn't an option. "If he had anything to do with her disappearance, then—"

"Rylie," Nathan interrupts. "Your grandpa didn't hurt my sister."

"You don't know that."

"I do." His voice is firm. "I know for certain."

"How?"

"Because I did his landscaping that day, and he never left the house. And Thea took him dinner that night, because he wasn't feeling well. She saw him too. He didn't hurt Lily because he couldn't have."

Rylie grips her necklace tight, her mind reeling. "But the recording . . ." She still hasn't told Nathan the worst part. The part about Ethan Langhorne. How he mentioned Lily's name on the unlabeled tape, how he said that he thought she "saw" him, that she *knew*. But Rylie can't show Nathan that one—she can't show him what's on the other side. The part about *her*.

"This is what you've been afraid to tell me?" Nathan's eyes are watering, and he coughs, clearing his throat. "Look, all I want is to know what happened to her, no matter what. And maybe your grandpa wasn't racking up any good-conduct medals, but that doesn't mean he would hurt Lily. He couldn't have. If it was worrying you, I wish you'd said something sooner."

"I wish I'd done a lot of things sooner." All the other things she's wished for come to her all at once. *I wish we still had the people we love around us. I wish we'd stayed friends. I wish everything could be the same as before.* But wishing won't change anything. She cut Nathan out of her life when her grandpa cut her out of his. It was self-preservation, but Nathan didn't know that. And then more of the truth is tumbling out, all of it swirling together.

"I'm sorry for not answering when you called me last year." Rylie forces herself to look at him. "I guess I thought it'd be easier not to talk, in case you brought up my dad, or my grandpa even, and I . . . I didn't want to go there."

It hurts to swallow. It almost hurts to breathe. "But if I'd picked up, then I would've known about Lily. I could have been there for you."

Nathan stiffens, visibly moves away from her. The way he's staring at her now—it's glacial, icy. It's like a chasm just split open between them. It's what she thought would happen when she told him about her grandfather.

"Rylie," he says. Her heart skips when he says her name, and she doesn't want it to. "What's this about?" he asks. The chasm's growing wider and wider every second.

"What do you mean?"

Nathan starts twisting the leather bracelets on his wrist again, his eyes conflicted. "I mean, you don't owe me anything. I'm not saying that. I know it's been a long time since we were close. So I'm not expecting . . ." He stops, takes a deep breath. "You said you came here to be more open with me, but you're not. So what's the deal?"

She *can't* show him the tape, but if she does, then he'll understand . . . "You're right," she says. It's hard to swallow. "The tape I mentioned, the recording of my grandpa, it—"

"Really?" Nathan cuts in. "You think I want to hear about a tape right now?" He stares up at the night sky for a second like he's collecting his thoughts, and when he turns back, the chasm is in his eyes too—they've gone distant.

"This whole act about not speaking for four years— I mean, I went along with it, since we hadn't actually hung out, but we *talked* to each other, Rylie. You can't deny that."

What? She almost loses her balance on the ridge. "You lost me."

"The last time we talked wasn't four years ago, Rylie. It was just last year."

The night air feels colder now. "You called me. I didn't pick up." She still remembers it, the shock of seeing his name flash up on her phone. She stared at it—almost, *almost* picking up. And then it went to voicemail. "You didn't leave a message."

Nathan lets out a bitter laugh. "Rylie, we talked for *hours*," he says, but he's wrong. He was upset last year over Lily, and now he's confused. "Either that or I talked to your twin."

"Nathan?"

They both stiffen. It's Thea, her voice drifting up from below. Nathan doesn't even say anything. He just stands and walks down the slope of the roof, all the way to the edge. Rylie doesn't want to follow him, but it isn't her roof and she can't stay up here alone. She hurries after him, almost slips.

"Sorry, Thea," Nathan calls out. "Are we being too loud?"

"It's late," Thea says. "It's time to come inside." She's standing in the driveway, her long white hair blowing in the wind. Her eyes find Rylie's. "I think you need to see the doctor, Little Lee. I think you need help."

"Thea . . ." Nathan's voice goes soft as Rylie feels a hardness clamp over her heart. Thea must have heard everything, all of what they said to each other, and she's not wrong either. She's not wrong about needing help. Rylie's chest goes tight. The cinch knot is back inside of it, squeezing tighter and tighter.

"Is Lily up there too?" Thea suddenly asks, and Rylie goes still. She glances at Nathan, but he's not looking at her; he's looking at Thea like he's trying so hard to keep it together.

"No," he answers. "She's not."

"Oh," Thea says simply. "I thought I heard her." Then she turns to Rylie and smiles at her, a gentle smile. "You should get home," she says, but her voice isn't gentle at all.

CHAPTER 25

THE JEEP'S HEADLIGHTS TURN THE road to grayness as
Rylie speeds away from Nathan's house. She lost him before
as a friend too, so she should be used to it, should have expected it even. Her phone is dark on the console—no texts
from him, nothing—and she pulls to a sudden stop, ignoring the blackness at the windows. Then she clicks on the
interior light, opens the hiking backpack, and dumps all the
tapes out onto the passenger seat. This time when she sorts
through the pile, she checks the labels on both sides of every
tape. And then she sees it.

A tape labeled MILLIE CALLAHAN on one side and E.L. on
the other, in writing so small, she missed it before. Maybe
she's missed other things too. She turns onto the highway,
and then shoves the tape into her grandpa's cassette player
as she drives.

At first there's only wind and footsteps. Someone's walking with the recorder.

"You've been following us." It's her grandpa's voice. "I
suggest you stop."

She waits for another voice, for Ethan's, but it doesn't come.

"Leave it. Just keep walking." It's her grandpa talking again, and then, a moment later, Ethan:

"Stop telling me what to do."

He sounds different from before. More confident, more sure of himself.

"Did you go like I told you?" her grandpa asks calmly.

"Why do you care?"

A sigh. "We've been over . . ." Her grandpa's voice is caught by the wind. "Every time."

"I know," Ethan says. "Every time I kill."

Rylie grips the wheel. *Every time I kill.* The cinch knot loops tighter.

"Right," her grandpa says. "So take me with you."

"Go to hell."

"But we're already there."

A sudden laugh; it's Ethan. "Relax, old man. I gave them your message."

Rylie turns up the volume, and even though she's speeding faster now, the gaps between the streetlamps seem to widen, the night shadows on the road growing darker and longer.

"If you listen to me, it'll be easier for you," her grandpa says. "Just take me with you."

"You think you know everything." Ethan's voice has a bite to it. A second later there's the sound of footsteps on the recording, fading fast. The wind keeps blowing hard on the tape, and then, right when she thinks it's over, there's a whisper, a single word: "No."

And then the recording cuts out. Lily's name wasn't mentioned. Rylie's name wasn't mentioned either.

Rylie lets out a breath and then keeps one hand on the wheel as she searches through the pile of tapes. But there aren't any others with Ethan's name or initials, and she suddenly wants to listen to her dad's playlist, she wants to drown out the voices that are echoing in her head. *Every time I kill*, Ethan said. So far he supposedly killed his roommate at the commune, then a gas station attendant, a hitchhiker at a rest stop, and an Enigma Tours driver. Where will it stop? And did it start with Lily?

An ache gets at her chest, and she tightens her grip on the wheel. Maybe Nathan didn't believe that her grandpa was involved with Lily's disappearance, but Nathan didn't hear him talking to Ethan Langhorne, or to the woman who told him that she wanted to kill her neighbors. And Nathan didn't see how much Amy Bishop and her mother were afraid of her grandpa either.

Rylie ejects the tape and flips it to the side labeled MILLIE CALLAHAN. Just then red taillights shine ahead, too close, and she jerks the wheel, barely missing a car stalled out at an intersection. The driver's staring straight ahead, oblivious to the green traffic light swinging on the cable. She keeps going, adrenaline racing through her from the narrow miss. Maybe she should listen to the rest of the tape without driving. There's a bright glow coming from a gas station just ahead, so she pulls in, parks toward the back. She tugs her phone from her pocket to shoot her mom a text: *On the way home, don't wait up*, and then she presses play on the tape deck. A moment later, the recording comes out staticky:

"I'm sure I did it." It's a woman with an Irish accent. It must be Millie Callahan.

"You're sure?" her grandpa asks.

"Yeah."

"Would you do it again?"

"It felt good at first, like a rush. But then . . . it felt like a nightmare."

"I warned you."

"I just want them to go away. I want them all to go away." There's silence—and then someone's crying. Millie must be crying.

"Did you read the book, Amelia?"

"Yes."

"And what did it say?"

The crying stops. Millie takes a breath, and then she says: "Shutters shut and open so do queens. Shutters shut and shutters and so shutters shut." She's repeating herself.

"Exact resemblance to exact resemblance," Millie whispers. It's like she's forgotten how to talk coherently. None of the words make any sense, but they sound so familiar . . .

And then Rylie puts it together. She knows what's coming next because she's heard it before—or seen it, anyway. Twice now.

The first time was on the yellow legal pad in her grandpa's

cabin. And the second time was in the Gertrude Stein book that Thea passed along to her, the one from the cardboard box full of her grandpa's things. It's still in the jeep—the box from Thea is still in the jeep.

Rylie grabs the box from the backseat and rifles through it. When she spots the book, she picks it up so fast that the spine tears in her hands. Then she starts scanning the pages, running her finger along the sections with red ink. She reaches the line—*What is the current that makes machinery, that makes it crackle*—just as Millie Callahan recites the same line on the recording. It booms out from the speakers in her lilting accent.

"If they were not pigeons what were they." Millie's voice is soft and beautiful, but the words are the opposite.

Rylie's eyes fall to the end of the page, and then she sees it:

Lily Lily Lily let Lily

Rylie shoves open the jeep's door and stumbles out, taking great gasps of air. The gas station's outdoor lights flicker, the bulbs coarsely humming. She takes another deep breath and leans against the jeep's cool metal, but Millie's voice is still in her head, and so is Lily's name. All of a sudden there are footsteps, rounding the corner fast. Just as she steps forward to look, something warm slams into her, knocking her down to the pavement. Her palms and knees hit first, hard, the gravel stinging her skin. She scrambles to her feet and glimpses a large shadow flitting past the gas station and into the desert scrub, into the darkness. She's shaking, her whole body is shaking, and for a moment she thinks of coyotes, but there's nothing now—whoever it was, or whatever it was, is gone.

Rylie glances back at the gas station. The attendant—an older man with thick gray hair—is pumping gas for a minivan. When he finishes he looks up from the island and meets her gaze as the minivan drives off. Now, except for him, the parking lot is empty.

"Hey," Rylie calls out. "Did you see someone run past here a second ago?"

The man studies her for a moment, then wipes his hands on his coveralls. "I'm closing."

"So you didn't see anyone?"

He stares at her. His eyes look odd in the fluorescent light. "You shouldn't be here," he says. "You should go home." This time his voice is softer, like he's concerned. It's dark and late, and he's probably worried about the news reports on Ethan Langhorne, the voluntary curfew that she has completely ignored tonight. She watches him walk up to the station and turn the sign to CLOSED, then disappear inside, the bell on the door jingling faintly. A moment later the lights snap off.

"A line distinguishes it," a woman says over her shoulder.

Rylie whirls, but there's no one there. "A line," the voice says again, coming from somewhere in the darkness, and then Rylie lets out a breath. The jeep's windows are wide open and she left the tape running. She gets in and slams the door, looking away from the rough edge of the missing side mirror.

"A dark place is not a dark place," Millie says. It's more

audio that doesn't make any sense, just like everything else. Unless . . .

Rylie starts up the jeep; the engine catches on the third try. If Kai thinks that the hexfoils and palindromes are some sort of message or code, then maybe Stein is a code too. She lets the jeep idle as she picks up her phone to call him, but it rings and rings, so she sends a text: *I need to talk.* And then she can't help it, she checks her text thread with Nathan again. Nothing. He swore that they'd talked last year, but he was wrong. She's sure of it. But then she thinks of the hike, how she can't remember it. And the drive with Owen was another terrifying blank . . .

Thea's warning echoes in her mind. *You need to see the doctor,* she said. How many people had told her grandfather the same thing?

Rylie glances down at her phone and opens her photo gallery, then finds the picture of Dr. Singh's contact card with the US Marine Corps logo—the eagle, the globe, the anchor—his full name below it, *Dr. Reginald Singh,* just like the footnote in Ben's thesis. Her *grandfather* was Dr. Singh's patient. The doctor will know something more about the memory loss, the missing time. He might even know what her grandpa was capable of. Whether he could have hurt Lily.

Her follow-up—the appointment she was planning to skip—is scheduled for tomorrow. She *has* to go now.

And then, just as she pulls out of the gas station and turns onto the dark highway, she hears it. One long, lone howl, far in the distance. It comes again; only, this time it doesn't sound like a coyote. This time it almost sounds human.

CHAPTER 26

THE NEXT DAY, RYLIE IS starving and regretting everything. Dr. Singh is behind schedule, so all morning she and Kai, who had insisted on coming in with her, camped out in the waiting room and read Gertrude Stein poetry. At some point Kai said he had to go and left with the book, telling her to text when she was done, but that was a while ago, and now her stomach is practically gnawing on itself. She heads to the front desk, ready to give up. "Do you know how much longer it's going to be?"

The man at the desk looks up her info again without smiling. The reason is obvious—the counter is piled high with cards and pictures. It's a memorial for Sara Mazur's mom. One of the candles even says I LOVE YOU, MAMA on the side, and Rylie glances away, her throat suddenly aching.

"It looks like they're finally ready for you," the man tells her after clicking out of his computer, and a moment later a nurse appears in the hallway to take her back. Rylie hurries past the counter, following the nurse to Dr. Singh's office. Last time she was here, she was groggy with painkillers from her fall on the hike, but now she notices that his office has a living-room feel, with its French doors and white shelves, armchairs piled with cushions, and the vanilla-scented candle that's burning next to the window.

"Ah, Rylie, welcome back." Dr. Singh slowly rises up from his desk and then reaches out a frail hand and shakes hers with surprising vigor. "I'm sorry for the delay. Today's been difficult. One of our staff . . ." He trails off, clearly not wanting to go into details about Sara's mom. "But we've never closed once in the twenty-odd years I've been here," he says, rallying.

Rylie sits across the desk from him, and the candle flutters as Dr. Singh lowers into his seat. "So how have you been feeling since I last saw you? You first came in after an injury on a hike, yes?"

She nods and then squeezes the pressure point near her thumb, trying to find the right words. "Yesterday, I had another . . ."

"Episode?"

So that's what he's calling it. She nods. "Another missing chunk of time."

"And?" Dr. Singh asks, clicking his pen as he turns in his seat and pulls out a file from a drawer. His calm voice reminds her of Ben, and maybe it's just his silver hair or his lined face, but he looks wise, somehow. He looks like someone who could understand her. "When did it occur, exactly?"

"Yesterday morning. I was driving. My brother was in the car with me." She closes her eyes, thinking of the screams on

Owen's Talkboy. "And then, somehow, hours passed. Hours I can't remember. I want to know why."

Dr. Singh clears his throat. "The *why* isn't certain," he says. "Missing time could be indicative of conditions like epilepsy, for example, or possibly something more serious. Your imaging and lab work were normal," he goes on, jotting down a note, "but we could consider an EEG to look for abnormal brain activity."

Rylie stifles the worry in her chest. "I actually came here to talk about my grandfather. He was your patient." She fiddles with the pendant around her neck, just to give her hands something to do. "I know it was a long time ago, but maybe I could see his file?"

Something passes over the doctor's face. He clicks and unclicks his pen without speaking. She stays silent, waits him out. That's how you get people to talk—her mom taught her that.

"I remember your grandfather," Dr. Singh finally says. "We were friends more than anything else. He came to me for advice and I tried to help him."

Rylie leans forward. "What did he want help with?"

Dr. Singh shakes his head. "I'm not able to discuss his file, just like I wouldn't be able to discuss yours."

But she already knows. "Anger issues," she says. "Aggression and memory loss." Her heart clamps tight. "Were you able to treat him?"

He glances toward the door, then back at her. "I'm afraid

I can't go into details. Have you been experiencing additional symptoms, Rylie?"

"But you just told me you were friends." It's a stretch but she presses anyway. "Did you talk about his . . . *issues*, as friends?"

Dr. Singh sighs. He picks a paperweight up from his desk—a copper anchor—and turns it over in his hands. "I understand he was your grandfather, but nevertheless—"

"We've met before, haven't we? I mean, way before my last appointment? When I was a kid." The more she stares at him, the more she sees it. The thick silver hair that was probably dark once, the kind eyes. His face is blurring into the face of the younger Marine in the photograph with her grandpa and Thea, the framed photo in the cardboard box. "You came over when I was little. You asked my grandpa some questions." She remembers it now, remembers drinking hot cocoa with Nathan on the patio while her grandfather and Dr. Singh talked in the kitchen. "That wasn't a formal visit, was it?"

And then—she doesn't know why he does it, maybe because he feels sorry for her, maybe because it was so long ago, or maybe because it really *does* fall outside his confidentiality pledge, but Dr. Singh starts to talk, his voice low as he leans forward.

"Informally speaking," he says, "none of the typical diagnoses seemed to fit your grandfather." He turns the anchor over and over, his eyes going distant. "I even suggested testing for lyssavirus, because of the aggression coupled with the hydrophobia, but the results were negative."

Lyssavirus, hydrophobia. She has no idea what he's talking about. "So you weren't able to treat him?"

He sighs. "I didn't try." He sets the anchor down. "I referred him to a colleague, and afterward he mentioned pharmacotherapy, but he didn't always take the proper dosage, Rylie, and the medicine didn't always work either."

"Could you—"

Just then the door swings open. "Dr. Singh," a sergeant says. "You're needed at the back."

Dr. Singh abruptly closes her file. "This can't wait?"

"They've just admitted another one." The sergeant's face is grave, and Dr. Singh stands. "Rylie, I'm so sorry," he says, his voice still low, still kind. "Would you mind rescheduling with the nurse first thing? Just follow us out."

"Wait," Rylie says, standing too, and Dr. Singh turns back. She has to ask him. "Do you think my grandfather could have . . . hurt someone?" *Killed someone.*

The doctor smiles at her, but it's a sad smile. "Don't we all have that capacity?" A moment later he and the sergeant are gone and Rylie is left staring at the empty office, at her paper file on his desk. Her *paper* file.

She has a minute, maybe two at the most. She hustles to the other side of the desk, throws open the tidy filing cabinet behind it. If her grandfather's file is still here, then maybe . . . She rifles through the Cs, and stops when she sees a familiar name. CAMPOS, IGNACIO. Why is Iggy seeing

Dr. Singh? She bites her lip, debating a glimpse, and then keeps going. But there's no CARUSO. Her grandfather's file isn't here, and any minute she'll be out of time. She hurries from the office and back into the waiting room. Leaving empty-handed wasn't her plan.

"Does Dr. Singh archive his older files?" she asks at the front desk, but the nurse holds up a finger as he answers the phone.

"They shred them after five years," a voice says.

Rylie turns, the scent of patchouli hitting her just as she hears the swish of a long skirt. It's Sara Mazur, holding a book and staring at her mother's empty workstation.

"Hey, Sara," Rylie says softly. Nathan asked her to talk to Sara, but she would have done it anyway.

"They keep them electronically." Sara's still staring at her mom's desk. "But unless it's your own file, it takes ages to get access."

"It doesn't matter," Rylie says. A file is nothing compared to what Sara's going through. "How are you holding up?"

Sara turns and sets her book on one of the chairs in the waiting room. "It was sudden," she says, pulling a piece of paper out of her purse. "She'd been complaining about a few things, but she was *healthy*."

Her voice breaks and Rylie gets it. She gets it, probably more than Sara realizes. "Do you want to talk?"

Sara shakes her head, working the origami paper in her hands. "I actually just came here to read." The bright light from the nearby doors is making her eyes look swollen. "I thought the book would distract me, and if I was here, I'd still feel like she was around."

Rylie thinks of her dad's songs, and then her own eyes start to sting. She nods at Sara's book on the chair—it's a trail guide for California. "Have you tried any of the hikes in here?" she asks, just to get Sara talking. "I mean, I know we did a hike that one night, but—"

"This is Lily's, actually," Sara says, and at the sound of Lily's name Rylie stiffens. Sara doesn't seem to notice—she just sits down next to the guide and vacantly flips through it. "I've gone through it before, but I can't decide which trail to do first." Her gaze goes to her mom's workstation and then back to Rylie. "Lily's notes make all the trails sound dangerous, even the easy ones. You hike a lot, right?" Sara holds it out. "What do you think I should do?"

Finally, a question she can answer. She takes the book. There's a flurry of handwriting all along the margins—Lily really did leave notes. Curious, Rylie flips to the index and finds the arroyo trail near her grandpa's cabin. She turns to the page, and her heart quickens. It's filled with notes too, the scrawl so messy that it's hard to read. One word is circled, and Rylie squints at it. The word is "cabin," but the rest of the writing is impossible to read. Anything else Lily thought about the trail, *or* her grandpa's cabin, is too hard to decipher.

"Did Lily have a hiking partner?" Rylie asks, not letting herself hope. "Or did she mostly go out alone?"

Sara keeps folding the origami paper in her hands. "She used to go with Bas a lot."

"Bas?" Rylie's heard the name before—she's just not sure where.

"Bastion," Sara says. "It's the name he went by, anyway. I think it was a nickname." She looks more like herself now, like talking about something besides her mom is reviving some part of her. "He's a little younger than us. But into desert conservation, which I respect."

Rylie stares down at the hiking guide, still open to the arroyo trail. "Do you have Bastion's phone number?"

"All I've got is this." Sara pulls her phone from her purse and scrolls through her photos. "Here he is. He's in the middle."

The photograph is of three people, or four, if you count the guy turning his back to the camera. No one's smiling, and Lily actually looks furious, like the picture has caught her off guard. A hiking bag's slung over her shoulder and she's standing between another girl and the guy who must be Bas, a stainless steel water bottle in his hand. His face seems familiar, like Rylie has seen him around Twentynine Palms, and his name seems familiar too. And then her heart speeds up again as it hits her. Bastion was mentioned in one of the recordings. On the tape with the blank label, when Ethan Langhorne talked about Lily, he also said: *Bas. I think he knows.*

"Bas talked a lot about saving the world," Sara goes on.

"Said he was into self-sustainability, communal living, that sort of thing. Nice guy."

Communal living. A prickle shoots down Rylie's neck. Now she knows why his face looks familiar too. He's been on the news, under a different name. He's the kid from the commune, the one who Ethan Langhorne supposedly killed. She pulls the phone from Sara's grip. Of the four people in the photo, one's missing and one's dead. She steals a quick glance at Sara. If she didn't recognize the dated photo of Bas on the news, now's not the best time to tell her. "Do you know who the others are?"

Sara points at the guy at the edge of the picture. "He called himself Z. I think after 'zephyr.' It means 'a gentle west wind'? But he wasn't that nice."

Rylie stares at him. Zephyr is mostly out of the shot, but there's still a glimpse of dark reddish hair, a scowl. His profile looks familiar too, and she tightens her grip on the phone. She feels close, so close. "What about the other girl? Do you know her?"

"Sort of. Her name's Amira, but she goes by Sparrow. She was with Z that day."

"Sara?" a nurse calls out, and she slowly unfolds herself from the chair. "I'll be right back," she says, and Rylie takes the chance to click into Sara's phone contacts. No Z, but there it is—the very first name in her list. Rylie quickly texts Amira's details to her phone and sends herself the picture too, before deleting the text thread. This is it. It's the link she needs, and Sara's had it all along. All along it was just a phone call away.

She eyes Sara and the nurse at the desk, but they're preoccupied and this can't wait. Rylie sets down Sara's cell and grabs her own to start the call. As it rings, she heads toward the door, her stomach tense with nerves. Maybe the girl can't answer; maybe she's missing like Lily. The line keeps ringing. Maybe the girl would pick up if she used Sara's phone? But then the call ends with an automated message: "You have reached a nonworking number."

Of course. Rylie feels like hitting something. Instead she takes a slow breath and clicks back to the picture that Sara showed her. Four faces, and two of them are gone. Lily is missing. Bas is dead. Rylie types Ethan's name into a search engine, clicks on a link to his prom photo, then compares it to the guy called Zephyr who's halfway out of the picture. It's too hard to tell, so she turns back to the waiting room. Sara's sitting down again, holding the trail book on her lap without turning any pages.

"What else do you know about him?" Rylie asks softly. "About Z."

Sara is quiet for a minute, like her mind's somewhere else. It probably *is* somewhere else. "Nothing, really," she finally says. "They'd been trying to hike somewhere that day. Lily wanted to go, but the others weren't that into it. It was a hut or a lodge or something."

Rylie stares, a memory itching at her. A *lodge.* There's only one lodge that she knows of around here. Datura Lodge—a place she went to with her grandfather, a long time ago. Another memory comes to her, and her heart misses a beat. Ethan even *mentioned* Datura on one of the tapes. Only, at the time Rylie thought he was talking about a person. She sinks into the chair beside Sara, and then she remembers last night too—the recording she played before stopping at the gas station. *Take me with you,* her grandfather said. He was practically begging Ethan. And he said, *what?* That Ethan went "there" every time. He must mean the lodge. Ethan went there every time he *killed.*

It's suddenly hard to breathe. "Sara," she says. "The place Z and Lily wanted to go. Was it called Datura Lodge?"

Sara slips her phone into her purse. "That sounds right. They said it'd be hard to find."

Rylie doesn't mean to tell her; it just slips out of her mouth—"I've been there before." The long-ago memory is taking shape. It was at night, and she was in the car with her grandpa and her dad, and her grandpa stopped suddenly, pulling over to the side of the highway even though nothing was around—just desert. He said that he stopped because of the water. A *miracle,* her dad called it, and it was: the moonlight was reflecting off the water, turning it silver. They got out to take pictures of it, and then a man appeared on foot and started talking to her grandpa. A few minutes later, they followed the man to a place called Datura Lodge. Then her dad waited with her while her grandpa went inside. The lodge was carved from rock, and they took a photograph of it. She still has the picture in the folder on her Nikon, even after all this time.

Datura Lodge. Ethan could be there now. He went there *every time he killed.*

"Sara?" It's another staff member calling to her, and Sara stands again and looks apologetically at Rylie.

"I'll be—"

"It's okay," Rylie says. "I've got to go anyway." She gives Sara a hug and then slips out of the office and texts Kai that she's ready, ignoring the message from Ben: *Don't forget the anniversary dinner tonight. You should see Owen's cake. It's nothing short of majestic!* And the one from her mom: *How did your doctor visit go?* Feeling impatient, Rylie texts Kai again. Kai drove her to the follow-up today—her mom had insisted on fixing the jeep during her lunch break, both the ignition and the broken side mirror—and now Kai's supposed to drive her back home. She already knows that he'll ask about Singh, but she's not telling him about Datura Lodge. He'd want to come too, but that didn't exactly turn out so well when they went to see the Bishop twins. This is her mess; she doesn't need to drag him into it any more than she already has. While she waits for him to text back, she works out a makeshift plan in her head. First home for the jeep, and then to Datura Lodge, to see if Ethan's there.

Telling the cops about the lodge is the other option— but they might not take the lead seriously enough. They might sit on it, and meanwhile Ethan Langhorne would be gone, and the truth with him. The truth about Lily, and her grandpa, and maybe even the truth about herself.

Rylie grabs her pendant and squeezes it tight. She's getting out her phone to text Kai again when it beeps. It's Lor:

Can you call me? I just got a weird text from Iggy.

"Rylie!" a voice shouts, and she turns to see Kai in the corridor. He's got his reading glasses on and the Stein book in his hand as he hurries toward her. "I didn't crack the code," he says, but there's the faintest hint of guilt in his voice, like he's holding something back. "What about you?" he asks. "What did you find out?"

CHAPTER 27

RYLIE CAN'T GET IN TOUCH with Lor, and she can't tell Kai her plan either, in case he tries to talk her out of it. She glances at his speedometer, wanting to ask him to drive home faster. She needs to grab the jeep, get to Datura Lodge before dark, and then back home in time for the anniversary dinner, but her stepbrother's hands are rigid at ten and two like he's following a driving license manual and his second-hand Volvo doesn't look up for life in the fast lane anyway.

"Thanks for taking me home," she says instead, and Kai glances over at her and raises a brow. His window is down, open to the late afternoon sky, and his black hair's blowing away from his face, making him look less Kai-like than usual, even with the *Labyrinth* T-shirt he's wearing. On his arm is another girl's face drawn in pen, and he catches her staring.

"Her name is Sophie Scholl," he says. "But she's not a girlfriend. And I'm not taking you home."

Rylie side-eyes him. "Very funny, Kai."

"It's not a joke."

"If driving me was a problem, Ben could've picked me up."

"I only said I wasn't driving you *home*." Kai merges onto the highway and heads away from the Sundown house. "I didn't say I wouldn't take you where you're going."

She hasn't told him where she's going, and she doesn't like the knowing look on his face. "Kai—"

"Sara texted me," he cuts in. "Said she was worried about you. I am too."

Sara texted him? "I thought you two just met."

"I heard about her mom," he says, his eyes flicking back to the road. "So I got in touch. Sometimes it helps to talk."

Rylie's throat closes up. "You don't have to tell me that."

"So I don't need to tell you what Datura Lodge is either?" Kai asks. "Why didn't you just say where you were going?"

She hates the stab of guilt she feels. "Because I didn't want you to stop me."

"So you were just going to show up there alone?" His hands tighten over the wheel. They look dark and bruised— there's a smear of ink across them. "You don't even know what it is, do you?"

"I do," she says quickly, even though she has no idea what he's talking about.

"Datura Lodge started as a secret society out of Los Angeles. A cult." Kai raises his eyebrows again like he wants a reaction from her. She won't give him one.

"You sound like a history teacher."

"The lodge supposedly became inactive in the 1970s,"

Kai goes on, ignoring her. "But some people think it just split off from the main order. Became its own thing. Got into rituals and all that." He glances into the rearview mirror. "Supposedly they even opened up a portal to hell in the desert."

Secret societies. Rituals. *Hell.* Rylie gets another glimmer of a memory. A hot summer day. Her grandfather loading them into his car. The promise of ice cream . . . Now she stares out the window, a dull uneasiness in her stomach as Kai keeps his course. "Well, I'm not joining up, if that's what you're getting at."

"What I'm getting at is that I'm going with you."

His argument is sound, but he's being a jerk about it and she refuses to meet his eye. Fog is shrouding the desert in a misty haze again, spreading so fast, it almost seems alive. The windows go gray like they're under water, and the inside of the Volvo starts to feel claustrophobic, like a coffin, and the bad feeling is in her chest because neither of them should be going to the lodge at all. She grabs the door handle, suddenly wanting out. The metal handle feels both cold and hot in her grip, and the whole car smells of mold. The stench is coming from the backseat. A sleeping bag is on it, next to a fluorescent hiking backpack she hasn't seen before. In its mesh pocket is a rolled-up map. A map she *has* seen before.

She plucks the map out and opens it. Kai's eyes narrow for a brief second before flicking back to the road, and then it becomes obvious. "After we did that last hypnosis, you told me you went to some of the places that were marked on the map," she says. "Was Datura Lodge one of them?"

When Kai glances at her this time, she sees how cloaked his gaze looks. She can't believe she missed it before—how calculating he looks. Like he has a stake in this. Like it's personal.

"I tried," he says. "It was one of the places I couldn't find."

She folds up the map, the unease in her stomach worse now. "Why do you care so much about going, Kai?"

"Maybe you're not the only one searching for something." He says it nonchalantly, but it still gets to her. The way he's holding the wheel too tight. The way he's staring at the road now like he can't look her way.

"What are *you* searching for?" she asks.

"I was going to ask you the same thing. Why the hurry to get to the lodge today?" Kai asks. He pulls his phone out of his pocket as he crosses over into the far right lane, the slow lane. The Volvo slows even more, almost like the fog is tugging them back to where they came from, but it's too late to go back—at this point it'd be too much of a time suck, even if she *did* manage to convince Kai to turn around. From the way his shoulders are stubbornly set, he won't be convinced anyway.

"Just tell me, Rye."

"Fine." If she gives him a little, maybe he'll give a little too. Maybe he'll admit why he's here, what he's looking for. "Because Ethan Langhorne might be there."

"This just gets better and better," Kai mutters, but he doesn't sound amused. "And if he really is a killer? If he's done everything they're saying about him? Four murders that they know of so far . . ." The Volvo slows even more. "You're just offering yourself up on a platter."

Rylie's hands turn into fists, the gauze from her bandages pinching at her skin. "I'm not offering myself up to anyone."

"Sure you aren't," Kai says. He reaches for the pen behind his ear and pulls it out, then jabs it back. "You're just the granddaughter of someone he confessed his darkest desires to, that's all. No big deal." His jaw is tense as he flicks on his brights, but they barely cut through the grayness.

"There's no way he'd recognize me, Kai."

"You know," he says, still staring ahead at what little road they can see, "I admire your courage." His smile looks like a grimace. "You like extreme sports, for God's sake. But this is something else, Rylie. This, what you're doing now. What you're trying to prove."

She folds her arms across her chest. "You don't know what I'm trying to prove."

"I have an idea," Kai says quietly. "I've made mistakes too, you know." He finally looks over at her, and this time he doesn't break his gaze. "You can't stop Ethan Langhorne alone, Rye."

She's not *stopping* him. "I'm just making sure he's there. I'm making sure we get answers."

"At the very least call Nathan."

It's the last thing she expected him to say. "You think I need a guy to protect me?"

"No, but he's trained for this sort of thing. Apprehending threats. Security forces."

He's right. She's heard Nathan talk about the simulations before, the drills at work, but she's also heard him talk about Lily. She's seen how much it hurts him. Plus, she and Nathan didn't really leave things on good terms last night. "We don't know for sure that Ethan's at the lodge. If he's there, we'll call the cops." She looks up, squinting at the fog. A road comes into view. "That's the turnoff. Take it."

"Rylie—"

"You insisted on coming even though you won't tell me why you want to."

"Because I care." Kai's watching her instead of the highway. "We're family, aren't we?"

She waits a second too long to answer him, and her throat feels tight again. "Turn *now*."

Kai suddenly jerks the wheel, and then they're on a gravel road, rocks rattling against the sides of the Volvo. But there's nothing around—just rock piles and desert. She stares down at the map. "We must have missed it."

Kai rubs at his hair. "Like I said, I couldn't find it before either. The map's wrong."

"Go back toward the highway."

He slams on the brakes, surprising her. "The map's *wrong*," he says again, but he starts reversing anyway, faster than he drove going forward. The dusky fog is all around them—not even the brights are cutting through. Rylie rolls down her window. They don't have much time. Even *if* Ethan's at the lodge, he might not be for long. They need to find the place.

"Holy shit," Kai says, and then she sees it in the headlights: the lodge rising up in the gloom, its large door painted black, half its structure built into the rock behind it. When Kai parks the Volvo, she shoves the map into her pocket and tries to gear herself up for what she needs to do.

"Did you ever check your Nikon?" he asks suddenly, fiddling with his phone. "After the drive with Owen yesterday."

"You're stalling. You're the one who wanted to come with me."

"That was before I knew why you were going." He holds up his phone. "The service keeps cutting out. What if we need to call for help?"

"We won't. Not if we're careful." There'd be no reason for Ethan Langhorne to recognize either of them. "Are you going to come in, or are you going to stay here?" She opens the car door without waiting for an answer. It's not that she doesn't care; it's that if she slows down, she might not go in at all. The fog makes her skin feel damp—almost wet—and she forces herself to keep walking, her phone lighting her path. Kai trails beside her, pulling down the brim of his Volcom hat.

"Are you really ready for this?" he asks.

"You thought we'd find hexfoils here," she says, changing the subject. "I don't see any."

"I don't either. But I see something else."

Kai stops walking and nods toward the dimly lit lodge just as she hears the humming noise. Hanging from the edge of the roof is a dark lump: a bees nest. Rylie eyes it. "The only person getting stung here is Langhorne."

"And people say my jokes are bad." Kai's grimacing again. "Don't pretend you're not scared when you are."

She's been very good at pretending. "If you don't have an EpiPen, you should wait in the car, Kai," she says, reaching for the lodge's door. Just as she does, it swings open, the bees humming louder as a tall woman wearing a bulky vest steps outside, her hands in her pockets as she looks them over. The woman's feather-shaped earrings are silver instead of turquoise today, and she's wearing long sleeves over the scar on her elbow, but it's definitely her, and Rylie's so surprised that she blurts out the first thing that comes to mind.

"You were supposed to wait for me yesterday. At the bakery."

The woman looks them both up and down again and then shakes her head. "I think you're confusing me with someone else."

"You told me you wanted to talk. About—" Rylie glances at Kai. About her bandages. About the scrapes and cuts underneath. About whatever was causing the missing time that plagued her grandpa, and now plagues her. It makes a strange sort of sense that the woman who cornered her at the bakery is also here at Datura Lodge. It's the same place where her grandfather used to go. It's the same place where Ethan Langhorne might be now.

"Hold up, you two know each other?" Kai asks, glancing back and forth between them.

"Kind of." Rylie can't look away from her. "You never told me your name."

The woman sighs. "Sloan Parker. We need to get inside."

Rylie nods. An invitation is better than barging in, and it will give them the chance to scout out Ethan Langhorne.

"There's just one thing." Sloan reaches inside her vest and pulls out a thin coil of rope. As she does, Rylie glimpses something black on her neck, something she didn't notice at the bakery. It's a circular tattoo. A *hexfoil*.

"Your hands," Sloan says. "I need to bind them."

Rylie steps back. "You're kidding, right?"

"Let's go." Kai touches her elbow like he's going to pull her away. "Let's go in."

Go *in*? Rylie shakes her head, but Kai's already stepping toward the lodge. "No way," she says.

"You don't have a choice," Sloan says simply, but Rylie *does* have a choice—she could be at the car in seconds. But then she thinks of Nathan and Lily, Ethan Langhorne . . . And her dad. He was here before too, a long time ago. He went to Datura Lodge and so did she, on that night they saw the water in the desert, and they both left in one piece. They left together that day.

"You're not tying us up. That's ridiculous."

"Those are the terms." Sloan lowers her gaze on Rylie. Her eyes have a yellow tint to them. "And not both of you. Just *you*."

Rylie forces herself not to flinch. Kai's jaw tenses up, but he doesn't protest. So much for that familial bond. Rylie looks down at the bandages on her arms and thinks of what's underneath, how Sloan claimed to have answers at the bakery. If Sloan takes them inside now, it might lead to more answers. It might lead to Ethan too. All they have to do is see if he's here.

Rylie lets out a breath. Then she holds her wrists out.

CHAPTER 28

RYLIE TENSES AS SLOAN TIES her wrists with the rope. The knot is efficient like a climber's, but tighter, and Rylie knows that she's made a terrible mistake. It feels like she's on a night climb and her headlamp has slipped and dropped— a glow that's falling, falling, gone.

"Go ahead," Sloan says, opening the door. Rylie shoots a glance at Kai before stepping through. Inside, the lodge is dark. The whole place has a *Stay out* sort of feel—it's the same off-limits warning she gets in her grandpa's house on Sundown. But Ethan Langhorne might be here. Ethan, and all the answers she has been searching for.

"Keep on going," Sloan says, nudging her.

The main floor is dark and lit only by a fireplace, nearly down to embers. Besides the armchairs next to it, the room is mostly bare, save for its walls. Hanging above the chairs is a huge painting of a winged creature with the head of a coyote. Rylie stares at it, the uneasiness back. Her eyes have adjusted to the shadows, and now the other frames along the walls are visible too. Some are of historic battle scenes, and others are photographs of forlorn, gaunt-looking people standing in front of mass burials. The largest frame holds a black-and-gray print. In it a dismantled cow and a jumble of human body parts are reaching toward the sky. On the opposite wall is a dagger collection.

Rylie doesn't know what's worse, the blades or the paintings. It's awful, all of it, and no one's here. Ethan's not here. She moves her wrists, and the bindings cut into her skin.

"This way." Sloan walks briskly toward the fireplace. Beside it is a small, discreet door. She opens it and then waves them toward an even darker part of the lodge. Rylie turns to Kai and fights the urge to run. In and out. They could do this.

"You coming?" she asks.

Kai is staring at the paintings. "Right behind you," he says, and she looks pointedly at one of the daggers on the wall so that he knows to take it.

"Let's go," Sloan calls out, heading into the dimly lit hallway. Rylie trails her bound hands against the wall as the hallway gets blacker and blacker. Then, ahead, is the faintest glow. Sloan makes a sharp turn, pausing briefly in front of a narrow stairwell made of stone before starting down. Instead of windows or lights, there are torches burning in its depths, *real* torches. Rylie slows. Just as her lungs start to feel as tight as the rope on her wrists, Kai steps in line behind her.

"Where are we?" he asks.

"Underground," Sloan says. "It used to be a mine."

At a sudden clatter of footsteps, Rylie leans into the

stone wall. A few people quickly squeeze past them, going in the opposite direction. On their necks are more circular tattoos—hexfoils.

"You'll understand soon enough," Sloan says. She doesn't sound very reassuring, and then everything becomes obvious: she's as nervous as they are. Rylie forces herself to keep going, forces herself to think of Lily. After what feels like another flight of steps, they finally reach the bottom of the stairs.

"This is . . ." Kai trails off as they both stare at the vast underground room. Its walls are carved out of rock, and rough pillars hold up the ceiling. Branching off at the back of the main cavern are several dark tunnels. The room's not just cavernous, it *is* a cavern, and it's lit by more candles and is thrumming with people hurrying past. Everyone seems as somber as their dark clothing, and their gazes linger on Rylie's bindings a little too long. She takes the chance to scan their faces for Ethan and then gets shoved forward.

"Move."

"I'm moving." Rylie steps toward the nearest wall, and Sloan points at a table and chairs under an archway.

"Sit."

"Quite the hospitality," Kai says as Sloan holds up a finger. Then she talks in a hushed voice to a man whose hexfoil is shaved into the hair on his scalp instead of tattooed on his neck. Rylie feels their eyes on her as she leans closer to Kai.

"We need to look for Ethan and then leave," she whispers.

Kai nods. "Those pictures they had upstairs," he says. "The Pontic Greeks. Guernica. They're all of massacres. Genocides, some of them." He pulls his pen out from behind his ear. "You were looking at *Guernica*. Picasso painted it after the Nazis bombed an entire village in Spain, killing over a thousand innocent people. Just for practice."

Rylie rubs at the bindings over her wrists and scans the cavern again, hoping to see Ethan in the crowd. "What else do you know about Datura Lodge?"

"It's mostly known for being into black magic," he says, watching her. "But I'm guessing you don't believe in that sort of thing."

Down here, she just might. "And you do?"

Kai tucks his hair behind his ears and then shrugs. "I don't know. To me this place has more of a European, underground rave type of feel. *Doomf, doomf, doomf, doomf.*"

He's trying to make her less nervous, but her laugh catches in her throat as Sloan pulls out the chair beside them. "All right," Sloan says, her dark gaze going to both of them and then settling on Rylie. "Let's talk. I know you have questions."

"Plenty." Rylie makes sure her voice doesn't shake. "Why tie my hands?"

Sloan nods toward her bandages. "Unlike your friend, you're marked."

"What do you mean?"

Sloan sighs. "You don't trust me. Without trust you won't understand."

"*Trust* you?" It's hard to believe what she's hearing. Rylie holds up her wrists. "What about this?"

"We're getting to that." Sloan raises a hand. "Eric?" she says, and the guy with the shaved head sets a ceramic cup on the table. She shoves the cup toward Rylie. "Drink."

"I don't think so."

Kai leans toward her. "If they wanted to hurt us, they could have done it already," he says quietly.

Rylie tamps down a wave of panic. They're fine; she's fine. Kai isn't tied up like her. He can help her, if she needs it. Her mom would call this a calculated risk.

"If you drink, the bindings come off. Then we'll talk." Sloan edges the cup closer. That yellow glint in her eyes is there again. It's a reflection from the candlelight; it has to be. Rylie turns to Kai, but his gaze flicks to the crowd, as if the game theory going on right in front of him isn't a big deal.

She lifts the cup. It's hot. She debates throwing it at Sloan's face and running, but that wouldn't accomplish anything now that swarms of people are between them and the door.

If you drink, the bindings come off. Drink, and she can finish what she came to do: find Ethan. Get the truth for Nathan. For Lily too. And for herself.

In one quick motion, she tips the cup back. The drink's hot, hotter than she expected, and it scalds her throat going down. Sloan checks the empty cup, and then nods and pulls a knife from her vest.

Rylie edges away, but Sloan's faster, and the blade flashes, snapping the rope free. Kai gives her an imperceptible nod like he knew she'd be fine all along. She feels like kicking him when his gaze goes back to the room, but he must be looking for Ethan. Or an exit.

"You'll need more soon," Sloan says to her, and it's not clear if she's talking about the rope or the drink. "That's the first thing you should know. It's for the darkness."

The darkness. Rylie tries not to look rattled. "What do you mean?"

Sloan nods toward her bandages again. "The second thing you should know is that we look for people like you. Some don't make it."

"Wait," Rylie says, holding out her arms. "Where are the scrapes from? Why aren't they healing?"

A shout comes from one of the tunnels, and Sloan glances up, her hand tightening over the knife. "What do you remember?" she asks. "From when you got them."

"She remembers coyotes," Kai says.

Sloan's eyes stay on Rylie. "You know that's not exactly right, don't you?"

Another shout comes, and Sloan stands. "Hold on."

"What's going on?" Rylie asks.

"Eric!" Sloan calls out, and the guy who brought the drink looks over. "Watch them," she orders, and Eric glares at them from across the room as Sloan takes off into the crowd. She seemed helpful at the bakery, almost protective, but she left that day without explaining anything, and she's disappearing on Rylie and Kai again now. All they really know is her name.

"Hey," Kai says, leaning in. "I'll distract the muscle; you look around for Ethan."

Rylie shakes her head. There's a bitter, almost grainy taste in her mouth from the drink. They shouldn't have come here. "Let's just leave."

"Then you'll have downed a mystery beverage for nothing." Kai pushes back his chair. "Wait for my signal. We'll meet upstairs if anything goes wrong."

She almost tells him no, but they've done the hard part by getting down here, and another minute of looking for Ethan won't hurt. She searches the cavern again, trying to track the faces that are hurrying through the shadows. And then, when Kai's already across the room, it comes to her.

Sloan. Sloan Parker.

She's seen it written down before, or part of it. One of the tapes from the cabin was labeled s. PARKER.

Rylie swallows hard, the hot drink churning in her stomach. Sloan knew her grandpa; Sloan told him that she wanted to kill her neighbor. Not just her neighbor, though. Every living thing, that's what she said.

Rylie lurches after Kai, feeling sick. They need to leave. *Now.*

"Kai!" she calls out. A few heads turn as she weaves through the crowd, trying to reach him. There's another distant shout, and then more people are running toward the tunnels, jostling her aside. When she looks up again, there he is, pulling up the hood of his sweatshirt, striding in the opposite direction of the crowd.

It's Ethan Langhorne.

He's less clean-cut than in the photos on the news, but it's him; she's sure of it. He's still moving against the crowd, head down, hurrying toward the stairwell like he can feel her eyes on him. Any second he'll be gone. She could find Kai first, or she could follow Ethan out alone, but if she doesn't go after him now, she might not get another chance.

"*Kai,*" Rylie hisses, and then she runs toward the stairwell, elbowing past more people with hexfoil tattoos. She rushes up the stairs, following the black hoodie ahead. Ethan's walking faster now; he must know he's being followed. Her hand closes on her phone in her pocket as she bursts into the hallway. Any minute he could turn around and attack her. Instead, he pushes the front door open and steps out into the fog.

Rylie glances back at the stairwell, hoping to see Kai's dark hair behind her, but there's no one there and it's now or never. If she lets Ethan go, the truth about Lily and her grandpa might go with him. But if she leaves Kai downstairs, then she's leaving him with Sloan Parker, someone they definitely can't trust. Kai or Ethan, *Kai or Ethan*, it's running through her head like a chant, and then, right below the framed print of dismembered body parts, she spots one of the daggers. She pulls it down from where it's hanging and shoves it into her back pocket. Kai will come looking for her any minute, and all she needs is a glimpse. All she needs to do is follow Ethan, let the cops know where he's going, what he's driving.

"Come on, Kai," she whispers. Then she grabs her phone and hurries out the door.

Authorities have found the body of an
unidentified female in a remote desert
location. Upon further investigation it was
discovered that the body had been dumped
near what appears to be a mass burial site,
where the remains of at least twenty other
individuals have been uncovered so far.
Anyone with information is urged to come
forward.

CHAPTER 29

THE FOG IS THICK AS Rylie steps outside, dialing 911 on her phone. It's not working, it's not going through, and then she hears the creak of hinges behind her. She whirls.

Ethan's standing between her and the lodge's door, his hood throwing shadows over his eyes. He's dropped the shy smile that was on his face in the prom picture the news likes to run, but it's definitely him.

"Stop following me." His voice sounds rougher than it did on the tapes. "You think I care about you?"

He must think she's someone else. Rylie suddenly *feels* like someone else, like this isn't really happening. Close by is a humming sound. The bees.

"Forget this secretive shit. I'm through with it." Ethan's hands are in his sweatshirt pockets. He can't see what she has in her own pockets. "Everything I've done, I've done for myself," he says.

"What have you done, Ethan?" She asks it without thinking, and when he steps forward, she smells the sweat on him. His eyes narrow on her bandages.

"You're kidding me," he says. "I know which one you

are." He smiles then—he almost looks nice, like he's just a normal guy and she's just a normal girl and they're saying a friendly hello. He even looks innocent: the splash of freckles over his nose makes him look younger than seventeen.

"Caruuuso," he says slowly. "Caruso-Evers, Rylie," he says, and her lungs clamp down. "I've seen your file. The lodge keeps one for everyone. They do now, at least." He smiles. "Especially for people like us. We're special, aren't we?"

If he's playing with her, she'll play right back. "I have my grandfather's recordings, Ethan. Or Z, or whatever you go by." Better to make him think she has something he wants. "They're with someone I trust." The humming gets louder and she glances toward the bees nest, fast, then back at him. She keeps her hand tight around her phone in her pocket.

"'Z' is what my parents called me," Ethan says calmly. "Do you know it's hereditary?" If he cares about the tapes, he's not showing it. "Do you know what you are yet?"

A chill crawls down her neck. "Do you know why I'm here, Ethan?" Now she sounds like her grandfather—answering a question with another question. Somehow his cadence is coming on instinct. But he got Ethan to talk before, so maybe it will work for her too. And she could record it—just like he did.

"You're here because of this." Ethan pushes up the sleeves of his sweatshirt. Bluish scars, thick and swollen, are twisting up his arms. "We're marked. We *belong* here."

Too late she yanks her own sleeves down. She doesn't

want him to see a likeness; she doesn't want him to know a thing more about her.

"We're the same, Rylie." Ethan smiles again, and it almost disarms her, how it lights up his whole face and turns it into something less hard and more dangerous all at once. "Let me guess, you're having trouble remembering? That's because it's a shock to the system at first. It gets easier. Pretty soon you can *never* forget."

The humming grows louder, and the edges of Ethan's black sweatshirt are fading in and out of the fog. Rylie blinks, trying to clear her vision. Whatever she drank in the lodge is starting to hit her. "Stay back or I'll yell."

"We're bad, both of us," Ethan says. He sounds too much like that unlabeled tape. It's like an echo in her head—everything he said about Lily on it, everything he said about *her*. "There's no sense in fighting it. We'll keep on hurting, keep on killing."

"Who have you killed, Ethan?"

He laughs. It's not a harsh sound—it's genuine laughter. It's warm like his smile, and it's all wrong because it makes her relax. "You're not one for analogies, are you?" he asks. "What about the Tibetan story of the well frog, have you heard it?"

He's trying to distract her. She keeps watching his hands—they're in his sweatshirt pockets again. The lodge is right behind him, its black wooden door looming through the haze, and then she remembers what Sara said at the police station, about how Ethan isn't working alone. The note he left for the cops pretty much said the same thing. "Has Sloan been helping you? Is she your accomplice?"

"My accomplice?" For a second he actually looks confused. *"Sloan?"* He laughs again. "No, Rylie." He steps closer, his hands still in his pockets.

"Once upon a time," he says patiently, like they have all the time in the world, "a frog from the sea decides to take a walk, and on the way he finds a frog living in a well. And the sea frog tells the well frog that life is so much bigger, if he'd just come out of his little home. And the well frog says, 'How much bigger? Twice this size?'"

Ethan pulls one of his hands from his pocket. He isn't holding anything; there's no weapon. The other hand is still tucked away, out of sight.

"And the sea frog tells the well frog, 'It's so huge, you'd never believe it. Come with me and I'll show you.' So the well frog follows the sea frog to the shore. And you know what happens? The ocean is so big, so utterly unbelievable to him, that his head explodes."

Rylie's trying to keep her eyes on Ethan, but shadows are moving in the haze; her vision's blurring again. "You're saying I won't believe the truth if you tell me."

"You already know the truth and just won't admit it."

"I haven't heard it from you."

Ethan glances toward the lodge and she quickly opens the recording app on her phone, then shoves it back into her pocket just as his gaze falls on her again. "You think I'm a threat," he says. "It's keeping you up at night." He takes another step. His eyes aren't blue like she thought before. One of them is green—it's heterochromia—and then all she can think about is her mom and especially Owen, what he's doing, whether he's worried that she's late coming home.

"You've heard Mojave Mix and ABC7 and Desert Oracle so you know what I've done, but you don't know *why* I've done it. You don't know what's driving me. You don't know about the darkness."

Her heart's going fast in her chest and the humming is even louder now. "Try me."

"Murder for a jar of red rum," he whispers. He smiles like he's enjoying himself, like he knows he's confusing her. "Figure it out yourself. That's how this works."

Murder. He's not even trying to hide it. She has to ask now—she has to know. "Lily Seguin," she says. "Is she alive?"

The smile drops away and there's a sudden intensity in his eyes. It takes everything she has to hold her ground.

"Do you know where Lily is?" Her heart is pounding loud, too loud. Ethan is strangely still. "Did you kill her like you killed the others?"

A bee's in the air, flying past her head, and then Ethan lunges. Rylie barely has time to move. She quickly lifts the dagger in a warning, but Ethan lunges again, knocking the blade from her hand, his hands grasping at her neck. He tugs at her necklace, yanks it back, and she gasps as he pulls it against her throat. She can't breathe, she can't reach him, she can't reach the dagger.

"More people will die, just like her." Ethan's breath is on her skin, and he's pulling tight as she tries to twist away, kick at him, scratch him, but her hands only hit air. "They'll disappear forever and it's my fault and it's your fault."

Breathe. Breathe. She tries to wedge her fingers between her necklace and her skin, but he only pulls harder.

"The darkness won't ever leave. Don't you get it? They're attracted to us. They *like* us."

Ethan yanks tighter and she can't get free of him, she can't get any breath. A distant memory flashes into her mind: Lily and Nathan wrestling as kids, Nathan in a choke hold. Nathan reaching to her for help. And then flecks of light are all around her, and the blood is rushing through her ears, louder and louder, and it almost looks like the fog is shimmering, there and not there, fading in and out, and right before her vision goes black, she sees a shadow next to her, she sees someone stepping through the fog. It's Nathan, it's *Nathan*, but he's not looking her way. She tries to call out but she can't and it takes everything she has to reach for him, the necklace digging into her skin, into her throat. Her lungs are empty, so empty, and then, somehow, her fingers graze his shirt and suddenly his head jerks and his eyes lock on to hers, and a split second later he's moving fast behind her and the leather snaps loose.

She hunches over, gulping in air.

"More people will die—" It's Ethan. There's the sound of fist on bone, and then something wet hits her leg and she hears footsteps, a dragging sound. She glances up, too fast, and sees Nathan in front of her, two Nathans; her vision is blurry. She can't see Ethan anymore, she doesn't know where he is, but the dagger is lying in the dirt and she picks it up, dizziness rushing over her.

"You okay?" Nathan asks, and she nods because she can't talk, her throat's on fire. He scoops up her pendant in a hurry and steps toward his truck.

"We need to get you to a doctor," he says. "We need to get him locked up too." There's a hardness in his voice as he steers her toward the passenger seat and helps her climb in. And there, lying in the backseat of the truck, is a body. It's Ethan. He's on his side, knocked out. A woman in fatigues is guarding him.

Rylie looks away, back at the lodge. "Kai," she manages to say, her throat burning—and then, through the fog, there's her stepbrother, waving and heading straight for them. She opens the door to let him in, but Nathan's already throwing the truck into gear.

"Follow us," Nathan calls out.

"I'll be right behind you," Kai calls back. He shuts the truck's door before it skids out of the sandy parking lot, gaining speed on the dirt road. Rylie watches in the rearview mirror as the fog eats up Kai and the lodge in seconds. The ache in her throat comes back full force, and so does the ache in her heart. Ethan Langhorne admitted to killing Lily, and he almost strangled Rylie too. For once she *wants* the missing time, she wants to forget, she wants everything to be a wide-open blank in her mind. But she's got it all recorded—everything he said is on the phone in her pocket. His entire confession.

"Nathan—"

"Stop talking," the woman in fatigues cuts in, leaning forward on the console. She gently pulls the dagger out of Rylie's hands. "Let me check you over." A second later cold fingers are on Rylie's elbow, and a penlight's in her face, shining in her eyes and making her blink.

Nathan glances their way, his knuckles pale over the wheel. There's a smear of dirt on his face and uniform. "Martinez, this is Rylie," he says. "Rylie, Martinez. She does a lot of surveillance work."

"We didn't even know about that place," Martinez says. "It's—"

"Later. Stay quiet for now," Martinez tells her, looking her over. "No bruising. No swelling either." She turns Rylie's face with her too-cold hands. "Stick out your tongue." Martinez's gaze is efficient, quick, but up close like this, she looks young, maybe nineteen or twenty, not much older than they are. "You look fine," she says, and Rylie nods. In the side mirror she sees that the skin on her neck is red but not bruised. She grabs her necklace from the cup holder and wipes the dirt off it, until the jade figure eight is clean, and then she ties the leather around her neck. For a second she wants it off, but she holds her hands still, keeps the pendant on. Ethan Langhorne won't ruin anything else for her.

"We should take him to base?" Martinez asks, but it's not really a question. Despite her age, her voice is commanding.

"Agreed," Nathan says, and Rylie shifts in her seat. Martinez is watching Ethan now, and Nathan's focused on the road, so Rylie clicks into her phone. She wishes she had earphones to listen to her dad. One of his songs is already running through her head. *Out among the rock and sand, they say to be careful for snakes . . .*

"That shouldn't have happened to you."

Rylie looks over. "It's okay."

"It's not." Nathan's voice is strained but quiet. "Kai texted me before you got there and told me what you were doing. I was on shift with Martinez. We should have been there faster, but I couldn't find it."

Anybody could have gotten lost. It's like the day she drove home from the bakery, how easily the desert turned on her.

"It was a pin on a map, and I messed up." Nathan's not keeping his voice down now. The old scar across his eyebrow looks wider, as if meeting Ethan ripped open everything painful, every reminder of Lily. "You were right there, all along, and I should've been there too. I should've made it in time."

But he *did* make it in time. Rylie wants to thank him, except her throat's closing up again, and now Nathan's looking her way, too long, and her throat feels even tighter. She wants to tell him to watch the road, watch the road before something else bad happens.

"Rye, I don't want to lose you again." Nathan's still not keeping his voice down, and now her heart's beating faster than it should be. "You make life better," he says.

You make life better. He said that before, back when she was thirteen. He held her hand on top of Trashcan Rock, the desert spread out below. He told her that life was better when she was around, when they were together. Side by side, just like now. His arm is resting near hers on the console, and their hands are so close near the cup holder. Even though they're barely touching, it feels like they've reached across the chasm that was between them and somehow pulled the land together again, back into place, making it whole again.

"Everest," she says.

"Denali." Nathan's smiling, almost.

A low groan comes from the backseat and Rylie straightens, tries not to flinch. But Ethan Langhorne can't hurt anyone anymore, and Nathan and Kai are fine, and she's fine too, she's *good*—no matter what, she did something good today. Now she just needs to get home; she needs Nathan to hear the recording she made of Ethan's confession; she needs him to know about Lily. But not while he's driving, and not with Ethan in the truck.

She keeps her gaze between the windshield and Ethan in the backseat, his fluttering eyelids, the fog at the windows, the headlights. If she just focuses on the headlights, she'll be able to keep it together. The remnants of another song are running through her head, her dad singing about how everything will be all right, how *it'll all be better in the morning, at first light.* It should comfort her, but instead, her throat starts to ache again.

It was the last song he ever wrote.

CHAPTER 30

RYLIE OPENS HER EYES. BRIGHT sunlight's streaming through the windows, and she pulls out her phone. It's late—almost one in the afternoon—but there aren't any messages from Nathan. Last night, after convincing him and Martinez to let her explain things to her parents on her own terms, and after Nathan was finally able to drive her home, they sat in his truck and she told him about using her phone to record Ethan. But she didn't tell him what Ethan said, and he didn't ask either. Instead, he asked for the audio file—he said he wanted to listen to it alone. And then he drove away and hasn't been in touch since.

Rylie sits up in bed and looks toward her balcony, at the blinding light seeping in. By now Nathan should have listened to it—by now he must know about his sister. Rylie can imagine him telling Thea, can imagine the two of them in Lily's room, Thea leaning against Nathan, Nathan holding her up. Then her mind goes to Owen and she's up and out of bed, heading toward his room. It's empty so she starts downstairs, but it's quiet too. On the kitchen counter is a half-eaten chocolate cake on a glass stand, sliced strawberries carefully arranged around its edges.

The anniversary cake. The dinner party. Last night when she got to the base with Martinez and Nathan, she texted a hasty excuse to her mom about skipping dinner, and the text that came back made her feel even guiltier: *You too? Kai's also out. He went camping.* Her mom's text explained why Kai hadn't followed her to base like he'd promised, and it filled in the blanks from the crackling voicemail he'd left, but Rylie had found herself missing him. He should have been there to see Ethan locked away. Watching him get thrown in a cell had been a relief. It was a relief to go home afterward too, and leave it all behind. When she finally slipped through the door, her mom and Ben had been sitting out near the pool with a bottle of red between them and towels slung over their chairs, her mom laughing like she hadn't in a while, and Rylie got away with just calling out a quick good night.

Now, after everything that happened, she wishes she'd hugged her mom instead, told her that she loves her. She wants to say the same thing to Owen—as soon as she can find him. Rylie slides open the doors to the patio and hears a loud bark. Castle's all the way at the fence, and there's no one else out back, but the fresh air feels good and she unravels her knotted braid, peering at herself in the shards of decorative mirror on the tabletop. There's no bruising along her neck from Ethan, no redness today. Her entire body is tired and sore but she'll be fine, just like Martinez said.

Rylie sinks into one of the patio chairs, the cushions warm with the afternoon sunlight, the pool a glimmering blue. Yesterday she almost believed Ethan when he said they were the same, that she was as bad as him. It's laughable now, with him finally in custody and the sun on her skin. It's over. It doesn't matter that questions are still swarming her head or that she's still wearing bandages. She slowly unwraps the gauze on her arms. What matters, what *really* matters, is that Ethan Langhorne isn't out there anymore, and that the truth about Lily isn't hidden with him. The news hasn't hit publicly yet, but it will soon, probably any minute. At least Nathan has answers now. Nathan and Thea both.

Lily . . . The truth cuts into her again. Lily's not coming home. Lily's never coming home. Then there are footsteps from inside the house and the back door swings open. It's Ben in his cycling gear, two steaming mugs in his hands.

"Thought I saw you out here. Up for some tea? I found this great blend at Italy Mine, that bakery you like?" Ben hands her one of the mugs, and Rylie murmurs a thanks and then takes a sip as an excuse not to talk. It burns her throat as it goes down.

"Got a lot on your mind?" Ben asks. He's looking at her over his glasses, really looking at her. "No pressure," he says, holding her gaze, "but I'm always here to listen, Rye. I hope you know that."

"I know." It's what she used to like best about him. A part

of her still wants to confront him about the thesis, but it seems so distant now, so *small*, compared to last night with Ethan. The tea churns in her stomach, and her discarded gauze is on the table like shed snakeskin, and then she almost tells Ben what happened. Not everything, just about Lily. She wants to tell him that she found out that Nathan's sister is dead. Ben would know what to say. He'd tell her that everything will be okay, eventually. He'd remind her that Ethan Langhorne is in custody and that he can't hurt anyone else. It's over.

"I know what's wrong," Ben says, and Rylie glances up from the table so quickly that warm tea sloshes over her hands. "Your mom wants to talk to you about it, when you're ready," he adds softly. "She tried to do what was best for you, Rylie. We both did."

So he already knows she was in his office, and he probably knows what she read too. "Is she here?" Rylie asks, and he shakes his head.

"She didn't want to wake you earlier. You looked like you needed the sleep," he says gently, and then all she can think about is last night again. "They had that budget meeting, so she's working through the weekend. We probably won't see her till later," he says. "Tomorrow they're starting all the closures."

Budget meetings, closures. It's hard to think about anything but yesterday, and Rylie suddenly wants to talk about it with someone who will understand. She steps around Ben and heads inside. "Is Kai still out?"

"Didn't he tell you?" Ben comes in behind her and shuts the patio door, Castle on his heels. "He's camping the whole weekend. I think he left after he picked you up from your doctor appointment yesterday."

"Camping the whole weekend," Rylie repeats flatly. Ben clearly has no idea that they took a detour to the lodge after her doctor appointment instead. Considering what went down with Ethan Langhorne and Nathan, she would've expected Kai to change his plans. *I'll be right behind you.* Didn't he say that in the lodge's parking lot? Then again, the tent was already in his car, the backpack too. Maybe after everything that happened, he'd needed to get away.

"I'm as surprised as you are. Kai isn't a big fan of the outdoors," Ben says, his eyes far away as he takes another sip of tea. "I think it's a step in the right direction, though," he murmurs. "We should all go together sometime. As a family."

"You're home, Rylie?" Owen appears at the top of the stairs—he must have been out on his balcony earlier. He starts heading down, his free hand on the railing, and then she sees that he's wearing one of her old climbing gym T-shirts. There's a slogan across it: IF YOU'RE NOT FALLING, YOU'RE NOT TRYING. "I thought you'd gone camping too," Owen says as he hits the bottom step. "Because you weren't in your room last night."

"Of course I was. You went to bed before I did, O," she reminds him, bending down to pet Castle. He flees behind Owen's legs, so she pulls out her phone instead and shoots Kai a text—*Call me asap*—and then hides the screen against her shirt as Ben follows her to the stairs. "It must have been cold outside last night, with all the fog."

"What fog?" Ben asks, and then her phone starts buzzing in her hand. But it's not Kai; it's Lor. Rylie picks up.

"Hey, I was just about to—"

There's heavy breathing on the line, and Rylie feels a tingle of worry. "Are you okay?"

"Just . . . turn on the news."

"Why?" The worry clamps tighter. "What's going on?"

"I . . ." That sound again. She's definitely crying. "Hang on, Rye. I'll switch to video," Lor says hoarsely, and Rylie hurries upstairs and accepts the video call. There's a brief glimpse of Lor's runny mascara, and then she aims the phone at her television. "Just watch," Lor says.

On the screen are the blue and red lights of a flashing cop car next to a burning gas station, a reporter with her mike beside it. "Late last night, a family-run gas station along Highway 62 exploded, leaving at least nine dead so far," the reporter says. "It's estimated that the explosion occurred sometime between eleven p.m. and one a.m. The public is demanding answers from an already overtaxed police force, who promise they're working around the clock to determine the cause."

"Did you get that?" Lor asks, and Rylie can barely answer because Ethan Langhorne's threat is running through her head: *More people will die . . . disappear forever.*

"An abandoned vehicle was found a half mile from the incident, no occupants inside," the reporter goes on.

"It's Iggy's car," Lor says, and Rylie feels like the breath's been knocked from her. "He works for a professor, his ecology professor? He never misses a shift because it's research on bees. You know it's Iggy's thing. But apparently he didn't show up yesterday or today, and the professor called my aunt. Then this."

"Lor—"

"They found Miles near the car, but he doesn't remember anything. Iggy's missing, Rye."

She feels her lungs go tight again. For the first time since going after Ethan, she thinks of the list she made with Lor and Kai, the list of missing people, the list of the dead. All the photographs that were in her grandpa's cabin, Lily's included. *Mackenzie Soren, Jed Hendersen, Juan Ramon-Ortez, Emily Okada, Odele and Robert Kucharski, Fern Childers Gallagher.* And now Iggy. The list didn't stop with Lily, it never stopped with Lily.

"Hey, Rye?" Owen swings her door open. "Can I come in?"

"In a minute, O." She quickly switches the call to audio and takes it off speaker, not wanting him to hear. "I'll be out soon, okay?" she says, shutting her door. "Lourdes, can you hear me?" she asks. Lor has always known what to say, ever since they met, and now it's Rylie's turn to say the right thing. "We'll figure it out."

"I hope—" Lor's voice breaks off.

"We'll find him," Rylie says. "We'll find Iggy."

But even as she says it, she can't get the list out of her

head—the list of names from the cabin; the nine people killed in the explosion at the gas station. Ethan Langhorne's threat is stuck in her head too: *More people will die . . . disappear forever.* But if Ethan was in custody last night, then it wasn't a threat; it was a warning.

Someone else is still out there.

Rylie's heart starts going fast in her chest, and she feels like she might be sick. There are others on her grandpa's recordings, people like Sloan Parker, Millie Callahan. People who want to hurt, to kill. It isn't just Ethan—he even said so in his note to the police, and he warned her yesterday too.

"Rye, you there?" Lor asks, her voice faint over the line. "The other day, Iggy told me . . ." She trails off again. "He . . ."

"Iggy told you what?"

Lor lets out a long sigh. "That if anything happened to him, to ask you about it."

"Why?"

"And the police," Lor says. "They asked me about you too. They said that Iggy called in about you. I told them . . ."

Rylie sinks onto her bed, feeling the breath empty out of her. She can hardly hear Lor; she can hardly hold the phone. *More people will die . . . disappear forever.* That's what Ethan said, and he was right, and now Rylie can't ignore what he said about her either. *We're marked,* he told her yesterday, flashing his scars. *We're the same. We're bad, both of us.* He said that everything was his fault, and *hers* too, and he also said something else, something about murder . . .

Murder for a jar of red rum. She shivers as she remembers it. *Murder for a jar of red rum.*

"I told them they were wrong," Lor finishes. There's not a shred of doubt in her voice, but there should be. Rylie can feel it crawling inside her, taking hold. "Hang on," Lor says, "I'm getting another call. Give me a minute."

The line goes silent and Rylie slowly sets down the phone, Ethan's words still echoing in her head. *Murder for a jar of red rum.* She feels like she's in a dream, a nightmare. Owen said that she wasn't in her bed last night, and now Iggy is gone, his car abandoned on Highway 62—the same highway she and Kai drove to the lodge yesterday.

It's just a coincidence; it has to be. But then she thinks of the map from her grandpa's cabin, the one that he'd marked with red pen. She took it from Kai's backpack in the Volvo; she still has it now—it's in her pocket from yesterday.

She picks her jeans up from the carpet and yanks out the map. Red ink is scattered across it; locations all over the Mojave are circled. Each time she lost her memory before, Kai looked for patterns, pointed out palindromes, hexfoils. Maybe there's a pattern here too. She grabs a pen from her desk and holds the map closer. In the mess of red ink she finds Highway 62 and then circles the spot where Iggy's car went missing, according to the news report. Then she circles the outer fringe of Twentynine Palms—the place near the bakery where she lost a chunk of time with Owen. And the first time her memory went, she was hiking near her grandfather's cabin. Three locations, three circles, three specific points; as precise as a route up a boulder.

She tightens her grip on the map. The three locations are in a line. They make a line. Then something else niggles at her memory: the Gertrude Stein book. *A line distinguishes it.* The Stein quotes are a pattern too. Rylie's brain feels like it's tingling, on the brink of understanding something that's just out of reach. The words echo in her head: *A line distinguishes it.*

"Lor?"

No answer. Rylie's still on hold. It feels like the truth is floating somewhere inside her and she just has to find it, put it together into something that makes sense. It's like the climber she once read about who fell a hundred feet and lived. He couldn't remember anything before the fall, but then he slowly reconstructed his memory, piece by piece. He said that it was like gathering up a dandelion that'd been blown apart in his head, and when he collected enough of the individual seeds, those floating white strands, it made an answer, one solid enough to hold on to. Right now her head feels like it's filled with dandelion seeds too. Each strand is a clue, and they're all there, itching at her mind. The line. The poetry. The hexfoils. The palindromes. And then it hits her and she nearly drops the map. Murder, red rum. *Murder for a jar of red rum.* It's another palindrome. It was some sort of clue from Ethan.

Rylie shoves the map into her pocket and then stares

down at her arms, at the scratches that won't heal. That's another thing she doesn't understand yet, another pattern. Every time she was near the places on the map, she saw coyotes. Or she *thought* she saw them.

She slides off her bed so fast, she accidentally knocks her Nikon to the floor. The Nikon that she *still* hasn't checked since the bakery.

"Rye, can I come in yet?" It's Owen, knocking at her door again.

"Just a sec, O. I'm still on the phone." She sets it down and then rips the camera from its case and turns it on. When the menu appears, she clicks on the most recent image, the one she took of Owen the day they went to the bakery, the day they got lost.

At first it looks like nothing. It's just Owen in the jeep, his body turned away from her as he sleeps, the window beside him gray with dusk and a view of the desert.

The desert, and something else . . .

Rylie almost doesn't notice it, the shadow in the background. At first it looks like it could be a Joshua tree, or even a smudge of dirt on the lens, except for the two shiny pinpricks of light in the middle of it. She stares at the blur of shadow and light and brings the camera closer. And then the pinpricks of light become glowing yellow eyes, and the dark smudge transforms into coarse fur in some places, hairless flesh in others.

She can't look away. The camera's shaking in her hand; her whole body's shaking. It's not a coyote in the shot—it can't be. The teeth, the way its mouth is frothing . . . Something Thea told her and Nathan one night comes back to her, something Thea said after they saw shadows running across the desert: *As long as humans walk the earth, there will always be monsters.*

Monsters.

Darkness, glittering eyes—the memory is rushing over her.

"Hey," Lor says, her voice loud over the phone, loud enough to pull Rylie back into the room. "I can't stay here and do nothing." There's the flare of an engine. "I'm on my way there."

"Lor? This is going to sound . . ." Rylie trails off. There's not enough time to explain. "Listen, avoid Highway 62. Take the back roads to my house."

"Why?"

Rylie clenches the phone tight. "Because I know what we need to do."

CHAPTER 31

A FEW HOURS LATER, RYLIE turns onto the gravel side road. The speakers crackle in the jeep; they're losing the station. "College student Ignacio Campos is still missing, and authorities claim that seventeen-year-old Ethan Langhorne, recently apprehended for multiple murder charges, has admitted to knowing his whereabouts. Langhorne is currently being transferred to . . ." The rest is garbled—Mojave Mix is cutting out but the lodge isn't far now anyway.

"We'll find him," Rylie says, her grip tightening over the wheel. They have all night to look. She told Ben she was sleeping over at Sara's house, to buy some time. Hopefully it would pay off.

"'Doubts are traitors,'" Lor quotes softly, staring out the dark window. Rylie tries Kai on the phone again—no answer—and catches Nathan's gaze in the rearview mirror. He nods, then looks away. He hasn't brought up Lily or Ethan, but he swore that he wanted to come when she stopped by his house earlier. No one has said anything about the gun he's carrying, not even Sara, who was at Nathan's when Rylie showed up. Apparently he'd been telling

Sara the news about Lily. Now Sara's sitting beside him in the backseat, working a piece of origami paper in her hands.

"My uncle would send a patrol car if we asked," Sara offers, and Rylie shakes her head.

"The lodge won't talk to us if we're with the police," Rylie says. "And the police won't want us talking to the lodge if they're working on a warrant."

"Agreed," Lor says.

Nathan nods. "At least the lodge shouldn't recognize me. I don't think anyone saw me take down Langhorne. Because of the fog."

"Nature was on your side yesterday." Sara makes a fold, and suddenly there's an arm, a pointed head. Then something that looks like a tail, and Rylie goes tense. She's trying to watch the road, but she can't stop looking at the rearview mirror, at the paper in Sara's hands.

"What's that supposed to be?"

"It's Guadalupe. A fur seal." Sara stares down at it. "They were almost wiped out." She lifts her chin. "They were saved."

No one would be saving them where they're going, not if something goes wrong. Rylie flicks off the jeep's headlights and then slows to a crawl. It takes a few seconds for her eyes to adjust to the dusky light, the shadowy hulk of Datura Lodge just ahead.

"I have to say something." She doesn't let her voice waver. "We might not find anything here. But Sloan . . ." Sloan Parker is her only lead. Sloan knew her grandfather—the recording is proof of that—and she was at the lodge with Ethan Langhorne too. Sloan might know where Iggy is and why people keep dying, like Sara's mom. And why Ethan warned that everything in Twentynine Palms would get worse, and why he was *right*.

"We're not backing out, Rye," Nathan says. Somehow he has guessed what she's thinking before she even says it, just like he always does. "This has to stop. All of it. Going to Sloan is the logical move."

Lor squeezes her elbow. "From what you've told us, it's worth a shot."

Rylie's eyes suddenly feel hot, and she blinks. Despite everything, Lor and Nathan still trust her, but they don't know the half of it. She hasn't told them the things that are too confusing to put into words. The strange photo of the coyote, the way the scrapes on her arms won't heal, the tape recording that talked about *her*. But she has to warn them. Because if anyone gets hurt today, it will be her fault.

"Just think about the risk." When she says it, she feels something lodge in her throat. "You don't have to come here, but I do. I need the truth." She clutches the wheel. "I need to know why I've been losing my memory." She makes herself meet Nathan's eyes in the rearview mirror, and then she looks at Lor beside her too. "I need to know what I've *done*."

For a moment the jeep is silent and the weight on her lungs feels heavier. She readies for Lor to recoil, for Nathan to act the way he did on the roof. But instead, he touches her shoulder. Then Lor grabs her hand and laces her fingers through hers, and in the rearview mirror she sees Sara wipe at her eyes and nod.

"We're here to help," Lor says, at the same time that Nathan says, "We're with you."

She wants to answer but her throat hurts too much. If she tries to speak at all, she might start crying, so she cuts the engine.

"Look." Sara points. "Kai must have got your texts earlier and beat us here."

Rylie stares. Near the lodge, parked in the same place as yesterday, is Kai's Volvo.

"Or he never left?" Nathan asks, and then he snaps his mouth shut. Rylie pockets the keys, the heaviness back in her chest. But Kai wouldn't have stayed here last night—he texted Ben that he'd went camping.

"He's probably waiting for us." Rylie grabs the box cutter she brought for the bindings, and then gets out into the cool air, shivering in her zip-up as she strides over to the Volvo. It's empty. Kai could already be out near the lodge, so she heads toward it, her boots crunching over the rocky path. But when she gets closer, she sees it: the bees nest hanging from the edge of the roof is calm, silent, and the door to the lodge is wide open.

She stops suddenly, Lor jostling into her. "Kai," she hisses. The others go still beside her. "Kai?" she calls out again, as loud as she dares.

"No lights. No vehicles, other than his," Nathan says

quietly. "Maybe he went inside because no one was here. Give me a minute to check."

He steps forward and disappears inside the lodge, and Rylie steps in after him, her senses on edge, Lor and Sara behind her. The lodge is completely dark. The scent of smoke is in the air, but the fireplace is cold when she touches it. She quickly scans the room. The frames, the armchairs, the Picasso print, the daggers displayed on the wall—everything seems the same as before.

"We need to find him." Rylie heads to the small door near the fireplace and opens it. More silence, more darkness. There's a clicking sound, and then the hallway lights up.

"Flashlight," Nathan says, jogging forward. They all make short work of the stairwell until they reach the cavern, their footsteps echoing as they step inside. The entire place is empty, the stench of smoke stronger now. Nathan aims his flashlight against the walls. "There's been a fire."

Rylie thinks of yesterday—the shouting from the tunnels, Sloan running. The way Ethan Langhorne snuck out quickly, not wanting anyone to notice him. The scent of smoke in the air right after they got him into the truck and drove away, leaving Kai behind.

Rylie switches on her phone light. Along the rock walls are streaks of black and gray, and there's more soot on the floor. The smoke gets at her lungs and she coughs, then smells something else. Something coppery.

"Guys?" It's Sara. She's looking at the ground, her back to them. When she turns, her face is pale. "Is that blood?"

Rylie stares down at the stain, gripping her phone tighter. Dread coils inside of her. Kai—his car is still here. Parked in the same place it was yesterday. When she *left* him.

"He's got to be here." Rylie hurries toward the back of the cavern without waiting for the others. Near the closest tunnel, her phone light hits something dark and thin. She takes another step. Everywhere her light shines, metal bars are stretching up between the ground and the ceiling. It's a cell. An empty *cell*. Its door is halfway open. On the ground beside it is a set of chains.

"Don't move."

Rylie goes still, but the voice is farther away, coming from the main cavern. She slowly turns. In the center of the cavern, Nathan's flashlight is pointing at a figure in a bulky vest. It's Sloan.

"You shouldn't be here," Sloan says to Nathan. "Check them," she orders loudly, and then a few people step out from behind her. More lodge members. One of them has a shaved head—Eric, the guy who brought the drink yesterday. Rylie crouches down, staying in the shadows.

"Don't touch me," Lor snaps, but a woman in a vest like Sloan's is circling her, circling Sara too.

"We came here to find someone. We'll leave," Nathan says in a steady voice. His hand is resting on his pocket.

Sloan steps closer to him, ignoring the beam of his flashlight. Today she's wearing short sleeves under her vest, but the jagged scar on her elbow is gone, completely healed—there's not even a mark on her.

"I tried to follow you yesterday," Sloan says to him. "You were with the girl." She turns to the other lodge members. "The one like Ethan Langhorne."

Rylie stiffens. *Like Ethan Langhorne.* Sloan is talking about *her.*

"She's nothing like Ethan," Nathan says. "He deserves to be locked up."

"He won't stay that way," Sloan says. "He never stays in one place for long." She nods, and the lodge members edge closer.

"What's going on?" Sara asks. "Why is there blood on the floor?"

They're not the right questions, but they're a start. Rylie tenses, waiting for an answer. Waiting to see if Sloan will answer at all.

"Someone got loose." Sloan pulls something out from her vest. It looks like a piece of cloth. "Tried to burn the place down."

Someone got loose. Rylie stays crouched, her mind racing, the panic rising in her chest. Her phone won't work down here. There's nowhere to run, no one to hear them shout. Kai isn't here and there's blood on the ground and Sloan has Rylie's friends cornered, all because of her.

"Mackenzie Soren," Lor says loudly. "Juan Ramon-Ortez, Emily Okada, Fern Gallagher." It's the list of names, the list of the missing. "Where are they?"

Sloan studies her for a minute. "Some of them stayed with us willingly," she says. "And some didn't."

The ropes and chains, the cell. Rylie's stomach goes cold. She came back for answers, but they've been right in front of her all along. *Datura Lodge started as a secret society*, Kai told her. Supposedly they do rituals, black magic even. And Ethan Langhorne and her grandfather aren't the only products of the lodge. The coyotes are too. Datura Lodge has to be some sort of backwater cult. They're into maiming animals, drugging people, maybe even human sacrifice. And she brought her friends right to them.

"Take them to the others," Sloan says.

The others. She could mean Kai. Iggy too. Then Sloan nods, and two lodge members suddenly grab Nathan. Lor and Sara are next. Both of them gasp, try to pull free. Sloan yanks a black hood over Lor, and a humming sound roars in Rylie's ears as a hot, tight fury rushes through her. She wants to scream, wants to do something. Stop Sloan. *Hurt* Sloan. She reaches for the chain on the ground. It's cold and hard in her hand. In her other fist is the box cutter.

"Don't."

Rylie whirls around as someone slips out from behind the cell, someone she didn't see before. The girl has shaved hair on one side and long black strands on the other. All the air leaves Rylie's lungs. "Lily?"

Her eyes are dark, so dark. "Is my brother armed?" Lily whispers, and Rylie gives a slight nod.

Then something sharp explodes against the side of Rylie's face and everything goes black.

CHAPTER 32

RYLIE OPENS HER EYES TO brightness. A shadow appears in front of her, and she pushes up to her elbows. Her vision's blurry—all light and darkness.

"Lor? Nathan?"

"They're not here."

Rylie sits up too fast at the sound of the voice. She blinks, rubs at her eyes. She's on a mattress. There's a small window in front of her, overlooking the desert. To her side is a white shelf. It's her grandpa's cabin—she's in his cabin somehow. She touches her forehead. It's throbbing, the skin hot and tender.

"You've been sleeping all day. I hit you too hard."

She turns, and dizziness rushes over her. Next to her is Lily Seguin, sitting on the edge of the bed. Her hair is longer than it was when they were kids, and it's thick on one side, shaved on the other. She's wearing jeans and a battered leather jacket, and there are faint lines around her eyes that didn't used to be there, but it's definitely Lily. Rylie rubs at her head again. The last thing she remembers is . . . *what?* Datura Lodge. The blood on the floor. The cell. Sloan.

"What are we doing here?" Rylie whispers.

"They think you can help them," Lily says, her voice low and gravelly like it's always been. "That's why they made me take you here." The mattress creaks as she leans forward and touches Rylie's shoulder. "How are you feeling?"

"Fine." Rylie stands and sways, feeling the dizziness in her head, her body. "Actually, that's a lie." A bitter taste is in her mouth; something sharp and grainy is on her tongue. She pulls it out—it looks powdery, like the shards of a crumbled pill. On the floor is an empty mug, and it reminds her of what she drank at the lodge. "You *drugged* me?"

Lily watches her for a minute with those eyes that look so much like Nathan's, so much like Thea's. "I medicated you," she finally says. "It was better than tying you up." She's talking just like she used to—blunt and even a little demeaning, as if Rylie should have already caught on.

Rylie wants to get angry, but all she feels is the dizziness, her head pounding in sync with her pulse, the sun too bright through the window. "I've been here all night . . ." And no one knows to look for her, since she told Ben she was spending the night at Sara's. "Where's Lor and Sara? Where's your *brother?*"

Lily stands, her eyes flicking to the bedroom door and then back to Rylie. "Datura is keeping them somewhere else."

"The lodge has Kai too, don't they?"

Lily crosses her arms. "Kai Okada came to *us*."

Rylie stares at her. She's got his last name wrong—but

something else is bothering her even more. It's the way she used the word "us." "So you're definitely with the lodge."

"They're not the enemy, Rye." Lily holds her gaze as she slips off her black leather jacket. Underneath she's wearing a tank top, and on her shoulders and neck is a thick crisscrossing of purple scars. Scars she never had before. Scars that look terrifying.

"These aren't what you need to be afraid of," Lily says.

What you need to be afraid of, not *who*. The cinch knot is in Rylie's chest, tighter than ever. She slowly unravels the bandages on her arms and looks down at her cuts, then back at Lily's scars. Lily, who always did everything first when they were growing up. Lily, who always *knew* everything first.

"Just tell me, Lil." The dizziness is making her head swirl. "Tell me how this all makes sense."

"We're not where you think we are," Lily says softly. She nods at the bedroom door. "You have to see it for yourself."

Rylie steps forward, and the room spins. And then, even with the door shut, she hears something coming from the hallway. The soft strands of a guitar, a voice: "And here we are in our little home, locking our doors to the night." Her dad's song. Someone is playing his song inside the cabin. "But I say don't believe what you hear, because the desert's where I found you."

Rylie swings the door open and stares down the narrow hallway. There's something out of tune about the recording, something *wrong* with it. The music cuts off.

"Need something?" a voice calls out. "Is she awake?" It's the voice she'd know anywhere.

"No," she whispers, and something snaps inside. Reality has finally broken away. She has lost her memory one too many times, and now it's coming back at her in a kaleidoscope of shapes, fractured and incomplete, the past and present mixing together.

"Lily?" the voice says, coming from the main room. "Little Lee?" And this time she knows for sure. It's *his* voice.

Impossible.

She rushes around the corner, and there he is. Her dad, holding a guitar and standing next to a telescope near the window. Her dad, looking right at her. Rylie feels herself go numb, her limbs seizing up, her mind seizing up, her heart splitting open.

"I . . . I don't understand."

"I don't either." He's watching her just as intensely. "Not really. Not when you're right in front of me."

It's *him*. The wrinkles at his hazel eyes, same as her own, and his curly hair, shorter than Owen's. He shouldn't be in front of her, but he is, and that means she's having some sort of hallucination, or a dream maybe, but it feels too real for that. It's too real to be a dream.

"I lost you." She stares at him, and only him. "I saw you die. I went to your funeral."

"I went to yours." His voice is raw. "Just this week."

Before she can process what he's saying, before she can process *any* of it, he takes two strides forward and pulls her into a hug. It's really him. He doesn't smell like tobacco, and he's thinner than she remembers too, but it's him just the same. Her breath gets trapped in her lungs.

"How?" she asks. "How are you here? Are we both . . ."

"We're both very much alive," her dad says, pulling away. He meets her eyes. "And it's not really me. I mean, I'm not who you think I am. I'm not the dad you grew up with, and you're not the daughter I raised." But it sounds like him. It looks like him. And the song he was singing, it was *his.*

But it can't be. Her dad is dead.

"You've crossed over," he says, and she steadies herself on the couch. The dizziness is back; it's inside her. Her mind is wild with half-formed thoughts: Her dad, who can't be her dad. Sloan Parker from the bakery who had a scar on her arm and Sloan Parker from the lodge who didn't, like they were two different people. And Nathan, telling her that he'd called her, that they'd talked *for hours,* when they hadn't talked at all. And then there's the strand that's been bothering her the most: what she saw on the night of the hike. When Kai did the hypnosis with her, she saw blood at the cabin. She saw a girl covered in blood, with a knife in her hand. A girl with her *face.*

Rylie reaches out and touches her dad's arm. She can feel the hairs on his forearm, the cords of muscle there. *Exact resemblance to exact resemblance . . .* He's real, he's alive, but it's not him either. He's like a twin, a double. And so is the cabin. The desk looks the same, but instead of built-in shelves, the walls have old sepia-colored maps hanging from them. Maybe this isn't really the cabin she knows. Maybe it's a double too, just like the man in front of her isn't really her dad—he can't be—but the thought won't stick, and then Stein's words come back to her: *If they were not pigeons what were they*. She has to make sense of it, she has to try, even though her head is pounding and nothing, *nothing* adds up.

"What do you mean by 'crossed over'?"

"Look out the window." Her dad hands her a pair of binoculars. "Go on," he says, but it's hard to do anything at all with him right here next to her, talking to her. His voice. She's wanted to hear it for so long, and every word is like a gift. Light's all around him from the nearby window; it's falling over his hair and shining on his shoulders and over his guitar. The light is casting his eyes gold too. "Look outside," he says.

Rylie turns, squinting out the bright glass. Outside is the stretch of rocky desert, the winding arroyo trail, the boulders, the mountains in the distance, and—

Water. There's water in the canyon. Just as she leans closer, a shadow flits past the window. She steps away. In the yard is a coyote, or something like it. Something larger, with flesh and fur along its back. Something more creature than animal. Something monstrous.

"Don't look at it straight on," her dad warns, and dizziness rushes over her again as she takes another step back. The creatures, the water in the canyon, *him*—it's all impossible. And then she thinks of what Lily said in the bedroom: *We're not where you think we are.*

Exact resemblance to exact resemblance. A line distinguishes it. It's all starting to make sense. The strands are coming together into the most fragile of shapes, but she can't say it aloud, she can't even think it, unless she frames it like a what-if. What if everything in front of her is real. What if everything in the hypnosis really happened. What if there are two of everything—two worlds that look almost, but not quite, exact—and she's been going back and forth between them. Crossing over.

Rylie throws up, right at her dad's feet. She straightens and wipes her mouth. Her stomach feels better, but her head's still spinning. Maybe she's imagining all of it—maybe there's something wrong with her and that's all this is. It could all disappear any minute. *He* could disappear any minute.

"It takes time to adjust." Her dad tosses a towel onto the floor and then gently reaches for her wrists, studying her scrapes. He's holding her wrists—it feels so *real*. He's tilting his head like she remembers him doing when he would bring out his guitar after grading physics papers, trying and failing to find the right lyrics. She wants him to take out his cigarettes like he used to, even though she always begged him to quit. She wants him to be exactly the same, but he's not.

"How?" Rylie asks as Lily steps into the room. "How is this possible, Lily?" There's still a sour taste in her mouth from getting sick. It can't be possible. "It's Datura Lodge, isn't it? They've drug—"

"Datura Lodge tries to help people like us," Lily says.

"People who aren't from here." She steps forward and puts her hands on Rylie's shoulders, guiding her back toward the window, toward the view of the desert. The view of water in the canyon.

Rylie turns to her dad, who's looking at her with something like pity on his face, and then she glances at Lily and she has to ask, no matter how crazy it sounds. "Did we grow up together?" All the questions are making her head ache even more. "Are you the Lily I know? Are you from—"

"The home you know?" Lily says softly. "The *world* you know?" For a moment there's a brief smile at her lips and then it's gone. "Yes, Rylie."

We're not where you think we are. "But how . . ." It's hard to believe she's having this conversation. It's hard to believe any of it. "How did we get here? And what does the lodge have to do with it?"

"The lodge is the reason I'm still breathing, Rye." Lily slips off her jacket and then pulls her hair to the side. Above the scarring on her neck is a fresh tattoo, raw and shiny at the edges. It's a hexfoil. "Without their help," Lily goes on, "people like us—"

"Usually don't survive," her dad finishes. His jaw tenses as he gazes out the window, deep in thought, and he looks so much like the dad she remembers. "Or our military gets to them, and then no one sees them again either." He turns quickly, and the maps on the wall flutter behind him. "So Datura patrols the area. We have to cover a lot of ground, but we've got vehicles for that. Lookouts too."

Vehicles. Lookouts. Rylie flashes back to the last hypnosis, to how she saw a truck appear, right when the coyotes had gotten so close. She steps forward and touches the map of the Mojave. "The line," she says, tracing the points she remembers from her grandpa's map. "It's where people cross between worlds?"

"We call it the rift here," her dad explains. "But people don't just cross over. It's not as simple as that."

"Then how—"

"We're attacked, that's how," Lily says sharply, like Rylie should be connecting the dots faster. "Sometimes we're attacked and left on our side. But usually we're dragged across."

"That's when the lodge intervenes." Her dad's voice is so much more patient than Lily's. "We try to stop—"

"The deaths." Lily turns back to the window and runs a hand over her scar. "They like to eat their prey where they feel safe."

Attacked. Dragged. Eaten. Rylie shuts her eyes, remembering the hypnosis again. The creatures on her Nikon, the coyotes that aren't coyotes. The creatures that are just outside the cabin. She shivers. "If they attack humans, why are they allowed to—"

"They don't," her dad cuts in. "They don't attack humans, not over here anyway."

Lily's eyes lock on Rylie. "They cross the line and attack *us*," Lily says. "People from our side. They're attracted to our scent, especially once we're bitten. And if we survive an attack . . ."

"You get an infection," her dad says. "It's something akin to your version of the lyssavirus, which is—"

"Rabies," Lily cuts in. "It's like rabies."

Predilection for violence. Memory loss. Rylie ticks off her grandfather's symptoms in her head. What else did Dr. Singh say about him? Something about a phobia, a fear . . . She glances at the window. The coyote-like creature is still there, watching her from just outside the glass. She gets the sudden sense that it's waiting her out, stalking her.

"What *are* they?" Rylie tears her eyes away, not missing the rifle in the corner of the room. There's one hanging above the door too.

"You don't have an equivalent." Her dad moves the telescope to stand beside her. "We call them grays," he says.

"They're almost like . . ." Lily glances out the window. "They're almost like werewolves."

Rylie steadies herself against the wall, another wave of dizziness hitting her. It's too much to take in. *Werewolves. Grays.* "So why did you stay here, Lily? Why didn't you come home?"

"I wanted to." Lily glares, her voice as sharp as her gaze. "I couldn't."

"Generally speaking, humans can't cross over alone." Her dad pulls a first aid kit from a drawer. "But sometimes we can *hear* the other world, your world," he says, and then Rylie thinks of Nathan again.

"Phone calls," she says. "You can—"

Lily laughs. "You can't deliberately call home. Believe me, I tried. But sometimes there's . . ."

"An interference," her dad says. "Like in the old days of party lines and cross talk?" He looks between them. "Never mind, you're both too young," he mutters quickly. "The point is, while an auditory interference is possible, it's unpredictable at best, and we can't actually *see* your world. We can't get there either."

"Most of us can't anyway," Lily says, and Rylie shifts under her gaze.

"What do you mean?"

"There are exceptions." Her dad takes out a cotton ball and douses it with rubbing alcohol. Lily might be in the room too, but it's hard not to look at him, not to watch his every move. "Ethan Langhorne is one of them," he says. "And you're the other. That we know of, anyhow."

"*I'm* the other?" Rylie bares her arms. "But I was attacked by grays too. I must have been dragged across."

"But you found the lodge after that. You crossed on your own." Her dad presses the cotton ball to the scrapes on her forearms, and they start to sting. "Sloan told me that you even took friends over. She said they made it to the lodge with you."

Rylie shakes her head. She can't think of her friends right now. She can hardly think about anything with her dad in front of her like this. "So the lodge is near the line, but it's only on—"

"Exactly," Lily interrupts. "It's only on this side. On our

side, it's just uninhabited desert," she says, and Rylie gets a flash of memory: Kai telling her that he hadn't been able to find the lodge himself—they'd only found it together, when she was in the car with him. But how did Nathan get to the lodge yesterday, how did he cross over without her? She touches the pendant around her neck, trying to think. Kai texted Nathan a pin of the lodge's location, but Nathan hadn't been able to see it at first, even though he'd been in the right place. He'd been standing right where Ethan attacked her. Rylie clutches the pendant, closing her eyes against the memory. The fog had been flickering almost, like maybe she and Ethan had been crossing back and forth between worlds as she fought to breathe. And somehow, while the fog was shimmering like that, she pulled Nathan across too.

"But why?" she asks as her dad starts cleaning the cuts on her other arm. The alcohol stings again and her throat is painfully dry but she ignores it. "Why can we cross over? How can we take people with us?"

"I wish I had all the answers." Her dad finishes up with the first-aid kit and then dabs on an ointment that cools her skin. "The lodge thinks the ability is hereditary. Anyone with an ancestor who had the infection can cross."

An ancestor with an infection, an ancestor who was attacked. Her grandfather. In the journals, he wrote about getting hurt in the desert. And Ethan's dad had scars too, all over his face and neck. They'd both been attacked, infected. They'd also both lived to have families.

"That's you, Rylie." Lily steps closer, her dark hair falling across her shoulders, hiding the scars on her neck. "You can cross. You can take me home, and everyone else who doesn't belong here," she says. "Those of us who are healed, anyway. The medicine takes time to work."

"Sometimes months, depending on the person," her dad adds. "You'd be going back and forth, Rye."

Months. Months of working side by side with him. Enough time to figure out if he smoked Lucky Strikes or considered ice cream a food group or played classic guitar by heart. She could help him; she could take everyone home like he wants. But something still doesn't add up. "There must be more of us. People like Ethan and me."

"There weren't many attacks in previous generations." Her dad puts the first aid kit away as Lily stays near the window, scanning the desert with the binoculars. "As the rift has grown," he says, "the attacks have increased."

"Wait, the line *grows*?" The dizziness comes back. "What caused it in the first place?"

"We don't know exactly. We've been trying to piece things together, little by little." He flashes a smile, almost like he's embarrassed, and looks over at the map. "We've guessed at the point of origin, based on where we found the earliest cases—infections, I mean—but we can't be sure." He taps the map. "We think this is the epicenter, for lack of a better term, but on *this* side there's nothing unusual."

Lily turns to Rylie. "Same for our side," Lily says. "I thought for sure the epicenter would be near the military base, but I know that area, and nothing's there. I used to work for this tour company, called—"

Enigma. "Nathan told me about it."

Lily nods. "Anyway, we focused on the strangeness in the Mojave. Went to all the weird historical sites, all the places where people had gone missing. We hinted at top-secret government experiments, black-budget defense projects. The tours really hyped it up." She nods at the map. "But there's nothing special around that specific point, just desert. The only thing out there is an old radio tower."

A radio tower. Rylie steps closer, a memory coming to her. A conversation she overheard, just recently. Someone was talking about a radio tower . . . She was in the kitchen, with Owen. And her mom. Her mom was talking about work, all the numbers she was going through. Accounting cuts for the base expansion. Rylie's mind starts to race.

"The earliest recorded case. Was it a leap year?"

Her dad rubs at his head the way he does when he wants a cigarette but knows he shouldn't. "Sure, by my math. Why does it matter?"

"It matters," Rylie says quickly. It feels like she's about to reach the last hold before the summit. The last hold before the peak, where everything becomes visible. Her grandfather tried to find a pattern, just like the lodge did, just like Lily did, but they never had access to the right information. The military base, the radio tower, the leap year . . . Her mom mentioned all those things—she was talking about a project she'd slated for closure. What else did she say about it? How the radio tower measured the earth's electro-magnetic field. By sending out a pulse . . . And a pulse would run in a line.

Her hands turn to fists. "I think you were right, Lily. About the defense project." But she wasn't right about all of it. If Rylie's mom was talking about it over breakfast, it isn't top-secret, black-budget kind of work. The military obviously has no idea what they created, or they wouldn't be cutting it. And then the final piece clicks into place and Rylie feels like she's slipping, about to fall. Her mom told Owen that she'd probably be shutting down the project *soon*, but what did Ben say yesterday? That her mom was work-ing late, getting ready for major closures. Closures that are scheduled for *today*. "And I think it's going to be shut down," Rylie rushes out. "Maybe even today."

"Shut down?" Lily and her dad exchange a look, and then he turns to her. "You realize that this is the news we've been waiting for, Rylie?" His face lights up with that crooked grin of his. "No more attacks. No more doubles. No more deaths." He pulls her into a sudden hug, and she doesn't want to let go. "If you're right about it closing, you need to get back," he says. "Both of you."

"Come with us." She doesn't care how desperate she sounds. "Cross over."

And then the impossible happens: her dad doesn't shake his head like she thought he might. "Maybe," he says, his voice thick.

"Shit," Lily swears, suddenly looking anxious. "We need to get the others."

Her dad stiffens. "The checkpoints." He picks up his keys, then throws a set to Lily. "You two drive ahead in the truck. I'll follow you."

Lily nods. "Come on, Rye."

Rylie doesn't want to let him out of her sight. But Kai. Lor. Nathan and Sara. The lodge has taken them somewhere else. She needs to reach them in time, she needs to cross back over with them. Maybe her dad would cross over too. Maybe she and her dad could get to know each other again. *Owen* could get to know him. She stops at the door, glancing back. "Hey, where's Owen? On this side, I mean."

Her dad tilts his head. "Owen? I thought your friend's name was Kai."

And then it feels like she really has slipped, like she has lost her grip and she's falling. In this world, in whatever place she's in, her brother doesn't exist. He was never born; he isn't alive here. She puts a hand on the wall to steady herself. She needs to go. She needs to get back to Owen, but maybe she could have her dad too. Maybe she could have them both.

"Okay," Rylie says. She could do this. *They* could do this. She swings open the door. "Let's hurry."

CHAPTER 33

RYLIE RACES INTO THE TRUCK as the gray stares at her from the shadow of the boulder. There's something hanging from its mouth—a thick, viscous saliva that's dripping onto the ground in front of it. Its eyes look hungry as Lily fires up the truck's engine, her dad quick to get into the jeep parked next to them. Dust rises in the air as both vehicles pull out, speed down the road, and then hit the highway. Seconds later, a row of military trucks passes by and Rylie's lungs clamp down as she thinks of the checkpoints. "Where are the others? How far are we going?"

"To the house on Sundown," Lily says.

"You're kidding."

Lily opens the console between them and searches through it as she drives. "Your grandfather, or his double anyway, started Datura Lodge," she says, glancing back at the highway. "He and Sloan established a lot of safe houses too. They're kind of a legend over here."

Rylie shifts in her seat. Her own grandfather was the furthest thing from a legend, but he did try to help, in his own way. He tried helping everyone on the recordings:

Ethan Langhorne and Millie Callahan and Sloan Parker's double from the bakery, and all the others who'd been attacked and then left on their side. Maybe he wasn't able to do much, but he tried, he spent his life trying, and something breaks away in her chest, like a tiny corner of her heart has softened.

"So when the cavern got burned yesterday, the lodge moved everyone to another safe house?"

"You always did catch on quick." Lily hands her a small plastic container. "Open it."

"You always did like telling me what to do," Rylie says, twisting off the lid. Inside is a pair of contact lenses.

"Wear them in case we get pulled over. Everyone has a golden tint to their eyes here."

The contacts burn as she puts them in. "At least gold's my color."

"It pairs well with desert chic."

The banter is good—it has always been Lily's way of easing pressure, but Rylie's feeling it in her chest anyway. She blinks, her eyes still burning from the contacts, and glances at the jeep behind them. Her dad's tailing them, staying a few cars back.

"The government here watches the line too," Lily says, as if she knows exactly what Rylie's thinking, just like Nathan would. "They have a few guard posts up and some checkpoints where they look for anyone like us—anyone who doesn't belong here—but they're stretched pretty thin. We'll make it."

Rylie glances at the side mirror again. The jeep is small in the glass, and all she wants is more time with him.

"He'll cross over with us," Lily says, like she's somehow reading Rylie's mind again. "He took Rylie's death pretty hard. She was his only family."

She was his only family. Another Rylie—the girl she saw on the night of the hike, covered in blood. "What was she like?"

"A lot like you." Lily slows at an intersection. They're getting so close to the house now, so close. Rylie tamps down the hope in her heart.

"So, impulsive and overly protective?"

Lily smiles. "She always did what she thought was right."

"How did she die?"

The light turns green and the truck surges forward. "One of us—someone from our world—went rabid," Lily says. "That's what I call it at least. Anyway, the guy broke loose about a week ago and hurt a bunch of people. Rylie stopped him."

"Stopped him?"

Lily glances over. "She'd done it before, stopped someone who'd gone rabid, but this time she didn't make it." Lily's jaw goes tight. "She stopped him, but she died too. They both did."

Rylie stares out the window at the desert, not really seeing it. It makes sense now, what Ethan Langhorne said about her on the recording, how she'd killed before. It was the other Rylie, and she'd been trying to stop someone who'd gone *rabid*.

"Does everyone have a double here? Does Ethan?"

Lily shakes her head. "This place is similar," she says, "but there's infinite room for variation too." She opens her window, and fresh air starts blowing into the truck. Her black hair whips back as they drive. "Think about it. One minor change, one small decision, can have major ramifications. Maybe not at first, but little by little. Ecosystems can be altered. Cities brought down."

And grandfathers could stop at red lights instead of speeding through them, and people could live. Her dad could live. She glances back at his jeep again. "What else is different here?"

Lily lets out a rough laugh. "You don't want to know," she says, just as there's a crackling sound over the wind, and then: "I'm going to fade back a bit more." It's her dad's voice, coming through a speaker. Rylie notices a walkie-talkie wedged between the seats and pulls it out.

"Stay close, okay?" she says into it.

"Roger that. We're almost there." Her dad sounds way too carefree, like he's almost enjoying himself, and her stomach clenches.

"Don't worry. If we were going to get pulled over, it would've happened already." Lily glances at the jeep too, then back at the road. "You know," she says, her voice softer now, "I'd almost given up on seeing my brother again. And now he's here." Her hands are too tight on the wheel. "I hope he forgives me."

Rylie turns, confused. "About what?"

Lily winces. "I left him a note. Between working for Enigma and following your grandpa around, I figured out that something in the desert wasn't right. And then I met Ethan, but he didn't tell me everything, not at first." She sighs. "I came looking for it, Rye. That's when I was attacked."

Rylie shakes her head. She reaches out to touch the scarring along Lily's neck, but stops herself. "None of this was your fault."

Lily's jaw tightens again. Then she finally nods. "I know that."

"You'd better."

Lily looks over at her. "Or what?"

"Or else," Rylie says, just like she used to when they were kids, and Lily laughs. It's a good sound. They need some good right now.

"Fair enough. Seeing my brother again still feels like a second chance, though."

"So does this." Rylie nods ahead, at the next turn. They're almost to the Sundown house. She lets out a breath, feeling hope spread through her as her dad gives a little whoop on the radio. Lily grins and flicks on the blinker, but just as they're turning into the neighborhood, just as the house comes into sight, blue lights flash across the truck.

"Shit," Lily swears.

"Don't stop."

"I have to, or—" The tremor in her voice works its way

into Rylie's chest as Lily slows, pulls over. An unmarked SUV parks beside them, and a soldier strides out.

Lily makes sure her hair is covering her scars, and then she rolls the window down. "Everything all right?" she asks.

The soldier seems young and a little jumpy, like she's a new recruit. "I need to see the usual," she says, peering in at both of them. "Arms, necks, sides. Got ID?"

ID. Arms, necks, sides. Rylie tries to act casual. Behind them, her dad's jeep is still visible, and the soldier gestures for him to wait.

"Here," Lily says airily. "We're kind of in a hurry." She hands over two cards, and that's when Rylie notices the white smudges on the soldier's hands. It's chalk.

"You're a climber too?" Rylie asks. The soldier glances up, her golden eyes slightly softer now.

"Sometimes. Not as much as I'd like."

Rylie's heart quickens—she can work with that. "We're headed out to Trashcan today. Just need to grab our gear first. We're trying to catch the last of the daylight."

The soldier looks out at the setting sun on the horizon and nods. "You *are* in a hurry then," she says. "I still have to follow protocol, though."

In the side mirror, Rylie watches the jeep edge closer. Lily's slowly rolling up her sleeves like she's stalling, like she's just waiting for Rylie's dad to do something stupid, so Rylie pulls up her own sleeves first. Panic has her by the throat, but she forces herself to say it anyway. "Got these the other day." She bares her arms like she's proud. "If you're not falling, you're not trying, right?"

"Always get back up," the soldier says quickly, as if she can't help herself. She nods at the scrapes, a small smile on her face now. "Okay, why don't I run these IDs and then you two can get your gear." As she walks back to the SUV, Lily picks up the radio.

"She's running them," she whispers.

Her dad's voice is firm through the speakers: "We can't take that chance, Lily."

"We *can.*" Rylie grabs the radio. "Lily has legit IDs, right? Our doubles." It's out of her mouth before she can take it back. The other Rylie isn't around anymore. The other Rylie is dead, and the soldier will know it any second.

"Little Lee?" her dad says. The jeep is close behind them now, close enough to see her dad's face. He's looking her way with that crooked smile again. "Take care, Little Lee."

"Don't."

"It'll be fine, okay? I promise." There's a revving sound, and the jeep suddenly veers around them, swiping the SUV. Seconds later, a siren roars, and then the soldier is speeding after the jeep.

"Stop!" Rylie grips the radio. Her throat aches. "Please."

The SUV rams the back of the jeep, and her dad drives into the rocky desert, off-roading. The jeep bounces over sagebrush, and the radio crackles again. "Out among the rock and sand, they say to be careful for snakes," her dad belts out. Ahead the jeep swerves around a boulder and keeps going, the SUV skidding to keep up. "But I say don't believe what you hear," he sings, "because the desert's where I found you. . . ."

Rylie slams her fist into the console. "We need to *do* something."

"We need to get the others." Lily's eyes are shiny and the jeep is almost out of sight. Rylie feels her heart split in half, all over again.

"Go home, Little Lee," her dad says. "That's what you need to do." His voice is clear through the radio, steady too. "I wasn't going to come anyway."

She shakes her head. "I know you don't mean that. I know what you're doing."

Her dad laughs, but it's a sad laugh. "This is how we save each other. Go home."

CHAPTER 34

THE SUNDOWN HOUSE IS LOCKED, its steel shutters down. Lily glances over her shoulder and then shakes the door handle as Rylie waits on the porch, her stomach in shreds. A security camera attached to the roof turns, blinking, as the door suddenly swings open. Cold fingers close over Rylie's arm, and then she's yanked inside, into darkness.

A match flares. Sloan Parker is beside them, no feather earrings and no vest today, her face lit up by the flame.

"You're lucky you made it," Sloan says, locking the door behind them. Her glare is hard and assessing, just like Rylie's mom's would be. "Is it true? Is the rift going to close?" She's standing so close that her breath flits against Rylie's cheek, and the yellow tint to her eyes is unmistakable now. She's definitely not the same woman Rylie met at the bakery. She doesn't have any scars. This Sloan is from *this* world, and she's been trying to help.

Rylie straightens her shoulders. "I think so."

Sloan nods, gives what must be the closest thing she has to a smile. "Good. We've been getting people ready. Come on."

Sloan doesn't turn on any overhead lights, but the candle in her hand is flickering over boxes of food and barrels of water and stacks of newspapers near the fireplace. The house looks nothing like the one Rylie's been living in, but a part of her still expects to see Owen or her mom or Ben. There's an emptiness here without them—it's like the house has been drained of something vital. She misses them suddenly and fiercely, and then she thinks of her dad again and her heart aches even more as she's led into the kitchen.

"Downstairs," Sloan says, gesturing at the pantry door with the candle, its flame sputtering.

"There's a basement on this side," Lily explains, but Rylie slows anyway, trying to hide the throbbing in her head, the dizziness that's back.

"Where are the others? Kai and Lor and—"

"Take care of yourself first. You need medicine." Sloan's standing close again, so close, the tattooed hexfoil on her neck looks like a flower covered in dew; sweat's glistening over it. "*Go,*" she says.

Rylie opens the pantry door and is surprised to find a ladder leading down to an even darker hold. She hurries down, her hands quick on the rungs, and then drops to the concrete floor at the bottom. A door swings open—Sloan must have hit a switch—and when the light hits her eyes, she bites back a gasp.

She's in a basement like the one in the cabin, but it's so much larger. On each of the walls is a huge painting: a blazing red circle with sharp petals inside—it's a hexfoil.

The basement stretches the length of her grandpa's massive house, and she can hear the hum of a generator. Cots are everywhere, people are everywhere, and Sloan's at her side, Lily on her other. Ahead are a couple of kids playing with dolls, some men and women praying, others chanting— "A dark place is not a dark place, a dark place is not a dark place."

"Medic," Sloan says. "This girl needs attention. Right away."

A woman who must be the medic hurries over to Sloan and whispers into her ear, and Rylie catches part of it. ". . . not much left."

"Give her a half dose, then," Sloan tells her. She turns, raising her voice. "Anyone who wants to go should get ready," she calls out.

"I'll go help them," Lily offers, hurrying off and leaving Rylie with Sloan.

"Don't they all want to go?" Rylie glances around the basement, at all the dirt-streaked faces on the cots. At the bandages, the wounds, the scars. The people who went missing, snatched away from everything they knew. People who were attacked. People who escaped and *survived*.

"Some of them like starting a new life on this side," Sloan says, her gold-flecked eyes looking over the basement too. "Others aren't finished with their treatment yet, and they don't want to take any chances. They want the infection out. I can't blame them."

The infection. The rabies-like disease. *A predilection for violence.* Rylie glances at the hexfoils on the wall and stares at the redness of their circles, how they resemble a shield, how they stand for protection. Then Sloan nods like they've reached an understanding and hustles through the crowd, all muscle and determination, as the medic finally hands Rylie a pill.

"Take this. It'll help you with the darkness. At least for a little while," the medic says, whatever that means, and maybe it's her churning stomach or the kindness in the woman's voice, but Rylie doesn't hesitate. She swallows the pill dry and then glances up as another lodge member starts ordering people into lines. Just past them are her friends, and it feels like she's seeing them for the first time. Nathan's in the far corner of the basement, talking to a lodge member who's handing out flashlights, and Lor is helping a woman on a cot pack a small bag. Beside her, Sara is pulling origami animals from her purse and giving them to a couple of children who are putting on jackets. Sara looks up and waves just as Lor turns and spots Rylie, then starts rushing Rylie's way. A second later Rylie is pulled into a rough hug.

"You'll never believe where we are," Lor breathes.

Rylie hugs her back, her eyes tearing up. "I know." If she weren't in a basement below a house that resembles her grandpa's but isn't really his—not the house she lives in, at least—she wouldn't believe any of it. She hears someone clear his throat, and then she turns. It's Iggy, Lor's cousin. He's *here.*

"Rylie." Iggy nods, his voice hoarse as he steps forward. His glasses are broken—they've been duct-taped together, and bandages are wrapped around his arms. "The last time we talked, I really wasn't myself, and—"

"The lodge found Iggy yesterday," Lor cuts in. "He was here when they dropped us off," she explains quickly. "And he told me he's been seeing Dr. Singh. You know, your doctor? Because he got attacked when he first moved to the desert, only it was so weird that he couldn't tell anyone about it, and then he figured out the same thing had happened to you, because of your bandages. And then he got attacked again. Only, this time he—"

"Mind if I get in a word?" Iggy asks, then pauses. "Actually, you pretty much just summed it up as dramatically as possible," he says, elbowing Lor affectionately.

" 'The web of our life is of a mingled yarn,' " Lor quotes, just as Rylie catches Nathan's eye across the room. On his face is that almost-smile of his, and then she feels someone step beside her. It's Lily, her arms folded across her leather jacket.

"He's missed you," Rylie says softly, nudging her forward. She watches as Nathan stops in front of his sister. They both stare at each other for a second, and then Nathan's moving first, hugging Lily close.

Rylie's eyes sting, and she thinks of Owen as she turns away, just as a red Volcom hat at the far end of the room comes into view. *Kai.*

She hurries over to him. He's sitting on an unmade cot,

hunched over his notebook. His dark hair is shielding his eyes, and she's not even sure he's breathing. "Kai?"

"I'm glad you're okay," he says, but he doesn't look up. He's not staring at the notebook; he's staring at the ink on his forearm. It's another face, but there's something familiar about it. She's seen it before.

"Who is she?" she asks curiously.

"Emily Okada," Kai says.

Emily Okada. Rylie stiffens. Emily Okada was on the list they made with Lor—the list of missing people, the list they put together from the photographs in her grandpa's cabin. Mackenzie Soren, Jed Hendersen, Juan Ramon-Ortez, Odele and Robert Kucharski, Fern Childers Gallagher.

And Emily Okada. The history professor who went missing in Black Rock Canyon a few years ago. On a camping trip. When the piece clicks into place, it feels like it's pinching at her heart. "Emily's your mother," she says softly. "I should've asked you about—"

"I should have told you." He rolls up the notebook, squeezing it tight.

"So she's not here? You're still trying to find her?"

Kai raises his head, and the look in his eyes is enough of an answer. "She *was* here."

He sets his hand on the blanket of the cot, tenderly, like there's someone underneath it, and then Rylie understands everything. This was his mom's bed, this cot.

"Oh, Kai—"

"They told me that her injuries were too severe," he says,

and Rylie's heart stammers, but she doesn't look at her own scratches. She keeps her eyes on him. "She was in a coma for a while, I guess," he says, his voice breaking. He looks up at her, then back down at the cot. "I was too late getting here," he whispers. "I had an idea of what might have happened to her, because of . . ." He shakes his head.

"Because of my grandpa," Rylie says softly. "You met him before he died, didn't you?" Her stomach sinks with the weight of what she's finally putting together. "You came to the desert when my mom asked Ben to treat my grandpa."

Kai looks at her with red-rimmed eyes and then nods. "I came out a couple of times. I met Lily too, before she crossed."

"And they told you about the line?"

"No, but they told me that people like my mom were getting *taken*. They said that it wasn't the sort of thing they could go to the media with, not without sounding crazy." He pulls off his hat and rubs furiously at his hair. "No one was onto it, not the police, not the military. And then Lily disappeared, right around—"

"My grandfather's death."

"Yeah." Kai opens the notebook on his lap and flips to the beginning. It might be small, but it's filled with pages and pages of notes and clippings—just like the black Moleskines. "I didn't really know much at first. Then we found those things at your grandpa's cabin. The photos and the maps. The recordings."

A shrill whistling sound cuts through the air—it's Sloan at the front of the room.

"The guards change out in ten minutes. Whoever's going needs to be ready," she shouts, and Rylie ignores another lurch in her stomach. A couple more people line up, but Kai doesn't even act like he's heard her.

"If you knew some of this before, why didn't you just tell me, Kai?"

"Tell you *what*?" He shrugs. "What could I have possibly told you that you'd believe?"

She can't drop it. "How do you know until you ask?"

"So you're saying that if I'd sat you down and said, 'Rylie, we just so happen to live in an interdimensional world full of inhuman creatures, and oh yeah, there's a cross-over point in the desert that people are yanked into against their will,' you would've believed me?"

"No, but—"

"Rye, I hardly knew you." He puts his hat back on. "And I hardly knew anything at all at first. Not until you found a way into the cabin's basement."

He has a point, but she does too. "If you had just said something earlier, told me about Lily and my grandpa . . . maybe we could have figured all of this out a lot faster."

"Maybe." Kai shrugs. "Or maybe this is the sort of thing that people have to figure out themselves, or they'll *never* believe." He stops on a page and points at a sketch of a coyote. Next to it is another drawing, this one of something hairless and crouched, like in the photograph she took. Not a coyote, a *gray*.

"I've been adding to my notes since I got here yesterday. I want to figure it all out. I *need* to figure it out." He shakes his head, his Volcom cap shading his eyes. "It's the stuff nightmares are made of, right?" Kai tosses the small notebook onto the pillow and then stares at the cot like he can't believe it's really there either. "I would have done anything to be here with her, Rye." He rubs the ink on his arm until it smears, the face blurring. "I would've traded places. She was my home."

Rylie's throat catches. *We're your home now.* That's what she wants to say. *We're your family.* And then she thinks of her dad. She scans the basement, but he's not here, he's not in the line of people at the door. Some of them are crying, kissing the others goodbye. Lily's hugging each of them, and some of them even reach out and touch her hexfoil tattoo, like it's some sort of parting gesture. But Kai, Kai will *never* have a chance to say goodbye. Rylie stares back down at the cot and the notebook on top of it, filled with his research on everything he'd been searching for, everything he hoped would help find his mother. She knows what it feels like to hope so intensely like that, to cling to it, and she knows what it feels like to finally let go, too.

She picks up the notebook and carefully turns to a new page. Then she takes Kai's pen from him and writes down what she learned about the rift, the experiment on base, the lodge, the grays—she leaves nothing out, holds nothing back, even as he reads silently over her shoulder. She can't give him his mother and she can't give him hope, but she can give him this. She can give him what she knows to be true. When she looks up from the paper, his eyes are shining.

"You're coming home with us, right?" Rylie grabs his hand and pulls him to his feet. "Owen can't lose you," she says. Her throat clamps tight again. "And I don't want to lose you either."

Kai smiles, surprising her. "Of course I'm going home," he says. He picks up his notebook and shoves it into his back pocket. "Wild coyotes couldn't drag me away."

Relief hits her and she looks away, her eyes watering up too. "Just maybe don't bring your guitar," she says. "Or you know, consider some singing lessons."

"Bard lessons. I'm in."

"Then we'd better hurry. I hear those fill up fast," she says, just as a high-pitched alarm rips into the room.

"It's time!" Sloan shouts over the crowd. "Let's go," she barks, looking straight at Rylie before turning to herd people out. Rylie hurries forward, making sure Kai is beside her. She watches Lily slip through the door, Nathan right behind her.

"Lily knows how to get to the line from here," Sloan says to Rylie. "It's five minutes on foot, and you've got twice that time before the guard post is manned again. If you reach the road, you've missed it."

Rylie stops. "You're not coming with us?"

"As like an escort?" Kai asks, lingering in the doorway as if he's not sure he wants to leave either.

Sloan shakes her head. "If the rift's closing, we don't want to get pulled across too."

Rylie looks past the door to where Nathan's waiting outside. His holster's empty—the lodge must have taken his handgun. She doesn't see any grays around the house, but she can't help but think of Kai's drawing, and what Lily said earlier, how *they're attracted to our scent.*

"Don't we need any weapons? Just in case?"

"Believe me, we need the weapons more," Sloan says grimly. "We'll cover you." She looks Kai and Rylie up and down, then squeezes their hands. "Beyond that, you're on your own."

CHAPTER 35

THE AIR IS COOL AS they head away from the Sundown house and into an overcast sky. Lily leads, setting a quick pace over the rocky ground. "This way," she whispers, glancing toward the guard tower in the distance. Its lights are off, even though a hazy fog is creeping into the air.

"Is it always foggy here?" Kai asks.

Lily shakes her head. "Usually just around sunrise and sunset."

"Weird."

Sara shoots him a look. "Not *weird*. Just different."

"A lot of things are around here," Lily says. "The climate, the ecosystem."

"The grays," Rylie says, just as she spots a shadow through the fog. She keeps walking, tries not to flinch. Nathan notices the shadow too.

"Everyone keeping up all right?" he calls out.

There are a few nods—the group is quiet, tense. Rylie looks over, recognizing most of them. Some of their names are on the list she made with Lor and Kai. Mackenzie Soren, strong and athletic, still wearing her LA Lakers hat over a head of curly hair, her shoulders hunched, jaw set. Juan Ramon-Ortez, a white-haired man at the back, slower than the others but keeping pace. Fern Childers Gallagher, a skinny fourteen-year-old in shorts, a bandage wrapped around her thigh. The others from the list didn't make it—Kai's *mom* didn't make it—but three kids joined them. The smallest, a towheaded girl, is held by Lor. The other two are flanking Sara, origami animals tight in their fists. Iggy is walking next to a fierce-looking woman with a cane who wasn't on the list, and there's a man with scarring on half his face. All of them keep glancing toward the nearby guard tower. Its windows are still dark.

"We'll be okay," Lily says. "The lodge is watching us. They're always watching."

"That sounds ominous," Kai says, trying to break the tension, but no one laughs. Everyone's breathing heavily now, probably just wanting to get to the line as fast as possible. Rylie keeps her strides long and even, like she's just on a normal hike, like everything is normal. Her head starts pounding again, and then Nathan's at her side, his fingers grazing her hand.

"We'll make it back, Rye," he says, and for a moment it feels like they're *really* just on a hike, and that she's going to be okay, they're all going to be okay. Nathan's stride is easy, almost relaxed, as if the flicker of hope in her chest might be spreading to him too, that hope mixed with dread.

"Thanks for not giving up," he says quietly. "You found Lily."

Lily turns at the sound of her name. Her eyes look as alert as Nathan's. "I owe you," she says to Rylie.

"Don't get ahead of yourself. I haven't brought us home yet."

"But you will," Lily says. "You're like Ethan."

Like Ethan. Rylie tenses. Her headache feels like it's thudding right behind her eyes as Kai steps closer, listening. "So you knew him, Lily?" he asks, and she nods.

"I saw him hanging around Rylie's grandpa a lot," she says. "And then, later, he even spent some time with the lodge, but . . ." Lily's mouth forms a hard line. "But it wasn't his thing. He left before he was fully treated."

Nathan nods tightly. "He's the main suspect in a murder spree now."

"Do you think he did it?" Kai asks, still looking at Lily. "Or was it the grays?"

Lily slows. Her eyes are on the fog, the desert scrub just ahead. "I don't know." She shakes her head. "The aggression, when it comes, is like a darkness inside. And Ethan's treatment was taking longer than the rest of ours. He didn't stay long enough to finish it."

Rylie stares at Lily, her stomach churning. "But I didn't either." That feeling she had in the lodge—that feeling of not being able to control herself—it could come back.

"You know what Miles and I love most about the bees?" Iggy asks. He's watching her warily. They all are. "Their venom is a protective mechanism. That's its function. That's how they protect themselves against predators."

He's trying to make her feel better, but now she's thinking of something else, another thing that makes her stomach twist. She slows a little, listening. It's quiet except for the footsteps of the group, their ragged breathing. "I always saw bees near the line before," she says. "I don't see them now."

Lor catches up to her. "You wouldn't be able to tell, anyway. The mist is getting thicker."

"It'll be gone as soon as we cross," Lily says. "We'll be there any minute."

Rylie feels everyone's eyes on her again, so she picks up her pace, pulling to the front. *A line distinguishes it.* Just visible ahead is a stretch of boulders, sagebrush, a dirt road in the distance. The fog is turning everything hazy, but she can see it in her mind, the line she traced on her grandpa's map. They just need to walk across it. She starts jogging, trying to speed up the process. Nothing happens.

"Hey, there's a light," Lor calls out.

In the direction of the guard post, a bright light flares, and someone in their group lets out a gasp. "It's okay," the woman with the cane murmurs, and the two older girls link hands with the younger kids, hushing them.

"The fog is our cover," Lily says quickly. "They probably can't see us."

"Which means the lodge can't see us either," Kai points out. He glances at Rylie and then looks away just as fast, like he doesn't want her to feel any pressure, but it's too late.

"What do you need to do to get us across?" Nathan asks.

His brown eyes are patient, trusting. She'd give anything to feel that same trust in herself.

"I don't know," she says. The cinch knot is back in her chest. "It always just . . . happened."

Lily's face goes tight. "Maybe your mom already closed the line."

Rylie feels the knot in her chest grow. If her mom already closed it, she'll never see her again. She'll never see Owen again either. She shakes her head. "We're getting across."

"That experiment you just told me about, in here," Kai says. He pulls the notebook from his pocket and hits it against his palm. "You said it measured electromagnetic rays of the sun. So maybe it doesn't work during the day."

"Rylie?" Sara's voice comes floating through the fog, her white-blond hair barely visible. "I hear something."

A pattering sound. First just behind them, then everywhere. All around them, shadows are moving through the fog.

"Stop," Nathan calls out, and everyone goes still. There's a growling noise, too close. Then, through the mist, a leg. A tail. More pattering sounds. More growling.

Grays.

"Don't look at their eyes," Lily whispers. There's another growl, and then the flash of a gray. They're being circled.

Rylie goes on edge. "Lift the kids onto the nearest boulder. We'll put our backs to the rock."

"No," Lily snaps, and beside her Iggy holds out his

lighter like it might keep the grays back. "We need to run. We need to *cross*."

"To cross?" someone calls out ahead. Rylie can't see who's talking through the fog but then she hears a laugh. "It's not dark yet." The voice, the laugh—it sounds too much like *him*—and now there are footsteps behind her. "It won't work, Rylie."

She whirls, but he's not there. She only sees more fur and flesh weaving in and out of the hazy mist, and it's suddenly cold, so cold. Tiny pinpricks of light start appearing in the gloom. First just a few, then more, and more.

"Look away from them!" Lily shouts, but Rylie's already looking away. She's looking at the shadow stepping out from behind the boulder. Not a shadow. A head, a black sweatshirt. His hood is up, but she doesn't need to see his face. She already knows who it is.

"Ethan," she breathes. She glances back to warn the others, but everyone has gone strangely still. Nathan has a rock in his outstretched fist, but he looks dazed. Lor is motionless, staring at the same gray as Iggy, the lighter clenched in his hands. Sara is crouched near another gray, her eyes wide open, unblinking. Kai is next to Sara, his whole body stiff. No one's moving except for Lily, who's swinging a stick at the closest gray.

"If you look directly at their eyes when they're hunting," Ethan says, "they immobilize you. You might remember the feeling."

Rylie tightens her fists. Of course she does. Everything

in the hypnosis really happened, and now it's happening all over again. *Ethan's* happening all over again.

"Get back!" Lily shouts. It's not clear if she's talking to the grays or Ethan. "Get away!"

"But we're different, aren't we?" Ethan says to Rylie, his eyes still on her. "The paralysis doesn't affect us as much." He suddenly smiles. "Ever heard that joke about not needing to be fast, just faster than the person you're with? Which is a good thing, because the grays tend to follow us around." He steps closer. "They like the smell of our blood."

"Why are you here, Ethan?" She has to stall him. Whatever he has planned, she has to stall him. Then she has to figure out how they're going to get away from the grays and cross when the sun sets. She scans the ground for a stick, a rock, anything.

"Get *back*!" Lily shouts again.

"What about a hello, Lil?" Ethan says, finally glancing over at her. "Or at least a 'Welcome back' or something?"

"Why? You've *never* helped us," Lily spits. She's swinging the stick faster now. "You only care about yourself."

"I helped with the Bishop twins."

"You took them across and that was it." Her face is twisted in a grimace, and she's working hard to keep the grays back. "Then you gave up," she hisses. "You quit trying."

Ethan stops smiling. "You don't know what it's like, Lily." His voice is softer now—he actually sounds like he wants to convince her. "The treatment worked on you."

Rylie edges toward Lily and the others. *Think.* She needs

to think, she needs a plan, but it's hard to focus on anything but Ethan. There's a humming sound at her ears, a humming sound inside her. She can feel her blood running through her veins. She can feel her body going tense, everything inside her ready to attack, to hurt. "Get back," she grinds out.

Ethan turns. "Get used to that feeling," he says after a moment. "The medicine doesn't cure people like us." He tilts his head, feigns concern. "Didn't they tell you?"

Rylie allows a quick glance toward Lily. She's still holding up the stick, doing her best to keep the grays back. The grays who are getting so close to her friends, so close to the kids huddled on the boulder. They need to cross over, but Rylie can't think, can't see a way out of this.

Lily swings the stick, just missing a gray. "Don't listen to him!"

"Lily's going to say anything she can to use you," Ethan says. "That's what the lodge does."

Anger moves through Rylie, swift and hot, and her vision narrows. Ethan doesn't step closer. He doesn't have to. He's the only thing she can see, the only thing she can focus on. Her head starts to pound again.

"Do you think it's all going to go away once you're home?" he asks. "You think everything will go back to normal? You think you'll be *good* again?"

She can feel the wrongness inside her—she can feel the infection thrumming through her, the fury leaking into her veins, swarming her every thought.

Ethan actually smiles. "I knew we were alike."

"We're crossing over," Rylie says. The humming sound gets louder at her ears but she ignores it. "You can't stop us."

"Why would I want to stop you?" Ethan's smiling again like he's two steps ahead of her. This whole time he's been ahead of her. "You only tried to lock me up, after all."

"That's your fault." It's hard to watch both him and the grays. "And we didn't just try. We put you in a cell."

"But I didn't belong on base, so they had to transport me last night." He steps closer. She doesn't trust him this close. "Good thing Highway 62 passes through the line, right?"

The realization almost hurts. "You escaped by crossing over."

"No thanks to you," he says, a bitterness in his voice. "Afterwards, I went back to look for you at your house, but I must have just missed you."

"What a shame." Rylie forces herself to turn away. She makes herself focus on the grays instead, on Lily, on *crossing*, but Ethan steps in front of her and pulls something out of his pocket. It's a small black box. No, not a box. It's a recorder. A battered Talkboy, glued and taped together. *Owen's* Talkboy. She sucks in a breath.

"Not in the best shape, is it?" Ethan holds it out like he expects her to take it. "He showed me how it worked, before . . ."

"Before what?"

"Before I killed him."

It feels like she's plunging downward, like the ground has dropped away. "You're *lying*."

Ethan hits a button on the Talkboy, and then she hears Owen, she hears his voice. "Rylie? Rylie?" There's a gasping noise, then: "Rylie, help me!"

The tiny thread of hope she's been holding on to snaps away completely, leaving her in a free fall. Everything seems so far away: Lily calling to her, the grays bearing down on her friends—everything's fading into the fog, fading away with the last of the daylight. Everything's fading but Ethan. He's in front of her, he's the only thing she sees, and she can *smell* him. She's watching a vein pulsing at his neck and she's breathing in his scent, and the whole world is getting darker, sharper.

"So here's the question," Ethan says, his eyes narrowing. "Can you ever really go back? Do you want to live in a world where your brother's dead, or live in a world where he's never been born? It's a tough choice, I gotta say."

Rylie feels the rage seep into her, and then she's rushing forward. She knocks Ethan against the boulder, hard. It feels good to slam him back, but a half breath later he twists sideways and grabs at her necklace, pulls tight. Pulls so tight, so hard, just like he did before, but this time she's ready. She elbows his side, and he grunts but doesn't let go, and a second later he's yanking tighter and she can't take in a breath and she doesn't want to, not without Owen, but her lungs are begging her to breathe, begging her to move, to fight, to *live*, and she needs to, she needs to hurt Ethan again. Everything inside her needs to hurt him. A flash of a memory: *The medicine didn't always work.* Another flash: Dr. Singh, leaning forward, listing symptoms. *Hydrophobia,* he'd said. Fear of water. *Water.*

Rylie spits in Ethan's face, and he lets go, recoiling back. He trips on a rock and stumbles, and it's just enough. She charges forward and shoves him to the ground, pinning her knees against his chest, pressing down on his neck. He grasps at her but weakly. His eyes are glazed. He must have hit his head, and it's so easy, so easy to squeeze. Ethan's hand drops away and goes to his pocket, to the black box there. The Talkboy. She presses down harder and hears him choke.

"Rylie, Rylie?"

It's Owen again. It's her brother's voice. Beautiful Owen, and in front of her Ethan's face is purple and red and he's gasping, he can't breathe; her hands are still clenching his throat, pressing harder. Owen wouldn't want this. Owen would never want this. Her grip loosens. *Owen.* She pulls away and crawls back from Ethan, horrified.

"How?" Ethan's voice is hoarse. He's staring at her and not moving, like she's a gray, like she has him paralyzed. "I can never stop," he says. "No matter how hard I try, I can never stop. Tell me how you did it. I have to know."

Her brother would give him that too. "I thought of the person I love most in the world. In all the worlds," she whispers. Owen. Owen, who's gone.

"Rylie!" Lily calls out. "Please get up!"

She straightens. The grays are closer now. Lily's barely

keeping them back. Ethan moves suddenly, and too late she sees the knife, but instead of swinging it at her, he slits his own palm. The blood comes, bright red and fast, and then the grays turn, all of them at once, and suddenly Nathan's letting out a yell and Kai and Iggy are moving forward with a flame and Sara's rising to her feet and Lor's lifting up a rock, and they're all shouting with rage and fury and *life*.

"Move," Ethan says, raising his bloody hand as the grays rush toward him. "Run!" he shouts, and then he's on his feet in the same moment Rylie is. She sprints into the middle of her friends just as the creatures dart around her, running away from her, running toward Ethan and away from the line.

"Everyone go!" Rylie shouts, and together they sprint into the fog until suddenly it's gone.

CHAPTER 36

WHEN THE FOG CLEARS, THEY'RE on the stretch of desert behind the Sundown house. It's a crisp, cool night. The stars are out. The stars are everywhere.

Rylie stops running. It feels like her head is splitting open, her heart too. There's a thick stickiness on her skin from where the grays touched her, brushed past her. She looks back toward the others. "Did everyone make it across?"

"We made it!" Lor grabs Iggy and starts jumping up and down as Rylie watches on numbly. They didn't hear what Ethan said. They don't know about Owen.

"We're heeeeere, not theeeeere," Kai sings, linking elbows with silver-haired Juan and the woman with the cane. Beside them, Sara's on her knees, hugging the kids who came across. The older girls are crying, and the man with the scars is staring up at the night sky with his hands raised in disbelief, or maybe in thanks.

"We're actually here," Lily says softly. She holds out her arms and spins until Nathan laughs, and his laughter sounds so happy, so *full*, and then Rylie thinks of Owen and turns toward the house. Her lungs seize. A cop car is in the drive-way, blue lights splaying across the garage door.

"Owen," she whispers, and then the front door bursts open. She stops, staring.

There he is, he's standing in the doorway, and for a second she wonders if she's in the right place, the right *world*. But there are his curls, his baggy climbing-gym T-shirt, Castle by his legs. "I hear someone, Dad," Owen says in his overly excited voice, and then Ben appears beside him, peer-ing out into the night, and Rylie has never been so glad to see them. Both of them.

"Kai?" Ben calls out, heading into the dark yard with Castle and Owen. "Rylie?"

She rushes forward to meet them halfway. Castle starts running in circles and barking, like he knows exactly how she's feeling as she pulls Owen into her arms. "Spaghetti O," she says. "You're here." He's here, he's alive. The person she loves most is right here, and it's enough. That love saved her. It has always saved her, even when she thought he was gone.

"Of course I'm here," Owen says, his eyebrows furrow-ing. "But someone came to the house last night asking for you, and Ben thought he looked like that guy on the news!"

"I wasn't sure, so I didn't call the police at first," Ben says. He shoves his hands into his pockets like he's embarrassed, and then pulls out his cell. "But when you weren't picking up your phone this afternoon, and when Kai wasn't either, I . . ." He suddenly notices the others and frowns. "What's going on?" he asks. "Where did all of you *come* from?"

"That might be hard to explain," Kai says. Rylie watches him quietly, thinking of what he lost. What they both lost.

"We were worried about you, Rye," Owen says, and she's almost brought to her knees. This whole time, she thought he was gone, because of Ethan. Ethan let her think Owen was dead. Ethan Langhorne, the commune killer, the bee-keeper. In the end, he wasn't a monster. In the end, he helped them. He helped them get back to Owen and her mom and Ben. Back to Twentynine Palms.

Rylie looks toward the house. Lights from the cop car are flashing over its roof, its tall pale stucco, and nothing about it has changed, but it seems different now, like a place she might want to live. Like a refuge.

"All right, I just called Eve," Ben says, slipping his cell back into his pocket. "I couldn't get ahold of her before, but—"

"Did she do it?" Rylie cuts in. "Did she finish the closures?"

She can feel everyone around her suddenly go still. They're all waiting on Ben to answer, but he doesn't seem to notice. Instead, he just laughs. "Yeah, I caught her on her work phone," he says. "You know your mom stays on schedule." He shakes his head. "She's not concerned about *work*, though, she's concerned about you and Kai. I can't believe it took me so long to realize—"

"We're fine," Kai says, his voice unusually rough. "Actually, we're better than fine. We're glad to be home." He steps forward and hugs Ben, and Ben looks halfway shocked and then hugs him back, so tight that Kai lets out a mock groan.

"What the hell is going on here?" A police officer strides out of the house with his radio in hand. It must be Sara's uncle, the police chief, because he jogs over to her first. "Sara?"

"We'll tell you everything," she says. "Or we'll try, anyway."

"Is that who I think it is?" The chief eyes Lily, then turns to Iggy and the others. "You *too*?"

"I think you're in for a very late night," Lily says. "Someone call Thea for me." She looks halfway giddy, like she's running on adrenaline. They all are, probably.

"Can we get these people inside?" the chief asks, already picking up his radio, and Ben's eyes widen before he starts nodding. "Of course, of course. Anyone hungry? Thirsty?"

Rylie hears fast footsteps, and then Lor is there, throwing her arms around Rylie and kissing her cheek, and Kai's got an arm around Rylie too, and when they both finally pull away, there's Nathan, his gaze on her, those warm brown eyes that she knew before and that she's only just getting to know now.

"We need some Skittles to celebrate." He smiles, and it hits her right in the heart. "Or the seven summits?"

"All of it," she says, and when she reaches for his hand, it feels like a current crackling, like two worlds colliding. Together they head toward the house, toward the place that finally feels like home.

ACKNOWLEDGMENTS

What a trip this book has been, and a long one too, filled with stops and detours that eventually led to the place I'd been searching for all along. I'd like to thank my agent, Catherine Drayton, for not giving up on me, and thanks to Claire Friedman and the rest of the InkWell team as well. Many thanks to my editor, Monica Jean, for not giving up on this story, and for the insight you brought to its pages at all the right moments. And my sincerest thanks to everyone at Random House who helped bring this book to the shelves, especially Lydia Gregovic (for stepping in with such generosity, enthusiasm, and editorial care), Krista Marino (for opening the door), and Beverly Horowitz, Angela Carlino, Ken Crossland, Tamar Schwartz, Colleen Fellingham, Bara MacNeill, Caroline Kirk, and the entire RHCB Marketing and Publicity team.

Special thanks to Jack Hughes, for the extraordinary cover I never could have dreamed up myself. My thanks to Roza Shanina (1924–1945) for the title, which first graced the pages of her diary. I intended for her story to be a bigger part of this book, but in truth she deserves a book of her own.

Writing can be a solitary task, so I'm grateful for all the

writers I've met along this journey, especially Marit Weisenberg, Katie Nelson, Emily Bain Murphy, and Darcy Woods. Ditto to my artist friends, for bringing inspiration into my life when it was needed most: Erin Hunter, Nancy Borowick, Danielle Evans, I'm thinking of you. And same for my book mates Joel Naoum, Peter Durston, and Mark Harding. (Mark, your read in the final hour deserves some serious applause.)

Thanks always to my oldest and dearest: Kristin Irwin, Katie O'Neill, Courtney Parker, and Hank Spangler. And my thanks, also, to Randy Clawson, for the invaluable read, and to John B. Dickens for the Marine Corps fact-checking, and for your military service.

Thanks to the friends who made a writing life less lonely: Justine Williams, for your equal parts good attitude and badassness; Iku Hoover, Sandia Boardley, and Christina Darkazalli, for sharing stories in Guam while running after toddlers in the sand; Catherine Deist, for your humor and energy; Simone Gorrindo, for your solidarity (I will be forever grateful that we crossed paths at MiM!); and last but not least, Gabrielle Copans, for being such a thorough reader and an easy, breezy, beautiful friend.

My unending thanks to Caroline Graham, for just being you, and for hearing the call of my 52-Hertz heart all those years ago. And heaps of thanks to Shady Cosgrove for always saying the right thing (and for all the writing things!).

Many thanks to my mom and dad, who not only read this book several times but stepped up to watch the girls while I revised it. Thank you to my brother Steven, who's ever ready to cheer me on, and to my brother Brent, for the medical advice and the endless conversations around plot (turns out you're a book doctor too!). And thanks to all the supportive, generous-hearted people in my life who I'm lucky enough to call family (here's looking at you, godparents, aunts, uncles, cousins, second cousins, in-laws, and sisters-in-law). I am grateful, always.

All the thanks to my husband, Jack, for your encouragement from the start till the end, and then some. Life would be a lot less beautiful without you and our daughters.

And finally, thank you, thank you, readers. When I was a kid, I wanted to become a writer because of the magic I felt while reading books. I hope this book gave you a little magic too.

ABOUT THE AUTHOR

Tara Goedjen never stays in one place for long. She has worked for a publishing house in Australia and as a tennis coach in Spain, and she wrote *No Beauties or Monsters* on the island of Guam and in the desert of New Mexico. Now she lives and writes in a rainy corner of the Pacific Northwest. She is also the author of *The Breathless*.

taragoedjenauthor.com